THE
PERILOUS GODS
BOOK TWO

WHEN THE WINDS SING

Also by L.D. Colter

A Borrowed Hell
The Halfblood War
While the Gods Sleep
Where the Shadows Dwell

THE
PERILOUS GODS
BOOK TWO

WHEN THE WINDS SING

L. D. COLTER

SOLARIS
NOVA

When the Winds Sing

First published 2025 by Solaris Nova
an imprint of Rebellion Publishing Ltd,
Riverside House, Osney Mead,
Oxford, OX2 0ES, UK

www.solarisbooks.com

ISBN: 978-1-83786-714-1

A CIP catalogue record for this book is available from the
British Library.

Designed & typeset by Rebellion Publishing

To my brother, Jeremy – non-fiction writer by day,
fiction writer at heart

Foreword

I REJOICE ANY time a writer—let alone an excellent wordsmith like L. D. Colter—chooses to incorporate Slavic folklore into their fiction. These characters are seldom seen in Western literature, and when we do encounter them, they're often depicted with all the accuracy and authenticity of Ivan Drago in *Rocky*, a Russian boxer portrayed by a Swedish chemical engineer.

There is good reason for this, however. There are heaps of material on Greek and Roman and Egyptian pantheons, but few reliable records about the Slavic deities. Any writer who undertakes the task of telling their stories must labor without a safety net.

Just how scarce are the records? We know that Perun was the equivalent of Zeus or Jupiter, a mighty thunder god at the top of the food chain. By comparison, we don't know much about Stribog at all. It's not even certain that the two were parts of the same pantheon.

These gods were worshipped by the Slavic tribes before the Varangians—Vikings—conquered the region and established city-states that eventually consolidated into Kievan Rus. No significant written records have survived, and much of what we know about the history of Kievan Rus comes from the *Primary Chronicle*, the manuscript written several centuries later. It was authored by a monk named Nestor, whose principal goal appeared to be lionizing Christianity and its early adopters rather than accuracy.

Thus, our glimpse into Slavic religions and mythology comes from oral storytelling, where old tales and rituals survived and changed over the centuries in an uneasy balance with Christianity. Many of the spirits the Slavs used to worship became known as devils, others were relegated to fairy tale characters. As for the pagan gods? Those were not tolerated by the Church and therefore sent to the dustbin of history.

Like all verbal stories, Slavic folk tales shifted and changed with every telling. The versions of Koschei the Deathless and other mythological staples as we know them today are largely from the seventeenth and eighteenth centuries.

Consider Baba Yaga. She is an old character, likely as old as Perun. But would a seventh century Slav recognize her modern depiction? Baba Yaga is often—but not always—described as a hideous old woman with features such as a bony leg or iron teeth. She's simultaneously an evil witch to be defeated, and a guardian of the forest and of the old ways to be placated. At times she serves as a guide to the underworld. That's a lot of jobs for one senior citizen! Colter chose to base her on a possible pre-Christian portrayal as someone who acted as a guide or teacher of young children, though not a particularly benevolent one.

Today, the most recognized attribute of Baba Yaga is her home: She lives in a hut on chicken legs. Or does she?

The idea of this hut is almost certainly more recent than Baba Yaga herself. Most experts agree that the "legs" are wooden stilts. The structures raised on one or more stilts in swampland were common among people in Finland, Karelia, and Siberia. They were built that way to reduce dampness and avoid rot. But when did the Slavs come into contact with this technology? Was it brought by the Vikings too?

The hut legs may have nothing to do with chickens, either. The Russian term "*курьи ножки*" sure does sound like "chicken legs," but the word "*курѣ*" means both "rooster" and "hut rafters" or "hut stilts." (Dal's *Explanatory Dictionary of the Living Great Russian Language*, 2nd edition, 1881.) Don't worry—everyone gets it wrong. There's a "no harm, no fowl" joke in there, somewhere.

So, you see, depicting these characters well is difficult work, and may require an entire wall of cute kitten motivational posters that say, *Hang in there!* (Well, the cute kitten posters can't hurt, anyway.)

But, as common wisdom goes, every challenge is an opportunity. Such ambiguity is license for a writer to add to the canon, to fill in the blank spots in the most interesting way possible. In this book, Colter resurrects the old gods in her own unique manner that still feels respectful of the lore. Let her be your guide into the deep dark forest of Slavic folk tales. You are certain to enjoy the tour!

Alex Shvartsman
Award-winning writer and Russian-to-English literary translator

PART ONE

Chapter One

A SHARP AND tangy scent of ozone seeped under Alex's motorcycle helmet, a single breath of warning before the heavy drizzle ripened to a cold, drenching deluge. Gray streaked the air. The landscape muted around him, blurring into a background of clouds and mist as rain bled down over the coastal redwoods and red barns and faded green pastures along the rural road.

He reduced his speed to adjust for the slick asphalt and gusty winds. Winter rain was a familiar companion in this northwestern corner of California, but he'd always viewed weather as an integral part of a whole rather than an annoyance to rail against. Even his parents passing away on wet winter days hadn't bound his grief from those times to gray skies and chilly rainfall. Nature, in all its forms, brought him a measure of peace that little else in his life had ever equaled.

Negotiating a curve in the road, a bearded, grandfatherly figure came into sight in the field on his left. The man was standing maybe a hundred feet from the road, flying a kite. The cheap drugstore model with its paper skin, light wooden skeleton, and tail of rag cloth shouldn't have been able to fly in this weather any more than if he'd tied a wet wool sweater to his string. Yet, it not only stayed aloft in the storm but sailed strongly, fifty feet or more above the road.

The entire scene defied both logic and physics. Alex searched for a rational explanation for the man, the activity, or the aerodynamics of the kite and came up blank. Raindrops as large as teardrops splashed his visor and dotted his vision as he lifted his head to follow the kite's implausible acrobatics.

A solitary car passed, traveling in the opposite direction. With no other traffic in sight, he eased off the throttle for a better look. The garbage bag rain jacket over his secondhand leathers flapped with decreasing violence as he decelerated. The cold had penetrated his layers and his fingers felt numb inside his gloves, so the old guy must have been freezing. The gray wool suit hung dripping from his torso, and the woolly black hat perched on his head offered no protection for his face or neck. Alex saw no structures in the field and no car parked along the road. He couldn't guess where he'd come from as none of the widely scattered farmhouses nearby were within comfortable walking distance for the weather.

The man held the spindle of twine with both hands, locked in battle with the kite that strained to break free and soar east. Alex drew level and saw a flash of white teeth and the man's shoulders shaking with laughter while the kite bucked high above the road, directly overhead.

Lightning streaked the sky, rare and unexpected at the coast. It filled Alex's vision. The white kite vanished against the bright flash, as if morphing into pure energy. And where the old guy held one string, the afterglow of the flash and the moisture on Alex's visor created the image of hundreds of strings, thousands, shimmering between the man's hands and the sky. Thunder boomed, loud as a bomb detonating.

He lifted one gloved hand to wipe his visor just as a brutal blast of wind hammered into his side, unbalancing him. Grabbing at his bike's handlebar again, he overcorrected, swerving left then right. The gust reversed direction, like some ocean monster inhaling to hurl another blast. Above him, the kite plummeted on a sudden wind shear and the vertical wooden strut shot toward him like a crossbow bolt. He braked and veered to evade it. His back wheel lost traction on the wet road.

The motorcycle toppled to the right as the kite hurtled toward him. A second before the strut would have speared him, the kite jerked horizontal, scooping the air and flying parallel to the ground. The sound of vibrating paper momentarily eclipsed the noise of his motorcycle peg scraping the pavement as the kite arrowed toward the old man, who must have yanked the line.

Alex tried to kick free of the bike, but it skidded out from under him before he had a chance. He slid less than a yard, tearing the garbage bag from his shoulders and scuffing his pride worse than his jacket. Lying in a puddle, half on his right side, his brain took a moment to assess the impact. Drizzle pattered on his helmet—the heavy rain having stopped as suddenly as it had started—while he confirmed he'd sustained nothing worse than a bruised hip and shoulder.

Shaky and amped on adrenaline, he pushed to his feet and cursed himself for an idiot for falling over at low speed in the middle of an empty road. He felt more like a high school kid who'd tripped on the stairs than a thirty-two-year-old ex-con who'd dumped his motorcycle. Flipping his visor up, he glanced reflexively at the field to see if the old man had witnessed his fall. He hadn't. He was preoccupied with a younger man who stood face-to-face with him, gesturing angrily.

The new person's sudden appearance was as startling as his clothing: a round fur cap and a gold-embroidered tunic of white cloth over white leggings with tall brown boots. Ignoring his bike lying on the centerline, Alex stared at the pair, struggling to make sense of the bizarre elements playing out on this peaceful stretch of road.

He bent to the kill switch on his bike and turned the

engine off, only half paying attention to what he did. It seemed impossible he could have missed seeing another person out there, especially someone who looked like he was dressed for cosplay. Ripping the remains of the garbage bag from his waist, he tucked the torn plastic into a saddlebag to throw away later. A distant grunt came from the field, and he looked up to see a fight in progress. He watched, stunned, as the younger man hit the older man in the face.

The unexpected violence fired electricity along Alex's already heightened nerves. His fingertips and lips tingled. He straightened slowly, feeling lightheaded.

It was out of the question for him to wade in and break up the fight. He couldn't. Not after the way things had gone to hell in Missoula. Those few moments on a quiet street outside a bar were all it had taken to set the events in motion that had ruined his life. He was on parole for felony assault and alarms were ringing in his skull, telling him to leave now before anyone saw him here.

He ignored the warning bells and continued to watch the two men, transfixed. The old guy looked a bit like his grandfather, who had developed dementia in his late seventies. If this man suffered from something similar, it might explain why he'd been out in the middle of nowhere in the rain.

Alex scanned both directions along the road, hoping for someone else to come by and stop the fight. There were no cars in sight. Calling 911 should have been the obvious solution, but things weren't that simple for someone like him. Reporting a crime had the potential to go sideways for an ex-con, and GIS and digital ID technology meant that calling anonymously was a thing of the past. He might be questioned. His parole officer might be notified. And if one of the men got badly hurt—or worse—he could end up a suspect.

Nothing. *Nothing* would ever be worth the risk of ending up behind bars again.

The old man not only managed to stay upright but fought back. The one in the tunic punched him in the gut. Alex stared hopefully at the empty road a second time. Making sure his motorcycle was in neutral, he hauled it upright, rolled it to the side of the road, and booted the kickstand down. Suppressing his concerns about the altercation, he squatted to block both men from sight and quickly checked the gas tank for leaks or damage.

He told himself the grunts were the wind, though the wind had died to a breeze. The ocean surf beyond the trees at the end of the field, then. He stood to see the two men still grappling but not as unmatched as he would've guessed. Neither appeared to have a weapon. Neither looked badly hurt. Three years ago, he would have intervened anyway. Not anymore. Prison had changed everything. Worst of all, it had changed him.

He flipped his visor down and straddled the bike. Any minute now, someone would drive by; someone who could call the police without repercussions. He turned the key in the ignition. The engine ground without turning over. A smell of gasoline wafted to him. He swore again.

His phone vibrated. It was bound to be Fen texting him to see why he hadn't called yet. If his ex-best friend's message yesterday meant what Alex hoped, he might soon be on the path to getting his conviction overturned. After practically begging Fen for help the past few months, the last thing he wanted was to undermine the tenuous reconnection it'd taken him so long to build. Looking unreliable—not calling this morning when he said he would—wasn't helping.

The flooded carburetor on the ancient Honda would take at least five minutes to clear. More time for the situation in the field to fall apart. More chance someone would see him sitting there, assume his involvement. More chance he'd miss Fen, because calling him from here while the two strangers fought a hundred feet away would be entirely too weird. His chilled hands sweated inside his gloves. He checked the road in both directions again. Other than the distant surf and a light breeze, all was silent. Against his will, he looked back at the field.

The old man was climbing the short embankment up to the road, smiling. He held his kite frame with his left hand and rolled the last of the string onto the spindle. He showed no sign of pain or injury, and the other man was nowhere to be seen. Alex's stomach lurched as he pictured the guy in the tunic and leggings lying stabbed or strangled somewhere in the tall grass. He needed to get off his bike, be ready to fight or run, but doubt and confusion pinned him in place.

"You are all right?" the man asked him. His sodden suit—the same color as the dark-gray clouds above, the same color as his eyes—had a thick weave and a dated look. His voice was deep, and he rolled his r's in a familiar accent that carried on it memories of Alex's parents and grandparents. The fuzzy, black ushanka hat, ear flaps folded up and tied at the crown, was identical to the one his grandfather had brought with him from Russia.

Alex lifted his visor again. "Where's the other man?"

"What other man?"

"The one you were fighting out there."

The man pursed his lips. "You are not all right. You hit your head?"

"Are you trying to tell me you weren't just in a fight with another man?"

"You need to look?" The man jerked his head back toward the field. "See for yourself?"

The likelihood that this old guy was lying and that a costumed man had suddenly appeared in the field, fought him without leaving any mark or injury, and disappeared again was looking very slim. Alex's call to Fen took a back seat to his need to know if he was losing his mind.

"Yeah. I think I do."

He could settle the question in a couple of minutes and still have time to at least text a quick explanation before driving the last mile or so to work. He removed his helmet and hung it on the handlebar. The soft rain drummed on his hair.

"I'm Stribog. Orel Stribog," the man said as Alex followed him back down the embankment. He moved confidently and with an unexpected spryness. Alex adjusted his guess at the man's age down by a decade.

"Alex Orlov."

"Orlov. Good name."

Alex hadn't spoken much Russian since his grandfather died three years ago, but he knew that Orel and Orlov were both derived from the word for "eagle." His last name had tumbled out because of that connection, and he wondered now if he'd introduced himself to a killer leading him to the spot where he'd left one person dead already.

His gut told him no. He'd known killers; this Stribog didn't trip the same warning flags those men had. And if he was wrong, he was at least thirty years younger, he'd stayed fit in prison, and doing time had taught him to hold his own against worse than this man. All the evidence seemed to point to Stribog being right, though: Alex had been in a wreck, hit his head harder than he thought, and had imagined the second man.

Stribog led him to a culvert where a stream flowed under the road and out into the pasture, meandering its way to the nearby ocean. Two strands of wire sagged low over the culvert. They climbed easily over the old fencing just as a car finally passed them. Alex glanced up, still jumpy, then wished he'd kept his face turned away. Even if there'd been no altercation here, at the least he guessed they were trespassing.

The wet grass swished at their calves as they negotiated the embankment down to the pasture. The boggy smell of saturated soil and crushed alfalfa rose from the field and mingled with salt air off the ocean. They traced Stribog's muddy footprints back to the flattened patch where Alex had first seen the old man.

As a forest ranger in Montana, Alex had tracked injured animals through the wilderness; he'd stalked poachers and illegal trappers who'd tried to hide their tracks. He read the signs now in the sopping wet grass as easily as he could read a trail map. There was only one set of footprints in the area where Stribog had been standing. There was no blood. There were no drag marks or footprints leading away from the trampled grass. No dead body lay nearby. No unconscious person.

"There was no one out here with you?" Alex asked anyway.

"Why would anyone be out here in the rain with me?"

"Why *were* you flying a kite in the rain?" he asked.

"Winds are good. Why were you riding motorcycle in rain?"

Alex didn't answer.

"Ah, good thing we came back," Stribog exclaimed. "My pin." Something gold and metallic, about the size of a fingernail, glittered in the muddy grass near his toes. He bent effortlessly to pick it up and rubbed it with one large, rough thumb. Alex saw the pin was molded in the shape of an eagle.

"Here, hold this." Stribog held the kite out, needing his hands free to reattach the pin.

As Alex reached to take it from him, Stribog lunged. One hand grabbed Alex's shoulder in a crushing grip. With the full strength of his other arm, Stribog punched the kite into his stomach.

The kite vanished.

Alex doubled forward, gasping. Bones shifted. Muscles and tendons stretched. His lungs squeezed dry. His chest and belly felt impossibly enlarged to the size and shape of the kite. He clenched his right hand into a fist, but his motorcycle glove padded the motion. His breath and strength had been knocked from him, and his lightheadedness and tingling came back redoubled. He couldn't inhale or exhale. Couldn't swing or run or fall.

"Definitely not all right," Stribog said. He jammed his hat back on his head. The gold eagle glinted at the front left. He bent to retrieve the kite that Alex must have dropped. "I think you hit your head."

Alex stared at the kite in Stribog's hands. He tried again to breathe as muscles and bones reluctantly shrank back into place. He didn't know what had just happened, but it couldn't have been the crazy thing he'd hallucinated. His chest ached but he managed to answer, "No."

"Yes, I think so."

Alex was forming a different theory. His job pouring concrete this close to Pelican Bay Prison must have set off some sort of panic attack. Lower Lake Road was hardly the fastest way to get from Crescent City to his job site, but he'd been coming this way all week to put a few acres of farmland and trees between himself and the prison where he'd spent two years and fifty-four days of his life.

The backside of the prison bordered Highway 101, making it nearly impossible to avoid when going north, but it lay well hidden from the highway behind a thick stand of redwoods. He'd driven past it on 101 many times with no problem. This week, his jobsite had been just north of the main entrance. Even though he'd taken a route well to the west to avoid it, he'd felt the facility crouched nearby. He'd been constantly aware of its presence while he worked a scant half mile away, close enough to conjure images of the check-in shack at the gate, the cluster of white buildings, the guard towers.

If this was a panic attack, though, it was the first one since the early days of his incarceration. And even at their worst, they'd never come with hallucinations. He didn't even know if it was possible for panic attacks to trigger delusions.

"I'm getting over a cold," he said.

Stribog raised his thick, white eyebrows but said nothing. They started back toward the road.

"You want me to call someone?"

"No. I'll be okay. I need to get to work. I'm late."

"I can give you ride." The man gestured up the road. Once pointed out to him, the mid-sized silver car seemed obvious. It stood parked on a dirt track in front of the gate to the next pasture, camouflaged by a dip in the gravel drive and the tall grass to either side. "Better than motorcycle in rain with bump on head."

Alex's fingers tingled so vigorously they stung. He wasn't sure if he'd be able to grip the throttle or brake. "No. Really. I'm okay."

They reached the road. He straddled his bike, mud caking his boots and bits of wet grass clinging to his leather pant legs. With shaking fingers, he turned the ignition key. The engine fired to life. Without pausing to text Fen, he pulled his helmet on, shifted into gear, and drove north.

In his mirror, he could see the old man standing in the road, watching him.

Chapter Two

WORK KEPT ALEX'S mind preoccupied for much of the day, but when he passed the site of his wreck on the way home, the questions and uneasiness rolled back in like mist off the ocean. Trying to tease the truth from his tangle of interchangeable doubts and certainties was like playing a game of Twenty Questions with no one to lead him to an answer by telling him if his guesses were right. By the time he pulled into the gravel driveway of his sister and brother-in-law's old farmhouse, he felt as unsettled again as when he'd driven away from the old man that morning.

Alina stood on the front stoop, pulling mud boots off her two boys under the shelter of the tiny metal awning. The house was quirky in that it had no designated front entrance. The narrow door facing the driveway opened into the kitchen, and the door at the right side of the house exited from the living room to a homemade back porch with steps down to a small, unfenced backyard bordered by tall Himalayan blackberry bushes.

Alex pushed in next to her, set his helmet and keys at his feet, and began unlacing his concrete-spattered boots.

"What happened to you?" Alina asked.

His hands stilled with one boot partially untied as he wondered how his sister could possibly know about the bizarre things he'd experienced today. "What do you mean?"

She shooed her stocking-footed five-year-old indoors behind his older brother, set their boots inside, and turned back to Alex.

"You're moving stiffly. You have a scrape on your wrist and scratches on your jacket and helmet."

Alina's skill for detecting the slightest sign of danger, injury, illness, malady, or distress had begun more than two decades ago with the onset of their father's terminal cancer. Their mother's cancer a few years later had honed it to a bright, sharp edge. Once Alina had children of her own, her talent had evolved into something almost preternatural.

He kicked off his low-top boots and looked down at his helmet. She was right. A couple of dull, gray scratches etched the shiny black surface. "I laid the bike down." He pushed his court-ordered ankle monitor lower until it no longer felt like a tourniquet gripping his leg. Avoiding eye contact with his sister, he rubbed the still-indented skin on his calf where the device had been riding just above his steel-toed boots.

"Alex." Her voice didn't hold anger or blame, only resignation. "Please. Winter's just getting started. Won't you consider getting a car? At least for days like this."

He straightened, looking down at her. Few people pegged them as brother and sister. Her, barely five foot six. Him, six feet. Her, blonde with sky-blue eyes. Him, brown-haired with eyes more gray than blue.

"This is Northern California. Winter is *all* days like this."

He and Alina had grown up in this corner of California. Far enough west to hear ocean foghorns and far enough north that San Francisco, a six-hour drive south, felt like central California. Winter rain could be nearly constant, tiresome at times, occasionally fierce, but most often it arrived as gentle, saturating storms that lasted days and lulled the landscape into a drowsy half-sleep. The rain today had alternated from drizzle to downpour and back again, never stopping. Winters had been drier than normal in the past few years, but this year was shaping up to be like the ones they'd known as children, growing up in Eureka, sixty miles south of here. The rain might end tonight, or it might continue day and night without letup for a week or more.

She let the subject drop and held the door for him. "Dinner's nearly ready."

He carried his boots into the kitchen, set them on a muddy towel next to his nephews' pull-on ones, and hung his helmet on a coat hook above. The humidity level in the kitchen could have rivaled a steam room. The house smelled like warm spaghetti sauce and boiling water and wet kids and wet dog, with the subtle undertone of mold that nearly every house up to twenty miles inland battled.

Bonkers, the family's golden retriever, ran at him wagging his whole body. The dog snuffled Alex's legs and drooled on his leathers from the left side of his mouth where he'd suffered a nerve injury to the lip.

"Don't let him talk you into letting him out. I just got his feet cleaned. Again."

Alex closed the door before Bonkers could make his escape and headed for the half bath off the living room. He hung his jacket and zip-off overpants on the back of the door and scrubbed his hands and face. Unbuttoning his shirt and the top of his jeans, he inspected his chest and abdomen where he'd remained sore all day. The weird fullness had persisted as well, leaving him feeling like he couldn't fully inhale. He saw no bruises or redness except a couple of minor discolorations where his hip and shoulder had connected with the road. Past experience told him there were no broken ribs, but he must have hit harder than he realized to still feel this sore.

"Did you reach Mark Fenster today?" Alina asked when he returned to the kitchen. She sounded as hopeful as he'd felt this morning.

"No. I got to work late because of the accident. I tried him at lunch and again before I left the jobsite, but I expect he'll be out of cell range most of the week."

He'd wanted to call last night when he got the text, except Fen lived in an internet-dead-zone cabin. The cabin Alex had lived in for the three best years of his life before selling it to Fen so he could pay his lawyers. With the one-hour time difference between California and Montana, their work schedules, and Fen's cell reception, the plan had been to talk while Fen drove from Missoula to Lolo. If Alex had been at work early, as he'd planned, he could have called right after Fen left the Missoula Ranger Station. They would have had about fifteen minutes before Alex's workday started and before Fen got into spotty reception on Highway 12 on his way out to patrol the West Fork Butte and Lolo Peak areas by snowmobile.

"I'm sorry. That sucks."

She didn't need to say more. Alina was the one person who got it. Who got him. Their years since junior high had swirled together like yin and yang. He'd been there for her through their teens, pushing down his own pain and fears about their parents' illnesses, to continually patch the holes in their lives, while every safe haven they'd known threatened to tear apart. And she'd been his sole support for each step of his arrest, trial, and incarceration while the job of his dreams, a girlfriend he'd loved, his best friend, his freedom, and his future all fell away from him as abruptly as leaves in autumn.

She stirred the simmering sauce. "What do you think his text meant?"

He'd been wondering the same thing since receiving it yesterday evening. *Saw someone you know. Leaving tomorrow for 1 wk WF Butte/LP. Call me 9:15am my time.*

"I don't know. I'm probably reading more into it than I should."

He'd asked Fen several times over the past three years to get in touch if he heard anything that might help him get his conviction reversed. The text had been cryptic, but Alex felt sure it had to do with his accuser, Steven Fabick. It had been hard to rein in his imagination over the past twenty-four hours: Fabick arrested on drug-related charges; caught in some lie to the police; Fabick getting beaten up again and the real attacker getting arrested this time.

Alina raised her voice for David and Jake playing upstairs. "Boys, come on. Dinner's ready."

Alex relaxed against the counter. She always called them ten minutes before the food was served. "Is Dan working late tonight?" he asked, to avoid spiraling into what-ifs about the text.

"No, I asked him to stop at the feed store on the way home."

"What still needs doing here?" He nodded toward the dinner-making process.

"You could slice the bread." She gestured with her spoon to the long bag sitting on the counter. "Put butter on the table. I've got the salad done. Oh, salad dressing."

He started with the bread.

"So, did you get hurt?"

She'd held off asking longer than he'd expected.

"No. I was hardly moving. I only fell 'cause I was distracted. Some old guy was flying a kite out off Lower Lake Road."

"It wasn't raining up there?"

"It was. Hard."

Talking out loud about this morning's strange events brought his focus back to the discomfort in his abdomen. The soreness filled an area starting at the bottom of his sternum, flaring out behind his lower ribs, and narrowing down to his navel. A diamond-shaped pattern. A kite-

26

shaped one. He set the knife next to the uncut portion of the bread and opened the fridge, as if physically distancing himself from the conversation might help him escape the confusion and doubts the pain triggered.

"How much longer is this job going to last?"

"We finished prepping the garage floor today and we'll pour the concrete tomorrow, but I think Frank has another indoor pour lined up for next week."

"That's good."

It was. Concrete jobs in winter didn't make for steady work, even with an established contractor like Frank.

"It sounds like we're going to be somewhere east of town," he said from inside the fridge while he rummaged past the overload of food she'd laid in for Thanksgiving. "Putting in a barn floor, I think. I get the feeling it's a small barn, though. Probably only a three-day job." He returned to the table with the butter and dressing.

"You're getting to know a lot about concrete."

"I guess so," he said.

She poured the noodles into a strainer. "It won't be forever." Her tone was even more forced and offhand than when she'd asked about Fen. "Once you're off parole, you'll have more latitude to look around for a job where you can use your degree."

"Associate degree," he said. "In Outdoor Rec. I'm not holding my breath for anything to knock my socks off."

His future was a topic she danced around as carefully as she might dance at the edge of a cliff. They both knew how remote the odds were that he'd ever get his conviction overturned. And if he didn't, his record would hang over any job application he put in, any home he tried to rent or buy, any relationship he tried to start, pretty much everything from here on out. Worse, though, he could never return to the job he'd loved and would give anything to go back to. Federal offenders couldn't hold gun-carrying enforcement positions, and certainly not federal ones.

He felt like he'd been playing verbal dodgeball with Alina since he got home, which wasn't like him. They'd always been open and honest with each other—but then, they'd had more practice talking about loss and pain than most siblings. It was the weirdness from this morning getting in the way now. He weighed how much he should tell her, if anything. Not being able to tell reality from imagination had left him shaken, and he didn't want her shouldering any more worry on his behalf than she already carried. Fortunately, the sound of a car pulling into the gravel drive ended their conversation. Saved by the Camry.

The two boys and Bonkers burst into the kitchen from one direction and Dan from the other, his arms wrapped around a large bag of dog food with a sack of wild birdseed hanging from one hand. The boys clung to his pants and climbed onto his feet, yelling, "Robot walk! Robot walk!" after Dan kicked his shoes off at the edge of the crowded towel and set down the animal feed. He obliged by making clicking and whirring noises while he walked to the table with exaggerated steps, knees lifting high, as he had every night for the past couple weeks of this ritual. The boys laughed with excitement. Bonkers ran circles around them, barking. Dan stopped by the table and rubbed his sons' heads.

"Been good, Boo Boo?" he asked his seven-year-old.

"Uh huh."

"How about you, Pee Wee?"

There was no answer.

"Hey there." Still nothing. He reached toward the closest of Jake's two hearing aids, secured to him by a cord that clipped to the back of his shirt. "Are his batteries dead?"

"No," Alina said. "He just doesn't want to tell you that

28

he had to change clothes three times today because he kept playing in the mud."

Dan put two fingers under Jake's chin and tilted his face up. "That true?" he said clearly.

"Yes."

"Was it fun playing in the mud?"

"Yes."

"Was it worth changing clothes three times?"

"Yes."

"Well, all right then." He pushed at both boys' shoulders, and they jumped off his stockinged feet.

"Sit down," Alina said to everyone in the tiny kitchen. "Everything's ready." The boys scrambled into their chairs opposite Alex. Jake lunged for a piece of bread and knocked his glasses crooked. Alina adjusted them and tightened the headband strap.

Jake's hearing problems had been evident in infancy, but the vision issues were more recent. Both were getting worse. Doctors felt the two things were unrelated, recessive genetic traits neither parent had been aware of that had converged on their youngest son. Alex had worried Alina might keep Jake in a plastic bubble for the rest of his life, but she'd impressed the hell out of him. She didn't coddle either of the boys or voice her habitual worries in front of them. She let them play and explore and be boys, though he could see the effort it cost her. Her children didn't see it, though, and that was the main thing.

There was no family left to ask if there were any more genetic surprises in store for the boys—or for Alex and his sister. He'd become Alina's legal guardian in Eureka when he'd been eighteen and she'd been fifteen. Their father had died first and then their mother—three years apart, from the same rare and aggressive bone cancer that action groups tried and failed to pin on the local pulp mill emissions. Their maternal grandparents had died before they were born. Their paternal grandmother had died in Palo Alto decades ago, and the grandfather that he and Alina had grown up with and adored had died nearly three years ago in assisted living in Eureka. A heart attack, the day after Alex's sentencing.

Dan's family was equally untraceable. He'd been born in Portland, but he'd been raised in Eugene by his adoptive parents, a Japanese couple who had waited years to adopt a Japanese boy. He'd never been able to locate his birth parents.

Dinner was the usual messy, jovial affair, and Alex found he wasn't ready to leave the comfort of family when it was over.

"Mind if I stay for a cup of decaf?" he asked, while helping Alina with the dishes.

"Of course you can. Here, I'll make it for you."

"How'd your transcribing day go?" Alex asked while she set up the coffeemaker.

"Boring." She smiled. "I got the foot doctor today."

"I'm sorry." He smiled too, though he was only half joking.

The whole family had picked up and moved to Crescent City so Alina could be close to Alex while he was in prison. She'd left a good accounting job in Eugene that had let her work from home except for in-person client meetings and where she'd earned a fair bit more than her current job. Dan had left a promising bank position for a much smaller bank with little chance of upward mobility.

Alex had tried to set them free three months ago, when he got out, but they said they felt settled here. David had started first grade last year and Jake was in preschool now. They sounded genuine when they told him they liked owning an eighty-year-old farmhouse more than paying rent in the higher-priced university town, and both swore they preferred rural life. Regardless of what they said, Alex could see what they'd given up for him. Everything here—jobs, schools, opportunities, even Dan and Alina's interracial marriage—was harder. They'd traded a progressive city for a small, economically depressed prison town where the other main industries of logging and fishing had all but shut down.

"Here you go." She handed him a steaming John Wayne mug.

He pulled out a chair at the table and placed his phone where he could see if Fen texted.

"Don't feel like you have to stay," she said, resting one hand on his shoulder as he stepped around the chair to sit. "You look like you had a hard day and I know you like your quiet and your space. And this"—she waved in the direction of the living room where the TV babbled and the boys played some rough-and-tumble game involving both Bonkers and toy cars—"is hardly peaceful."

"Sure. Thanks." He knew she only said it out of concern for him, not a desire for him to leave, but her worry that he wouldn't be able to relax changed the feel of staying. Besides, if he stayed, the conversation might return to the old man and his kite. "It has been a long day."

He said goodnight to Dan and the kids and left by the back door. Standing against the porch railing at the top of the short staircase to the yard, he sipped the coffee he hadn't wanted. Sounds drifted to him as Alina herded the boys off to their bath and Dan told her about someone named Juanita at work. He would have been glad to return inside and sit on the couch in the middle of it all, but his converted shed-cum-tiny-house-slash-cottage stood waiting for him in the backyard.

They'd surprised him with it the day he got out. Alina had planned everything, apologizing that it didn't have the solitude of his cabin outside Missoula or the wide-open spaces of Lolo National Forest, but hoping it would give him a semblance of the quiet she knew he cherished.

It was also a place he wouldn't have to worry about rent, since his legal fees and fines had left him with nothing. Even a chunk of the money he made working for Frank went to paying a daily fee for his mandated ankle monitor.

The soft drizzle turned to light rain. He dumped out the rest of the coffee and descended the steps to his cottage. The shed had windows on three sides and had been bolted to a concrete pad. They'd wired it for electricity, plumbed it for water, dry-walled, carpeted, painted, and lovingly decorated it. The bed was queen-sized and comfortable with a large white duvet. Cupboards and shelves had been installed. Along one wall stood a short counter with a hot plate, coffee maker, and a sink big enough to fit both hands under the tap. Beneath the counter was a mini fridge. There was a thin, knee-high space heater on the far side of the bed, and a small desk holding his laptop to the left of the door. Between the summer fog and the cool air off the ocean, air conditioning was a non-issue.

He had to use the bathroom in the house and he stored his few extra belongings in their spare closet, but Alina and Dan had thought of almost everything. And for the one thing they hadn't considered, he'd cut his own tongue out before he'd tell them how similar the dimensions were to his old jail cell, or about the uptick in what used to be mild, childhood claustrophobia, or how much he'd rather sleep on their couch. He hadn't even told his sister that he drove a motorcycle instead of a car to avoid the feeling of being closed in, worried that she might put two and two together about the cottage.

His claustrophobia had improved markedly over the past three months, and he could usually close the door now when he first came in. Tonight, though, the fullness in his chest had his nerves jittering more persistently at the closeness of the walls. He left the door standing open for the time being, set the mug in the sink, and slid one window half-open on the side away from the wind-blown rain. He checked his phone again but there were no delayed calls or texts he'd missed, and the area Fen had been heading into had almost no cell service. All he could do now was wait and hope that Fen didn't think he'd blown him off.

He pulled off his shirt and jeans, leaving his socks on to pad the bulky ankle monitor on his left leg, then took his small mirror off the wall. Alina had picked that out too, for its forest motif of black bears and pine trees. He propped the mirror against the bed pillows to get the angle right and looked again for bruising or redness on his chest and belly. He found none. He pushed at the sore margins with no increase in pain.

Planning an early night, he closed the door, leaving the window open. He reached across the bed to hang the mirror back on the wall. Pain receptors suddenly screamed from his collarbones to his hips. Dropping the mirror on his pillow, he looked down in alarm to see something pushing out against his chest and belly. His stomach bulged forward, like an expectant mother whose fetus had just somersaulted.

A second later, all was normal again. No movement. No pain. No deformity. Like it had never happened. Alex wiped sweat from the light stubble on his chin and upper lip. He stood stock-still, watching in the mirror, alert for any new sensations. Still nothing. He gently eased himself onto the bed, anticipation locking his muscles.

It was another twenty minutes before he risked standing and moving, tentatively reassured that the experience wouldn't repeat. He eased over to his desk gingerly and settled in for a long session of internet searches on abdominal distension, aftereffects of wrongful imprisonment, trauma from motorcycle accidents, psychosis, and hallucinations.

Chapter Three

ALEX WOKE TO a perfectly ordinary day. Climbing out of bed, he experienced nothing more than garden-variety soreness in his hip and shoulder, and his morning progressed without incident until David knocked a glass of milk into his lap at breakfast. If changing out of milk-soaked jeans was the worst today had in store for him, he'd take it. His anxiety ratcheted up a notch on the drive in to work when he turned onto Lower Lake Road, but the fields today were blissfully clear of kite-flying Russian grandfathers and violent men in tunics and tights.

The first of the concrete trucks showed up fifteen minutes after he got to work and soon enough the physical labor of leveling, floating, and finishing the slab took over his thoughts. As for the rest of the crew, Ida and Stan bantered nonstop, as usual, while Jaws worked in companionable silence most of the day. Their boss, Frank, chatted with the truck drivers and the concrete company field supervisor who dropped by, directed what little work needed direction, and spent much of the day on the phone to the batch plant, suppliers, and new customers.

As the workday wore on, Alex lost himself in the rhythms. The earthy smell of the wet "mud" of concrete. Sweeping long-handled tools across the surface, careful not to work the water up where it would weaken the surface of the slab. He'd give anything to be hiking through the forests of Montana instead, but at least this kind of work gave him a sense of completion. It was nice to look back and see what he'd accomplished over the day. And when they finished a job, he left behind an enduring testament to his labor and skill; a structure with a life expectancy likely to extend well beyond his own.

By the time Frank cut the arrow-straight expansion joints and Alex and the rest of the crew finished and broomed the hardening surface, the more questionable events of yesterday had taken on a distant and surreal quality. He chalked the weirdest of his memories up to a combination of stress over the unexpected text from Fen and working too close to the prison. Both things related to the worst few years of his life. It didn't have to mean he was losing his mind, even if they had triggered a momentary break with reality.

The job wrapped up early, and by half past three everyone was ready to start the weekend. It was too early to head over to the Whale's Tail for happy hour and too late to go home first, so he decided to run a couple of errands he'd been putting off. Twenty minutes later, he was headed for the checkout counter in the Dollar Tree with laundry soap in one hand and dish soap in the other when his phone rang. Thumbing the screen on, he saw the call was from Fen. He shoved the detergents onto a shelf of bagged candy and hurried outside to answer.

"Hey, Fen." He tried to keep his voice from rising into a register reserved for excitable schoolgirls.

"Hey, Alex." Fen's voice came to him choppy, the syllables carved out of his words. "Sorry I didn't call you back yesterday. I was— and out of the office in record time, and you know what reception's li— once you're on Highway 12."

"It was me that didn't call on time. Sorry about that. I ran into some delays on the way to work. I wasn't expecting to hear from you until you got back."

"I've had nothing but satellite cell to the office since yesterday, but I— to swing back up toward town this

morning for a lost hiker false alarm. A delayed text ca—
in from you on this phone or I never would've guessed I
had reception."

"Yeah, you're cutting out now. So, hey, before I lose you,
what was your news?"

"Let— get to a better spot."

Alex waited, praying the call wouldn't drop. He braced
himself for an anti-climactic newsflash. Maybe Fen had
run into a mutual friend of theirs. Maybe he'd run into
Anjali—hell, he might be calling to say she was getting
married or something. Okay, it probably wasn't news
about Alex's old girlfriend. He'd fallen in love with her
almost from her first day they'd met, and he'd thought
she loved him. She'd been about to officially move in with
him when he'd been arrested. And then she'd ghosted
him as soon as his trial had started. Fen had had the good
manners not to mention her since.

"How's this?" Fen asked, coming through clearly.

"Better."

"Good. Okay, well, you asked me to let you know if I
heard any news that might help you. You might like this
even more. I saw Julie Mosca in Bozeman the other day."

Alex felt a giddy, elevator-in-free-fall shock at the name.
Julie Mosca. The woman Steven Fabick had threatened
to hit outside the bar in Missoula that Wednesday night
three years ago when this whole nightmare started.

Alex, passing by, had called out reflexively. He and
Fabick traded words but nothing physical. Julie, Fabick's
girlfriend, left willingly with him. And Alex's life
had fallen apart only days later when Fabick regained
consciousness in the hospital after being attacked in his
home over the weekend. He'd told police Alex had beaten
him with a tire iron, leaving him for dead. Witnesses had
testified to the altercation on the street. Most damning,
Julie had backed up Fabick's court testimony—under

duress from Fabick, he assumed. And now Fen had seen her in Bozeman, not Missoula.

Fen continued, "They sent me down there to teach a one-day outdoor safety class at the college. I saw her walking into a convenience store while I was gassing up the truck. I can't swear Fabick isn't in Bozeman with her, but it was only about a month ago that Irene from the Missoula office told me she nearly collided with him when she was coming out of a store. And Mosca looked healthy, not like she did at your trial. I thought it might mean she'd gotten clean and moved away from him. I checked online and neither of them has a phone listed in either city, so nothing's for sure, but I thought you'd want to know."

Still reeling, Alex pressed the fingers of his free hand to his mouth. "Absolutely," he said, stroking the stubble on his chin and trying to dial down his enthusiasm. "This could be huge." His most-hoped-for scenario suddenly had the potential to become reality. If Julie *had* left Fabick, she might be willing to recant her false testimony. "I mean, I get it that she could be in Bozeman buying or selling drugs for Fabick or visiting a friend or whatever, but it sounds really positive. Thanks, Fen. Really. Thank you for this."

It was something Alex could never have learned on his own. Besides the fact that it would be undeniably creepy for Julie if the man she'd put in prison started keeping tabs on her, it would also likely have been a parole violation for him to try. On top of that, if he ever got to the point of petitioning for a new trial, the court needed to see him in the best possible light, not as some skeevy stalker. Fen had seemed more comfortable with his request once Alex made it clear that he just wanted Fen to keep an ear out. He'd gone to great lengths to assure him that he had no nefarious plans for Julie or Fabick and didn't want Fen crossing any lines either.

"I hope the information helps you." Fen paused. "I mean that, Alex. I really do."

For the first time in a very long time, there was no hint of lip service in Fen's tone. On top of that, they were talking about Fabick and Julie and the trial, and Fen wasn't cutting the conversation short, saying sorry, he had somewhere to be. Alex took a slow breath through his nose to ease the sudden tightness in his throat before he answered.

"Thanks, Fen."

"I'm sorry it isn't more. And, hey, I'm sorry I haven't been there for you like I should have been."

Alex shrugged reflexively. "Don't worry about it. Fabick came up with a pretty convincing story. Even I wouldn't have believed me." He smiled, though Fen couldn't see that any more than the shrug.

"No." Fen remained serious. "I shouldn't have doubted you. I knew you better than to believe what those two said in court, or at least I should have."

"It's okay." Alex leaned back against a section of warm stucco wall between the large store windows. He could hear in his voice the complexities of the three-year journey into hell he'd taken all but alone. That, and a profound gratitude to at last be believed by someone other than Alina. Still, he had to ask. "What changed?"

There was another pause, and Alex wondered for a moment if the call had finally dropped.

"I guess because you've been out for three months and you're still saying they set you up. You did your time. You could walk away from it all now, but you're still diving back into the shitstorm that ruined your life. I told myself before that I believed you, but that photo at the trial of you and her having coffee kept seeding doubt. That and Mosca testifying against you as well as Fabick. It kind of muddied the water just enough, you know?"

Alex pushed off the wall and kicked a pebble around on the sidewalk with the toe of his boot. Yeah, his best friend should have known him better than to believe he'd go after someone with a tire iron, even someone like Fabick. Same for Anjali and everyone else he knew. His sister had been the only one to never waver. Her and Dan, but Dan probably only because he would have risked divorce if he'd dared to doubt.

He stared up into the cloud-covered sky. For the first time in three years, this wasn't a phone text wave from Fen. This wasn't a humorous birthday card sent to the prison and signed with nothing but Fen's name. This wasn't Alex acting jolly and confident, trying to win Fen's trust back. This was the Mark Fenster who'd come to the hospital every day while doctors tried to prevent damage to Alex's toes after his snowmobile broke down in the backcountry. This was the Fenster that Alex took fishing the weekend before Fen signed his divorce papers, the two of them talking into the night around their campfire.

"I understand," he said. "I really do. Fabick tailored his accusation to fit with some pretty damning evidence. And it's not like my ace defense team did squat to disprove anything."

"They were complete shit." Fen chuckled.

Alex huffed a laugh. Fen hesitated again, and Alex suspected his friend was about to fall into a perpetual apology loop.

"Hey, Fen. It's okay." He emphasized his words to break through Fen's guilt and regret. "It's okay. I brought it on myself." He paced a short back and forth path on the sidewalk. "If I'd done what everyone else outside the bar did that night and minded my own business, none of this would have happened. And then me and my Savior complex when I see her in the store, right? Inviting her to coffee to fix her life. Whoever did take a tire iron to that little shit and for whatever reason, they were a lot more badass than me for Fabick not to give them up. And I dangled myself like a piñata in front of him. I made myself the perfect fall guy. He gets to pin a felony assault on me instead of ratting out whatever scary bastard did the deed, and he shafts me in the process for giving his girlfriend domestic abuse advice and telling her to leave him. Two birds, one stone."

"You're wrong, Alex. You didn't cause any of this. Not one damn bit of it. Those two are responsible. Not you."

He stopped pacing. "I am, though. I was an idiot from the get-go. If Julie *has* left him, she did it in her own time, for her own reasons, and on her own strength. I didn't need to share my sage advice on a topic I know shit all about. But there it is. They were co-dependent addicts. All I accomplished was telling her where and when to meet me so she could spill the beans to Fabick and he could stealth the perfect photo op to blackmail me, or whatever it was they had planned. And when he got beat to shit two days later, that photo came in handy in a whole new way."

He kicked the tiny pebble, sending it skittering down the sidewalk. The doors to the store pushed open and two people left. He turned in the other direction and lowered his voice.

"I've learned the hard way to stay out of other people's business, and I don't blame you or Anjali or the police or anyone else for not believing me. It's been nearly three years since my arrest and a lot of money, but it's okay. I'm back where I was in high school when my sister and I were on our own. And same as I was a few years after that, when I was fresh out of college. I'm here in California, I'm dead broke, and I'm working pickup jobs. And just like back then, I'm going to be all right. It's just going to take a little time."

"Yeah, well it sucks it happened to you, and it didn't help any that I was an asshole about it. And I just want you to know that I know that."

"All right, you owe me a steak dinner at The Anvil someday. Drinks and dessert too. That ought to cost you at least a paycheck."

"You're on," Fen said, and Alex heard the smile in his voice. "Okay. Don't take this the wrong way, but I really do have to go. Admin's going to look at my GPS any minute now and think I fell asleep in my truck."

Alex laughed. It felt good. "Trust me, I know how it feels to have Big Brother watching. You better get going."

"Talk at ya soon," Fen said, and hung up.

Alex thumbed his phone off and slipped it into its case. He had Fen back in his corner, and Julie Mosca had been seen in Bozeman—without Fabick. He felt more positive about the future than he had in a very long time.

THE WHALE'S TAIL sported the usual Friday night happy hour crowd when Alex showed up at half past four. The day had been warm and overcast with light, high-riding clouds for once, and opening the door to the windowless bar felt like walking into a cave. For the first few weeks, he'd found it hard to buy into the exuberance of the Frank Hill Concrete crew's Friday night happy hour— sans Frank Hill, who rarely joined them—when they so often worked Saturdays. Over the weeks, though, he'd come to enjoy the tradition. Still energized from his conversation with Fen, he felt especially in the mood for camaraderie.

Jaws and Stan were there ahead of him, sitting at their usual table in the middle of the room. A pitcher with a fresh, foamy head stood in the center along with a couple of spare glasses.

"Jaws just told me he's going to work crab season this year," Stan said, sloshing his beer glass toward the man as Alex took a chair facing the back of the room. "Can you believe that?"

"The old man and the sea, huh?" Alex said, pouring himself a beer. He'd never been much of a drinker but after the last couple of days, he was looking forward to a glass or four.

"Aw, you can both go to hell," Jaws said. "I can out-lift and out-work either of you."

Alex didn't doubt him. The man might be pushing mid-fifties, but the black hand wrapped around the beer glass was half again as big as Alex's, as were the forearm, biceps, and shoulder above it.

Stan laughed. Jaws cracked a smile too narrow to show his shark-like double row of teeth. The front row seemed to be mostly baby teeth, with a second row of adult teeth that had pushed everything in his mouth crooked rather than causing the baby teeth to fall out. Alex knew the man's real name was Mike Murphy, but Frank had dubbed him with the nickname and the moniker had stuck. Jaws didn't seem to mind. Alex guessed he'd heard worse.

"How about you?" Jaws asked Alex. "You ever thought about crabbing? Pays better and it's steady work in the winter. Season starts December 1st. I could probably get you on."

It might have tempted Alex if not for the tight spaces in the bunk rooms, galleys, fish holds, and engine compartments on fishing boats—pretty much everywhere except the deck. He shook his head, watching the bubbles lifting off from the bottom of his glass like little rockets. "Too cold for me out there." That was true too.

"And Montana winters weren't?" Stan said.

"It's a different kind of cold. And when it was bad, we could stay in the ranger station unless we were called out."

"And when you got called out?"

"It was fucking cold."

They laughed. He thought of the nineteen hours spent next to his broken down snowmobile.

"I'll bet even those bears froze their balls off," Jaws said.

"Bears have the sense to hibernate."

"I'd shit my pants if I came up on a grizzly," Stan said.

Alex had told them about a couple of encounters once they learned he'd been a forest ranger before prison. "They leave you alone as long as you keep your distance."

"Yeah, well, if you can handle bears and shit it's no wonder no one messed with you in the joint."

"I guess." He'd never said no one messed with him.

Alex hadn't even told them that he'd done time. He didn't much care for people finding out that he'd been incarcerated with some of the most violent criminals in the state. Frank must have told the crew before his first day at work, maybe as a heads-up for them not to piss him off or something.

Alex still wasn't sure how he'd ended up in the only supermax prison in all of California; a facility where forty percent of the inmates were serving life sentences. He suspected that someone in the justice system thought they were doing him a favor by sending him back to Northern California where he might have friends and family. Having been convicted of a violent federal crime, no place they sent him was going to be good, but nearly any prison would have been better. Only two things had gone in his favor there. He never did time in the "shu"—the Secure Housing Unit, solitary confinement for the worst of the worst—and his lawyer had eventually won a petition to have him moved from the general population to minimum security.

His time in minimum security hadn't been easy, but it had been better. Still, prison had marked him in subtle ways, and he resented the changes. He tried for the sake of Alina's family to curb the swearing that peppered his language these days, though working with a concrete crew wasn't helping that any. But a roughness to the timbre of his voice seemed as permanently stamped into his body now as his couple of new scars and two-plus years of memories of incarceration.

The front door of The Whale's Tail opened, shedding a bar of silvery light that crawled forward only a few feet before being overwhelmed by the murk. He looked over his shoulder to see Ida, the sole woman on their crew, making her way to the table. She was followed close behind by a concrete truck driver she'd been seeing, Jim-something. He was about to turn back when the door pushed wide again. Silhouetted in the light was an older man with a gray beard and a black, woolly hat. It was Stribog, holding the door for a tall, blonde woman entering with him.

Stribog and the woman walked through the center of the room toward Alex's table. The woman looked young, perhaps twenty, dressed in a fashionable, white cowl-necked sweater with bat-wing sleeves, and low-heeled boots under tight jeans. She walked like a model, telegraphing a self-confidence and power that managed to intimidate him from across the room.

Jarred from the good mood he'd been enjoying, he stared at the pair. The uncertainty and uneasiness of yesterday morning slammed back into place as abruptly as the times he'd woken from a pleasant dream to the harsh reality of his old cell. As they neared his table, Alex's stomach suddenly cramped. Pain shot through his solar plexus like he'd been punched hard from the inside.

They didn't stop or greet him as they walked past, but Stribog nodded once to him, and the woman met his gaze and held it. The two of them took seats at a small table against the back wall. The old man removed his hat, revealing a head of thick gray hair.

"Know them?" Jaws asked.

Alex hadn't shared the strange things he'd seen yesterday with any of his co-workers.

"No, not really," he said, trying to ignore the thumping inside that felt like a boxer throwing jabs up into his diaphragm. "I've seen him around is all." He pressed a hand over the soreness below his sternum.

"I'd say you've seen her around too," Stan said, commenting either on the look the woman had given him or the fact that Alex was still staring at the couple.

Stan, Jaws, Ida, and Jim all turned to look at her.

"No. Just him."

The cramping in his midsection finally eased up.

"Well, from her look when she passed, maybe she wouldn't mind running into you again sometime," Ida said, twisting back to Alex.

"I'm not into them that young." He took a long draft from his beer and topped it off.

"You're not getting out of it that easy," she said with a smile. "I thought all you ex-cons were crazy to hook up with a woman as soon as you got out. A hot, blue-eyed blonde? You ought to be fanning that flame, boy."

"You had a girl in Montana, didn't you?" Stan said.

"Woman," Ida corrected.

"Think you'll get back with her again?" Stan continued, unperturbed.

"No, that's done." Alex studied his beer.

Ida, reading his mood, reined Stan in by abruptly switching the conversation to whether the 49ers or the Packers would win the game this weekend.

Alex glanced to the back of the room where the pair chatted. Stribog had an umbrella drink in front of him, and the woman drank some clear liquor from a tumbler.

He tried to guess if they were speaking Russian, but they were too far away to hear over the classic rock coming through the overhead speakers and the general hum of conversation.

Alex felt certain he'd never seen either of them at this bar before. It could be coincidence, them coming here the same time as him, just like it could be coincidence his abdominal pain had started up again on seeing the old man. It could, but Alex felt sure it wasn't.

Stan, Ida, and Jim laughed at something Jaws had said, dragging Alex back from his thoughts. He rejoined the discussion, only occasionally glancing at Stribog and his companion. Their happy hour gathering maintained its momentum for another hour but, as usual, once drink prices went back to normal at six o'clock, things broke up quickly. First to leave was Jaws, then Stan, as they drifted off to find dinner somewhere where the food was cheaper.

"We're headed over to the Chinese buffet if you want to join us," Ida said to Alex, as she and Jim stood.

"Thanks, I'm going to hang out and finish my beer." It was his third, but he'd been nursing it.

He'd decided to stay at least until the woman finished her second drink. If she got up to use the restroom, it might give him a few minutes alone with the old man. If he didn't get a chance to talk to Stribog, maybe he could follow the pair when they left and find out where the old guy lived.

Or maybe not. Only a few hours ago, he'd assured Fen that he'd learned to stay out of other people's business. His ankle monitor pinching his leg made for a convincing reminder. On the other hand, the two of them showing up here had stirred up his pain and his suspicions, and for the sake of his sanity, he needed answers to both.

For all his machinations about a way to talk to Stribog alone, in the end, it was simple. The woman finished her drink, touched the old man on the arm saying something to him, and left. She glided to Alex's table.

"*On tebya zhdyot*," she said, then continued to the exit.

He and Alina occasionally bandied Russian words or phrases about, but it'd been a few years since a native speaker had conversed with him. He pieced it together as, "He's waiting for you."

Alex watched her over his shoulder, then glanced to the back of the room. A waitress momentarily blocked his view. Stribog paid her and she picked up both empty glasses. When she left, two full shot glasses stood on the table, one in front of Stribog and one in front of the other chair. The old man watched an animated conversation taking place at the bar. Alex studied Stribog's profile but found no clues in the one twinkling gray eye he could see, the weathered skin, or the slight smile beneath the heavy fronds of beard and mustache. He polished off his beer in three swallows, walked to the back of the room, and sat across from Stribog. Instead of being warm, the seat felt as cold as if the chair had just been brought in from outside.

"*Za tvoye zdorovye!*" Stribog said, wishing Alex health. He lifted his shot glass and tossed his drink back. Alex left his untouched.

"Why did that woman say you were ready to see me?"

"Why were you waiting to see me?"

"Who says I was?"

"We play question games now?"

"No. I don't want to play games."

Stribog clasped his fingers together and leaned forward. "Then what do you want, Alex Orlov?"

Vivid images from yesterday morning flashed across his memory. The costumed man in the field. The fight. Stribog flying a kite, from what had momentarily looked like a thousand shimmering strings, in the middle of a downpour. The kite vanishing. He didn't know which he wanted to validate more—that the things he'd seen and felt were real or that he'd had a prolonged dissociation with reality. What he wanted most was a third option, though he couldn't imagine what.

Alex bit his lip and tried to mold his feelings into words. "I want answers."

"I'm an old man. I must have answers to something." He grinned, showing his strong, white teeth.

Some intangible air of authority made the self-deprecation feel like an absurd hyperbole.

"That kite. Why were you flying a kite in the pouring rain?" He didn't feel like tackling the more important question of *how*.

"I told you, winds were good."

"Is that all?"

Stribog pursed his lips and shrugged. Alex waited but Stribog said nothing more.

He picked up his shot glass to stall, unsure how to continue. He muttered a more generalized toast in return, "*Budem zdorovy,*" and sipped his drink. It burned going down. He hadn't drunk hard alcohol since Montana. Numbing the judgment centers of the brain wasn't a smart move for someone on parole and now he was having a shot—tequila, he realized with surprise—on top of three beers.

"I was expecting vodka."

"It wouldn't go with my tequila sunrise. I like tequila sunrise."

Alex hesitated again, resisting the temptation to reach across to the hat on the table and toy with the curly black wool, so like his grandfather's hat that he'd played with as a child. He tried a new tack. "How long have you been in Crescent City?"

"A few days. And you?"

He never knew how to answer that question. Three months or three years; both were accurate. "A little while," he said. He wanted to ask about the woman, but it was tricky asking an older man about a younger woman. Wife? Mistress? Granddaughter?

"Did you come here from Russia?" he asked instead.

Stribog tilted his head in thought. "Yes," he said. Then "Yes," again, sounding more certain, but he didn't allow Alex time to question the hesitation. "And you are American."

Alex nodded. "My relatives emigrated here in the early nineteen hundreds, around the time of the Russian Revolution. They ended up in the Bay Area, a few hours south of here, in a big, tight-knit Russian neighborhood in Palo Alto. My parents met there, childhood sweethearts."

"And you speak Russian."

"I speak it okay. The community where my parents grew up was so traditional that my mom's parents never did learn English, and my dad's parents didn't speak it well. My mom's parents died before I was born, and my dad's mom died when I was little. When my folks moved to Eureka, my grandfather came with them. My parents spoke Russian at home sometimes, and we all had to use it with my grandfather."

The waitress stopped at the table to ask if they wanted anything else. Stribog shook his head.

"Where in Russia are you from?" Alex said when she'd moved on.

"This is what you want to ask me?"

They both knew the answer to that.

He met Stribog's gaze. "Tell me the truth. Was there another man in that field with you yesterday?"

"No. No man."

It sounded like part of an answer.

"And the kite..." He faltered, then pushed ahead. "It didn't... disappear for a minute?"

"You still have pain?"

"Yes."

"Anything else?"

Something large somersaulting below his chest last night, something pounding at his solar plexus half an hour ago. "No."

"Fever?"

"Not that I'm aware of."

Stribog pursed his lips again. "I knew a man once who said a *Tryasavitsa* had possessed him."

"I don't know what that is."

"One who can enter human bodies. Bring illness, fever, pain. Maybe make you feel like someone is inside you."

Alex toyed with his empty shot glass. "Yeah, I don't think I've been possessed."

"Me either. I think you fell off your motorcycle. Hit your head."

Right, Occam's razor. But Alex couldn't bring himself to believe the simplest explanation. He had wanted to, had worked to convince himself, but with Stribog showing up again he'd given up on denying that something more was going on. It all tied in somehow. He just didn't know how.

"So, this man who said he was possessed, what happened to him?"

"My daughter helped him. She knows about helping people. You working tomorrow?"

Alex shook his head.

"Come see my daughter. She'll have you *kak ogurchik*."

Something about a cucumber. Healed? Healthy?

"You know the Four Winds Motel?" he continued. Alex nodded. "Come tomorrow at one o'clock." He scribbled a room number on a napkin and pushed it to him.

Alex's grandfather had been a believer in folk remedies. He would have told him to go. Alex didn't believe in folk remedies, didn't believe he was possessed, didn't believe he had a head injury, and he very much wanted to believe he wasn't losing his mind. Maybe he'd get some straight answers from the woman tomorrow, and if not, at least he'd keep the old man on his radar. Meanwhile, if the pain got worse, he could always cough up the money and go to urgent care.

"And now," Stribog said, lifting his hat from the table and placing it on his head, "I must go." He stood.

Alex watched Stribog until he'd pushed out the front door and was gone. Crossing his arms on the table, he studied the empty chair as if he could piece together the puzzle of the man from the dust motes still swirling in his wake.

Chapter Four

ALEX PULLED INTO the lot of the Four Winds at five minutes till one and parked near the office. He scanned the faded red doors and peeling white paint along the single-story, L-shaped motel until he found 109. A grinning Stribog answered his knock and held the door wide for him to enter.

Gray afternoon light bled into the small room through the opening in the heavy, white, plastic curtains. Two beds with multicolored, polyester bedspreads jutted out from the left wall and a small television and old-style coffee maker with glass pot stood on a desk to the right. The dark, low pile carpet reeked from layers of fabric odor spray. No personal items were in sight, not even a suitcase—only the ushanka hat at the far end of the desk, its gold eagle pin shining dully in the gloom.

"Better today?" Stribog asked. He flipped the security latch across the doorframe and let the door swing shut on it, bracing it partially open.

"Not especially."

In truth, not at all. The pressure, shortness of breath, and odd heaving sensations in his chest had grown progressively worse last night and this morning. By ten, he'd given in and gone to an urgent care clinic, even though Frank offered no medical insurance beyond workers' comp. All he'd accomplished was receiving an unconvincing diagnosis of intercostal rib strain from his wreck, a prescription for extra strength ibuprofen, and a hefty bill for the office visit and rib x-rays.

"That's okay," Stribog said. "My daughter is good with these things, you'll see." He threaded the narrow path between the bed and desk then raised a fist and pounded on the wall. "Morana!" He gestured for Alex to take the desk chair. "Tea?"

"No, thanks," Alex said.

Stribog tore open the four black tea bags the motel provided and dumped the leaves in the basket, filled the little coffee maker with water, and hit start.

Having spent an hour in the urgent care waiting room this morning, there'd been plenty of time for thoughts of Stribog to cyclone around in Alex's head. He'd plugged the last name into the browser search bar on his phone, half afraid old Russian myths would pull up. Instead, he got pages of results on 9mm semiautomatic guns, the last thing an ex-con needed in his internet history. He'd quickly shut his phone off. He hoped he'd get some answers out of the old man today. Given their last two encounters, he wasn't holding his breath.

"I didn't get to ask you before, what brought you and your daughter to Crescent City?"

"An argument at home. Not with Morana. Someone else."

"You're moving here?"

"No. Not moving. This is temporary." Stribog tore the plastic cover from a Styrofoam cup on the coffee tray.

"Do you know someone here?"

Crescent City was a long way from Russia. In fact, it was a long way from anywhere. Eight thousand people lived in the city, the only incorporated town in the large, rural county of Del Norte. The county bordered the sparsely populated southwestern edge of Oregon and two other California counties that were just as rural.

"No. But I like the big trees." Stribog smiled.

Alex wondered, not for the first time, if the old man was quite right in the head.

The tiny coffee pot hissed like a steam engine and spat the final drops of tea in every direction except downward into the pot. Stribog filled his cup with tea almost as dark as coffee and swirling with stray tea leaves.

He lifted a packet of sugar and examined it. The blue hotel logo, four parallel wavy lines meant to represent wind, showed bright against the white paper. He flicked the packet with a finger. "Should be eight," he grumbled before tossing it back to the tray. He sat straddling the corner of the bed nearest the door, his cup clasped with both hands between his knees and an expectant light in his eyes.

Alex tried again to steer the conversation. "Yesterday, in the bar, when I asked if there'd been another man in the field with you—"

The door of the next unit thumped closed, and Morana swept in without knocking. Both she and Stribog wore the same clothes from last night, as far as he could tell. But where her thick blonde hair had been down at the bar, today she had it pulled into a loose bun, accentuating the long nape of her neck.

Cool air entered the room with her, and the chill raised gooseflesh on Alex's forearms. He stood as she crossed to him in three strides of her long legs, offering no word of greeting. The sleeves of the sweater flared like wings as she removed items from a small paper bag and reached forward to set them on the desk: a tin of mustard powder, a pint Mason jar containing a pink milky liquid, and a small, dark-brown glass bottle with the label turned away from him.

"Where do you hurt?" she asked without preamble, speaking in accented English.

"Here most of all"—he touched the four kite-shaped points—"but pretty much all in between. A doctor this morning said it's costochondritis from my fall, but that doesn't explain the things I've been feeling inside."

"Drink this." She uncapped the Mason jar and handed it to him. It smelled like sour cream.

"What is it?"

"Fermented milk. Some beet juice. Drink, then take off your shirt."

Alex looked to Stribog who smiled his congenial smile and nodded. If this was the price of getting information... He took a tentative sip, guessed goat kefir rather than cow's milk, and drank it in a few big swallows. Standing, he removed his jacket, pulled his T-shirt over his head, and sat again. Morana unscrewed the lid from the dark bottle. It lifted off to reveal a plastic applicator extending from the underside. The tip of the applicator dripped with dark orange iodine.

"Sit up straight."

He did, and she painted four lines linking the points he'd indicated, drawing a diamond on his chest across both skin and hair. The evaporating liquid pulled gooseflesh onto his forearms again and the chill in the room seemed to deepen. She then painted diagonal lines within the diamond, first one direction then the other, forming a net of orange stain.

Her speech had snapped like a brusque wind, but her silence as she worked felt easy and peaceful. It enveloped him and made him think of the stillness of a forest buried deep in winter white, and of snowy Montana nights alone in his cabin with cider warming on the wood-burning stove. He suppressed a shiver and attributed it to the imagery as much as to being shirtless.

She rested the knuckles of one hand below his left ribs, the iodine applicator still held between thumb and forefinger as she surveyed the pattern. The back of her hand felt cool, then icy. A moment later, the heater beneath the window kicked on with a noisy clatter, proof that the room was indeed chilly.

He'd had no cramping since arriving at the motel, but the deep ache had persisted all day. Until now, he realized. Focusing inward, he mentally probed his ribs and stomach, then his lower abdomen. Nothing. No ache. No shooting pains. And no pressure, though before, he'd felt pumped full as a party balloon.

The heater settled into a rattling hum. Morana recapped the iodine bottle and told him to get dressed again. He pulled his shirt and jacket back on, glad for the layers as well as the little gusts of heat wafting across the room.

"Sprinkle this in your boots." She handed him the tin of mustard powder.

This, at least, felt familiar. He'd done mustard packs on his chest as a child at his grandfather's urging, who had proclaimed them capable of healing everything from sore muscles to flu. It felt superfluous now that he seemed so much better, but he did as he was told.

"How do you feel?" Stribog asked as Alex pulled his boots back on and laced them.

He felt great but didn't want to sound like a revival tent attendee after a laying on of hands. "Uh, good. Better, I think. We'll see how it goes, I guess."

"You'll have no more trouble," Morana said.

"It's done, then?" Stribog asked in a tone that sounded uncharacteristically serious.

She nodded. "It's done. Tell him if you want. I still say no."

Alex, tugging his jeans down over his boots and the ankle bracelet none of them had mentioned, looked up at Stribog from his bent position. "What's done? Tell me what?"

"Inside you." He waved a finger toward Alex's chest. "He is controlled now."

"He? What, like that *Tryasavitsa* thing you mentioned last night?"

"No," he said, his seriousness deepening to severity. "My enemy is no mere *Tryasavitsa*. He is powerful. Too powerful. It is imperative he stay contained while I find what I have lost." The sternness lasted only a moment before his face relaxed into his normal, amiable expression. Alex wondered which aspect was the mask and which the real Stribog.

"Your enemy?"

"I fooled him into thinking I'd found what I came here looking for. He followed me, to take it from me. I pulled him into my trap, but one that could only keep him a short time. I needed a place that would hold him longer."

Stribog stood a hair straighter. He pointed to Alex's chest with a confidence and strength that made Alex wonder if he really had been able to punch a kite into him. Even his speech had changed subtly. Still accented, but his tone was more commanding, almost regal, and he wasn't dropping articles from his sentences anymore.

"You're saying you caught your enemy in your kite?" He glanced to Morana, expecting her to show either amusement or concern, but he saw neither. "And I just happened along and dumped my bike right then. And you, what, imprisoned this enemy of yours inside me?" Alex hadn't meant to smile when he said it; the old man had to be demented. Perhaps his daughter was playing along.

"You had taken that road every day that week, Mister Orlov. Mister Eagle." Stribog smiled. "Orel and Orlov, yes? Me, the strength to capture him. You, a place strong enough to hold him. Stronger now that Morana has quieted him and reinforced his confinement."

Alex turned to Morana. "You don't really expect me to believe that your father put some kind of spirit inside me, and that your kefir, mustard, and iodine sedated it, do you?"

"Of course those don't control him," she said, gesturing to the items on the desk. "They occupied you while I did what needed doing."

"You can't both be serious," he said, feeling mildly panicked. He'd wanted a third option for the things happening to him, but not this one. He faced Stribog. "I came here because I know what I saw, no matter how you spin it or how I try to convince myself otherwise. There was someone out there with you, and there's an explanation for where he came from and where he went. *That's* what I want to hear, not this nonsense about catching an enemy in a kite." He stood, feeling too vulnerable sitting. "Either that man walked into the field and I didn't notice him, or he'd been lying down in the grass when I got there, or something else that makes sense. But this? You can't feed me a line of bullshit like this and expect me to believe it."

"You also asked me last night if the kite had disappeared," Stribog said calmly. "Or do you forget that now? I think you worry about it still. I think you want to know why the pain pushes out from deep inside. Why it moves like a living thing."

The heater hummed and rattled into Alex's silence.

"Who are you really?" Alex looked from one to the other. "I mean, seriously, what are you two playing at?"

"I am playing at nothing. I am an old man looking for something I lost."

"And you came here from Russia, right? You lost this thing in Russia, but you and your daughter came all the way to Crescent City to look for it?"

Stribog shrugged. "I am from places with many names—Russia, that will do. It was not here that I lost my possession, but it is here I must look for it. My enemy wishes to find it first, and that he must not do. And Morana"—he shrugged—"she's *like* a daughter to me. But for the rest…a man in the field with me, the kite seeming to vanish? Yes, inasmuch as you can understand them, these things are so."

"I need to leave," Alex said, but made no move toward the door. "So, what now? For the sake of argument, let's say I believed you, which I don't. What do you think is going to happen from here?"

"Come back every two days," Morana said brusquely, "three at most. No longer. Sooner if you feel anything unpleasant. *Anything*," she emphasized.

"We are here if you need us," Stribog said. "Other than letting Morana help you, there's nothing you need do. Only wait." He stood and ushered Alex to the door with one hand pushing lightly on his back and one hand extended forward. Alex went willingly, anxious to be outside, in the open, away from the crazy.

"I am hopeful this will not take long," Stribog said as he gently impelled Alex past the door and out onto the sidewalk. "I find the thing I am looking for and then we release my enemy. We go home, you go home. All is well."

He gave Alex a cheery smile and a wave, and he shut the door.

Chapter Five

ALEX LEFT THE motel, his nerves jittery from the odd encounter and his questions still unanswered. The urgent care doctor had told him his pain should steadily improve and that ibuprofen would keep him comfortable in the meantime. Stribog and Morana told him he had a creature inside him, and he'd have no trouble for two or three days but that his pain would come back if he went longer without her help. By Tuesday morning he would know which, if either of them, was right. Till then, the best thing for his sanity was to try and move on and forget the whole experience.

On Sunday, the forecast called for nothing worse than partly cloudy weather, and Alex took a long drive through the redwoods north of Crescent City to clear his head and calm his nerves. Monday, he remained pain free. Frank started them on the barn pour and said he'd scheduled some new footings and foundations for a contractor trying to get a late project finished before winter ramped up. It would mean a couple of weeks of full-time work for all of them, rain notwithstanding.

On his lunch break, Alex dialed the office of Frazier, Tobares, and Betts. He'd tried to reach his lawyer on Friday after talking to Fen, but was told Lois Tobares had left early for the weekend. Expecting today to leave a message with her receptionist, he was pleasantly surprised to be put through. He updated her about Julie Mosca as succinctly as possible, but she didn't sound as excited at his news as he'd felt.

"Remember, your right to appeal has expired," she said. "There's a motion for appropriate relief created by a North Carolina statute for correcting errors made during a criminal trial. We could file a motion for that if we get new evidence, but Ms Mosca recanting her testimony on its own would carry very little weight. Witnesses do it all the time, and for all sorts of reasons. Juries are still free to consider all the previous evidence and come to their own conclusions."

"Wouldn't it depend on what she said?"

"Again, not necessarily. What we need is hard evidence, new and irrefutable evidence that we can present. I'm not saying I won't follow up on this. I will. I'll check into what you've told me and see if she's moved. If it appears that she's not still living with Steven Fabick, I'll make every effort to contact her. I'm just saying don't get your hopes up."

Too late for that.

He thanked her and hung up. And he damn well would hold on to any hope that came his way. Proof of his innocence wasn't going to fall into his lap. At least this was a starting place, and the San Francisco lawyer Alina had found for him while in prison had shown more moxie than his Montana lawyer ever had. She'd been the one to get him transferred to minimum security and the one who'd gotten his parole hearing moved up half a year by citing good behavior and suggesting a GPS ankle monitor for the first six months of his parole. Hell yes, he would be hopeful.

On Tuesday, Alex checked the time with increasing frequency throughout the workday. One o'clock came and went, then two o'clock. Seventy-two hours plus since Morana's voodoo at the Four Winds, and no sign of the odd cramps returning. At three o'clock, he sang along with the music in his earbuds as they finished for the day and started their cleanup. At four, he left work, exhilarated by the growing certainty that the weirdness of the previous week was behind him.

The journey from jobsite to home was only a fifteen-minute drive but once out on the rural roads he shifted, opened the throttle, and leaned into the rush of wind. His windscreen, gloves, and leathers dulled the effect, but speed still had the power to electrify his nerves and sharpen his senses.

There'd been another reason, besides claustrophobia, why he'd chosen a motorcycle over a car after prison. For more than two years, what he ate, when he showered, when the lights went off, and how he comported himself every minute of every day around every person—guards and prisoners alike—had been dictated by others. To have nothing now between himself and the unforgiving road provided him with a measure of control over his life. It gave his decisions meaning. The higher the speed, the higher the risk, the more his actions and reactions mattered. It had seemed a small but important victory in reclaiming control of his life. When he'd first driven down the coast, days after his release, he'd felt like he was flying. Today felt much the same.

He arrived at the house a good half hour before sunset. "David. Jake," he called out as he entered the kitchen. "Anybody want to go for a walk?"

Bonkers arrived at a run, cueing in on the all-important word and beating the boys by a margin of at least ten seconds. David appeared next with Jake a few steps behind, toy car still clutched in one hand. Alina was the last to the kitchen, her headset unplugged and worn at ease around her neck.

"You look happy," she said. "Something fun happen?"

"Nothing special. It was just a good day."

"Well, if you want to take the boys for a walk, your timing is great. Jake had speech therapy this afternoon, then I had errands to run before I picked David up from school. Now I'm late finishing work and the boys have been rampaging ever since we got home. I'd give Dan's right arm for some uninterrupted time between now and dinner."

"All right, boys, you heard your mom. Hurry and get your boots on so we can be back before dark." He grabbed a small paper bag from under the sink and scratched out a short list on a Post-it note for a woodland game.

About a quarter mile west of Alina and Dan's home sat the tiny county airport, a fact that had made their old farmhouse more reasonably priced—even though the airport saw only one commercial flight daily and the occasional private plane. To the north was the wild and brambly boundary of the ominously named Dead Lake, and east of the house, at the end of their short road, a long but narrow section of tall, widely spaced, young redwood trees ran between them and the northeast side of town. Alina didn't allow the boys to explore up toward the lake, but the woods were fair game as long as she, Dan, or Alex were with them.

Five minutes later, Alex, the boys, and Bonkers were following well-packed trails through the trees.

"Watch out, David. That's poison oak."

Alex steered Bonkers by his leash to the middle of the trail and took Jake by the hand. David obediently drifted into line behind his younger brother. Alex, David, and Alina weren't allergic to poison oak, but Dan and Jake were. Bonkers could collect about a pint of toxic oil on his coat in a single walk, and David could be nearly as oblivious as the dog about blundering into it.

"Okay. You both know what poison oak looks like, right?" He pointed to the shiny plant they'd just skirted. Both boys nodded.

"Jake wasn't paying attention," David offered, though he hadn't been either.

"That's okay. You have your list?"

David waved it like a flag.

"All right, the scavenger hunt has begun. When you've collected at least five of the items in your paper bag or it starts getting dark, we'll head back and make a forest picture for your mom."

The boys took off at a run.

"Remember, no more than three steps off the trail to get anything."

"Okay," David yelled as he ran.

Games and activities were the domain of seasonal rangers and camp hosts more than law enforcement rangers, but one of Alex's first jobs out of college had been working as a seasonal park guide in Shasta County. The scavenger hunt had been popular with grade school kids.

Within two minutes, David was hollering that he had a fern leaf in their bag. Jake, at his brother's shoulder, yelled the same.

"Hey. This way," Alex snapped, as both boys struck out again, headed away from the trail. They turned like marionette puppets in that quick, jerky way of children, and ran on down the trail. Bonkers barked at their excitement. Alex walked a few yards behind, close enough to see what they were getting into and far enough away to let them find things by themselves.

"Pine needles!"

"Good. Help your brother count out ten of them."

He waited on the trail while David counted and Jake dropped them one by one into their paper bag. Finished, the boys continued on and Alex started moving again, but a stitch in his side brought him up short on his second step. He splinted the pain with his free hand. "Dammit.

No," he muttered, as if he could mentally will the side stitch away. "No, no, no."

The boys were about twenty-five feet ahead and straying off the path again. He took a couple of deep breaths, focused on relaxing his muscles, and told himself it was a normal catch in his ribs. The spasm eased, but before he could move, a sensation like a bowling ball spinning inside his stomach doubled him over. He pressed his hand over the pain and felt the upper part of his belly push out and retract. "Oh, shit."

Sweat chilled his forehead and palms. He looked up and didn't see the boys.

"Clover," David said from somewhere behind a tree.

"Cohver," Jake echoed.

"Back thi—" Alex began, calling the boys back to him, but a new spasm took him down to one knee and turned his words into a sheep's bleat. The grotesque heaving and distension under his hand stripped away the last of his denials. The improbable had been eliminated and all he had left was the impossible, that Stribog's story was true. He pictured a mini version of the tunic-clad man from the field grabbing his ribs from the inside and shaking them, fingers stabbing through muscle and connective tissue.

Bonkers wandered off the trail, dragging the leash that Alex had dropped. He zigzagged away, sniffing happily. Alex scanned the area where he'd last heard David and Jake, noting that the spaces between the trunks were growing murky; they were losing light fast. Something moved ahead and to his left. He pushed to his feet and grabbed Bonkers' leash with a grunt.

With a hand still pressed hard against his upper abdomen, he took two jogging steps in the direction of the shadow he'd seen. With a start, he realized that the figure was one silhouette, not two, and too tall to be either of the boys. It traveled at an oblique angle to him, giving him no more than glimpses through the trees. The gloom, the pain, or the combined strangeness of his week tunneled Alex's focus to a single, all-consuming fear: that the figure would find the boys before he did. He pushed through the cramps and jogged toward the individual.

"I got five, but Jake only got four," David said from somewhere behind him. Alex spun, startled to see David to the right of the path.

"Where's Jake?" he panted.

Jake emerged from behind a tree only a few feet from his brother. Breathless, Alex waved both the boys to him and scanned again where he'd seen the silhouette. He saw only trees and gloom. No movement. No adult-sized figure.

Slipping Bonkers' leash grip up to his wrist, he grabbed each of the boys by a hand. Trying not to use them for balance, he hurried back to the house.

Alex opened the kitchen door, shoved the boys and the dog inside, and called to Alina that he'd decided to go out for dinner. Ten minutes later, he pounded on the door of room 109 at the Four Winds Motel. There was no answer. He pushed through the Scotch broom bushes beneath the window and cupped his hands against the glass. Peering through the wavy slit where the curtains met imperfectly, he could see the room was empty. Room 110 proved the same.

David and Jake were at home and safe, which was good. Not so good, the spasms and pressure hadn't let up. Given the time of day, Stribog and Morana might be at dinner.

He drove along the streets nearest the motel, looking unsuccessfully for the silver rental car in restaurant parking lots. Back at the Four Winds, Stribog and Morana still hadn't returned, and a light rain changed his mind about waiting outside for them. There was a diner across the street from the motel but if he became incapacitated or passed out there alone, he might end up in a hospital—something he couldn't afford and that wasn't likely to help him anyway. Giving up, he drove home slowly along quiet suburban streets, pulling over occasionally to let the worst of the cramps subside.

Back home, he looked up the number for the Four Winds. A desk clerk with a strong cigarette rasp answered. He asked her to try Stribog's room first then Morana's, but there was no answer from either.

To pass the time, he turned on his laptop and plugged in a search for Stribog again, keeping the focus tighter by searching "Russian names." This time, both Stribog and Morana turned up easily across multiple sites and with a variety of spellings. They weren't folktale sites, though. Both appeared in list after list of pre-Christian Slavic deities. Major gods were highest on the lists, with different ones listed for different regions or eras, he supposed: Dazhbog and Chernobog, Svarog, Rod/Deivos, Perun, Triglav, and more. But there, in each list, were variations of Stribog, God of the Winds, and Morana, Goddess of Winter and Death.

Perhaps prison had taught him too well to suppress emotion, or perhaps he simply had no physical or emotional bandwidth left after the past week of surprises. Maybe some part of him expected what he found. In any case, the implication that he'd been caught up in the affairs of ancient Slavic gods left him feeling nothing but numb.

Between waves of pain, he searched next for "evil spirits Russian" then "Russian folk medicine," while continuing to call the Four Winds Motel at fifteen-minute intervals. Finally, he tried "Russian exorcism."

The only thing close to his needs was an old-fashioned folk ritual that involved inhaling smoke from burning foul-smelling garbage until the victim vomited out the evil that possessed them. The cramps and impacts against his abdomen and chest were still coming and going, not worse, but not better either. The motel phone rang without answer. It seemed he had nothing to lose by trying the ritual except whatever remained of his lunch.

Alina and Dan kept a compost pile next to the garden. He brought a food-storage bowl from his kitchen, rolled up the sleeve of his flannel-lined work shirt, and shoved his arm in up to the elbow near the top of the pile, where the vegetables and the neighbor's goat shit were freshest and just beginning to rot. The earthy smells of the vegetable matter, the sharpness of the mold, and the pungent urine mixed with the manure certainly fit the bill for "foul-smelling garbage." Worse, though, were the textures in the semi-liquid slime from chunks of rotting zucchini, tomato, and other still-recognizable vegetables, the squish of moldy bread, and the firm deer-like pellets of shit.

After hosing the brown mucus stains off his forearm and hand, he grabbed a bundle of newspaper out of the recycling bin in the garage. For good measure, he scooped up a fresh pile of Bonkers' leavings with the pooper-scooper propped against the deck. He cleared a small spot under the eaves on the far side of his cottage—out of the rain and away from the main house windows—wadded the newspaper, added the refuse, and lit the paper on fire. The paper burned and the compost smoked with a reek that would make a skunk puke.

He leaned into the smoke and inhaled. Between the smell, the slime, the stomach cramps, and his willingness to vomit, the ritual worked quickly.

The paper burned up and the rest of the fire smothered in the rain. He threw the remains of the pile back on the compost heap, rinsed his mouth and face from the hose, and waited. He held little hope the "cure" would work. As expected, his spasms and occasional painful distension continued unchanged.

He called the Four Winds again, his desperation increasing. Holding the phone to his ear, a residual smell of compost wafted from his hand and nauseated him anew. The desk clerk gave dramatically exasperated sighs and groans when she realized it was him. There was still no answer in either room. Alex downed three of the prescription-strength ibuprofen pills from the clinic and debated his options.

The rain had stopped for the moment, but he wasn't sure he felt safe driving himself back to the motel in case his symptoms went from bad to worse. Glancing at the house, he thought of asking Dan for a ride, but there was no way in hell he would risk Alina finding out about any of this. By this time of evening, Stan would be about halfway into the twelve-pack he routinely picked up on the way home from work and Alex didn't have a number for Ida. He didn't know a lot about Jaws' home life except that he was divorced and rented a trailer at the edge of town, but the big man had mentioned once that he didn't usually go to sleep until one or two in the morning.

Alex tried his number and Jaws answered on the third ring. A TV played in the background.

"Hey, it's Alex."

"What's up?"

"You remember the old man and the blonde woman at the Whale's Tail the other night?"

"Yeah."

Alex briefly summarized his pain since his accident and condensed the weird encounter at the motel to Morana treating him with herbal remedies.

"I'm pretty bad again now. I've been calling and they're out. I want to go over there and wait for them, but I'm not sure I should try driving. There's a diner across the street that serves beer. If you feel up to driving me over, I'll spring for drinks. Dinner too, if you haven't eaten yet."

"Sure. I'll take you over there. And it's your decision, man, but if you're feeling that bad you think maybe you should see a doctor instead?"

"I tried that already. The guy's daughter helped more."

Nothing in town was farther than a few minutes from anything else. Alex grabbed his canvas Carhart jacket and waited at the end of the driveway. Jaws showed up in his rumbling, black, Trans Am muscle car, complete with gold firebird across the hood. Holding one arm tight across his belly, Alex hurried into the passenger seat and hoped Alina hadn't heard the car idling at the shoulder of their dirt road, or seen him get in, hunched over in pain.

They went to the motel first, but Stribog and Morana were still out. The diner had large windows along one wall and they took a booth with a clear view of the motel across the street. Alex tried to get some dinner down but gave up after a bite of hamburger and a few greasy fries. Jaws went to work on his burger, fries, coleslaw, and beer.

"Have you done any crabbing before?" Alex asked, feeling obligated to fill the silence while Jaws ate.

Jaws nodded, swallowed. "I did a season when I first got here, a couple of years ago."

"Must get some rough seas in the winter."

He shrugged his heavy shoulders. "I saw worse in the Navy. Crab boats here stay close to land. They come in if a big enough storm's brewing."

"You were in the Navy?"

"Thirty-two years. Lieutenant, junior grade, when I retired at fifty."

Alex did the math. "Signed up at eighteen?"

"Seventeen and a half," Jaws said, twirling his beer

glass. "I fudged my age on the paperwork and my enlister pretended not to catch it on my ID."

Alex didn't ask what had driven him to enlist at such a young age. "Thirty-year pension and a full-time job, man, you must be making bank. If I'd made it to my Forest Service pension, I don't think I'd be finishing concrete or working on crab boats. You should kick back, enjoy it. Open a bait shop on a warm beach and put your feet up."

Jaws gave a "whatever" twitch of his lips. "My first pension check, I got myself this." He indicated the heavy dive watch on his wrist with more dials than Alex could identify. "Since then, my pension's gone to my kids. And to my folks back in Kentucky." The way he said it implied every penny of it went to them.

"How many kids do you have?" And what else didn't Alex know about him?

"Four. My oldest was eleven, my youngest three, when I came home from a nine-month deployment to divorce papers on the kitchen table. The youngest one hardly knew me, the oldest one didn't much care to, and my wife already had a new dad lined up for them. I did another eighteen years in the Navy. Home ports kept changing so I didn't see them much." He took a swig of beer, swishing and swallowing to rinse between his sets of teeth before finishing the french fries. "They're all healthy, though. Doing good from what I hear. The money doesn't make up for the years I wasn't there, but I figure it helps them out."

It was a pragmatic and factual recitation, not unlike the manner in which Alex could summarize the years of watching both his parents die slow and painful deaths while he and his sister juggled caring for them with trying to get through high school.

"So what year's your Trans Am?" he asked, steering away from the personal line of conversation.

"It's a '79. Got it when I was about twenty off another sailor who'd bought it new."

"How do you keep it so cherry in this salt air?"

"I stored it covered in Illinois thinking I'd be out in a couple of years. Then I re-upped again, and then I stayed on till retirement. I only had it on base a few times, when I was mainland. Didn't really use it till I got out."

Alex told him about the classic truck he'd restored in high school, and they compared stories of rust care and scratch removal until a stomach pang brought Alex's attention back to the present. He stared out the window, hoping to see Stribog's car pulling into the motel.

Jaws finished his meal and swished-drank the rest of his beer. He'd picked up a couple of toothpicks from the holder at the counter on the way in, and his large, callused hands tore the tiny plastic wrapper on one now. He set to work, expertly guiding the toothpick between the rows of crooked teeth.

"Navy dentists did X-rays and told me the only thing they could do was pull them all and give me dentures."

Alex hadn't meant to stare. He'd seen the ritual before—at lunch breaks and at the Whale's Tail—but he'd always assumed Jaws hadn't been able to afford dental care.

"I… no… sorry, I didn't…"

"I didn't want dentures at seventeen, especially the ones back then that flapped when you talked. I still don't want 'em. They told me I'd never be able to keep my teeth clean enough to avoid losing them, but they were wrong." He smiled a rare, toothy smile, his sixty-plus white teeth gleaming against his black skin.

"Good for you." Alex meant it, as much for Jaws making his own choice as for succeeding at it. And for him having endured whatever it had entailed along the way.

He looked out the window again. Still no lights in the windows of 109 or 110. Still no car parked in front of the rooms. A new cramp roiled through his bowels.

"Hey," he said, when it passed, "are you okay with Jaws or do you prefer to be called Mike?" He'd thought to ask on occasion but had never found a natural way to broach the subject. He'd learned more about his co-worker in the last hour than he had in the last few months, and it seemed a good time to ask.

"I prefer Mike."

"You know Frank would quit with the nickname in a heartbeat if you asked."

"I'd ask if it mattered."

"Right."

Alex sipped at his water and ordered another beer for Mike. He changed the subject but found he had increasing trouble focusing on the conversation. His cramps, anxiety, and lack of appetite, coupled with looking out the window every few seconds, probably lit a blinking neon sign over his head that flashed "drug addict waiting for a fix." If Mike suspected it as the reason for the evening's outing, he said nothing and asked no questions about how Alex had met the two Russians.

"You doing okay?"

Alex nearly jumped and realized he must have been staring out the window again, deep in thought. "Yeah, I'm all right. Why? You need to take off?"

"I'm good. You're just looking kinda pale."

"It's the stomach cramps. They've been getting a little worse."

That could've won understatement of the year. The rattling and rolling had eased up a few minutes earlier and Alex thought maybe he was through the worst of it. He wasn't. A tearing had followed, like whatever was caged in him had given up on bashing its way out and had instead decided to claw a hole through him. He looked out the window again at the light Tuesday night traffic and the nearly empty motel parking lot, then back to Mike.

"Hey, I'm sure you've got better things to do than wait here with me. I thought they'd be back long before this. If you're ready to get home, I can always stay here and call a cab if they don't show up."

"I said I was good," Mike said impassively.

Alex picked up a cold french fry, dipped it in some ketchup, and set it down again. "I'll be right back." Mike shot him a concerned look. "Don't worry. I just need to take a piss."

He didn't want to get up but going to the head was a thing that could only be put off so long. He eased to the edge of the bench seat with one hand on the table and one on the seat back. A sudden, new tearing sensation doubled him over, forehead to knees. He opened his eyes a few seconds later and saw Mike Murphy's size thirteen boots toe to toe with him.

"I think I'd better take you to the hospital." The big man wrapped one hand around Alex's upper arm.

"I can't afford an ER visit. They aren't going to do me any good there anyway."

Mike sighed. "Tell me what to do."

The torn tissues burned like a line of fire just above his navel. Into the center of the pain came another hard thrust, like a mini battering ram. Alex let out a loud grunt and wrapped his forearm tighter across his belly. The thrust came again, harder.

Mike held a glass of water near his mouth, seeming unsure what else to do. "You're sweating buckets."

The waitress and a handful of late-evening customers were staring.

The thrust came a third time, followed by the feel of muscle giving way and skin stretching. Alex cried out.

Looking down in horror, something jutted beneath his T-shirt. He pulled his shirt up a few inches. A protrusion about an inch long and half an inch wide stuck out from the flat plane between the bottom of his breastbone and his navel. His skin stretched tight over a shape that was unmistakably an adult-sized fingertip, right down to the faint outline of the short nail, the fingernail bed, and the first knuckle. The sight of it left him reeling, confused, queasy.

"Yeah," he grunted. "Get me to a hospital."

Chapter Six

ALEX LET HIS T-shirt drop back over the ghastly deformity. During college, he'd gone shin to shin with an opponent in a soccer game and dislocated his kneecap. He'd looked down to see unfamiliar bony planes while the disc of bone that should have covered them jutted out from the side of his knee like a flag from a flagpole. He felt much the same now. Shock and tunnel vision battled with his ability to process the wrongness he saw.

"Hernia," Alex choked out the lie. "I got it a few years ago trying to wrestle a dead elk into the truck bed after my winch broke. Must've come back worse." The elk and broken winch were real, the hernia wasn't. He hoped Mike bought the story. He'd always been a terrible liar and he wasn't going to come up with anything better on the spot.

Mike threw a few bills on the table, put his arm around Alex's back, and helped him shuffle out the door. He unlocked the passenger side of his Trans Am and eased Alex into the seat. The car started with a growl. The man said nothing, but he gripped the steering wheel with both hands while they waited at the edge of the diner's driveway for traffic to go by. He gave a low rumble, not unlike his car, when the last car slowed in front of them to turn left, then gunned the accelerator before the other car was completely out of their way.

"Wait!" Alex shouted. "That's them." Mike hit the brakes hard enough that Alex braced his hands on the dash.

Mike looked at him. "I don't think an herbalist is going to help with a hernia like that. Your call, though."

Alex wondered if he heard a slight emphasis on the word "hernia."

"If she says she can't help me, they can always take me to the hospital."

The Trans Am shot across the street into a narrow gap between traffic. They bounced in the deep driveway entrance to the motel and Alex grunted.

"Sorry," Mike said.

Stribog and Morana were out of their car and walking to their rooms. They turned as the Trans Am bounced into the lot and parked next to their rental car. Alex struggled to open his door. Mike came around to the passenger side and helped him out.

"When did it start?" Morana said in her brusque fashion.

"About three hours ago."

"And you came to see me when?"

"Two or three hours ago. Right after it started."

"Not before? I told you two days. No more than three."

"We weren't here yesterday or today," Stribog said to her mildly. Morana rolled her eyes as if Alex's disregard for her instructions somehow overrode that. "We were delayed," he explained to Alex. "We've been away since we saw you Saturday."

He reached to take Alex from Mike, gripping one arm in a strong hold, but stopped and closely examined the big man's face. Mike stared back pointedly when impolite crossed the line into rude. Stribog draped Alex's arm across his shoulders and helped him up onto the sidewalk.

"It's bad," Alex said. He nodded down at his T-shirt tenting out an inch or more under his open jacket.

"You gonna be all right?" Mike asked, still on the other side of him.

"Yeah. I'm going to be okay now. Thanks, man. Really, thank you. I owe you."

"I'll tell Frank you won't be in tomorrow."

"You never know," he panted. "I might surprise you." He tried for a smile but failed. He lifted a hand in farewell as Stribog opened the motel room door.

Morana flipped on a light while Stribog lowered Alex onto the bed, taking most of his weight easily. If Stribog and Morana really were gods, it would explain Stribog's strength and spryness, but the thought of being in a seedy motel room with two Slavic deities refused to feel anything but ludicrous.

"It hurt all evening. This happened about fifteen minutes ago." He lifted his T-shirt and Morana sat on the edge of the bed for a closer look. Alex stared at the protrusion with her, getting a better look than he had in the diner. At least two inches were sticking out now. The first knuckle showed clearly. The entire fingertip jutted like a mast pole on the deck of his belly just above his navel.

"You shouldn't have waited so long," Morana said. She pressed her cold hands to his lower ribs and upper abdomen.

"We weren't here anyway," Stribog said to Alex in a stage whisper, giving him a wink. "It's good we got back when we did."

"Take it out," Alex said to Morana. "Whatever this thing is, I want it out."

"Not yet," Stribog answered for her. "To let him out now would be dangerous for us all."

Alex's fear-fueled anger erupted. "Look, I don't want—"

"Shush," Morana snapped, pushing at his shoulders. "I'll make him quiet again."

Alex bit back his retort to Stribog.

The sweat of fear and injury that had pearled on his forehead and neck dried when the cold seeped from her hands into his bare skin. Gooseflesh rose on his forearms. The chill deepened, seeming more intense than the last time she'd touched him. The bitter cold sank inward, into his bones, and deeper, into his organs. He exhaled and watched to see if his breath would vaporize into mist. It didn't.

And still Morana held her hands against his abdomen. Calm crept through him. Not a comforting calm, as before, with the memories of his Montana cabin. A helpless calm, in the mugging way anesthesia had taken him when he'd had surgery on his knee after a second kneecap dislocation in college. In the seductive way that cold and frostbite had nearly claimed him when he'd gone out in a storm to search for lost cross-country skiers and his snowmobile had broken down. His mind drifted into the cold with his body. It floated on an icy tide, his thoughts slowing, until at last they slipped beyond the cold, beyond the room.

Morana's hands lifted, startling him back to full awareness. She glanced at Stribog and nodded once.

Alex lifted his head cautiously and examined his exposed belly. The protrusion remained, pointing angrily at the ceiling.

"It's still there." His words were laced with panic.

"Yes," Morana answered. "He came very close to escaping."

"Can't you fix it?"

She looked offended. "I did."

"No. This." He pointed at the foreign finger covered in his own flesh.

"You think I am village healer? I pit my power against his and I win. He sleeps." She gave a single amused snort, the strength of her accent and dialect decreasing again with her anger. "And you too. I didn't make you sleep, and you did anyway."

Alex moved tentatively to sit up, afraid to contract his stomach muscles. He pushed himself up with his arms.

His chest and abdomen ached as if he'd spent the whole evening vomiting instead of just once, but the acute tearing pain of being clawed open from the inside had vanished. He slid his legs off the bed.

Thinking of the anatomy of countless animals he'd seen gutted, he looked down at the finger. "This thing is just under the skin. If it punched through muscle and connective tissue, how did the pain go away?"

Stribog answered for her, his voice calm but his accent strong at first too, perhaps reflexively matching Morana's. "Could man like one you saw in field with me fit into my kite?"

"No," Alex said emphatically, feeling vindicated for all his earlier disbelief.

"Could he fit there?" Stribog drew a circle in the air indicating Alex's chest and belly.

"No," Alex said with the same certainty.

"No," Stribog said. "And yet he does because he is not a man. He is no more tied to the form you saw than I am to this one, or Morana to hers. It hurt when I forced him in, yes?"

"Yes," he said, uncertain now where this was going.

"And it would hurt very much more than this"—he waved at Alex's midsection—"if he were to force his way out on his own. What happened here"—he pointed to the finger—"*represents* him trying to get out. It hurt, yes, but in the same way his form is not real, neither is this. When I remove him, he will be sleeping, this will go away, and all will be well. If rules of flesh applied to him, how could I put him there? How could I get him out again without harm to you?"

A dark doubt about how this all might end for him occurred to Alex suddenly, and fear flared his anger again.

"Look, I never consented to any of this." His voice echoed overly loud in the small room. "Your fights have nothing to do with me. I don't want to be a pawn in your games. Take this thing out and put it, I don't know"—he looked around the room—"in your fridge or something. Throw it in there and strap the door shut. I mean, you're telling me it was in a kite, for god's sake." He saw the irony in his choice of expression too late.

"You're right, you didn't ask for this," Stribog said soothingly. "But no, we can't put him there"—he waved vaguely toward the mini fridge—"or anywhere else. Even my kite was a risk for those few minutes."

"But why me? Why am I involved in any of this?" He thought of his luck these last few years, or lack of it. Could this much shit in his life really boil down to nothing more than wrong place, wrong time?

"I told you before. There are reasons you were chosen for this. Orel and Orlov. Strong, like eagles. I tell you also, I will involve you no longer than I absolutely must." Stribog took off his suit jacket and tossed it onto the bed. "But you are involved, Alex Orlov, whether you wish it or not." Removing his hat, Stribog rubbed at the eagle pin with a thumb then placed the hat on top of the jacket. "Tomorrow, when we go out, I think you should come with us, eh? Another set of eyes will be a good thing. Maybe we will find faster this thing I lost."

"What?" The shifting conversation had Alex's emotions swinging as violently as a carnival Tilt-A-Whirl. "I can't go with you. This is your quest, or whatever, to deal with. I have a job I have to show up for." And a parole officer who might hear about it if he didn't.

Morana ignored his protests and addressed Stribog. "Yes. Good. We can't risk being gone again when he re-awakens." She indicated Alex's midsection.

"Your friend said he will make your excuse at work," Stribog said. "We need to be together when you need Morana's help again. I spoke truly when I said letting him loose now could endanger us all."

"Him. What *him*?" Alex's volume increased again. "I want answers, damn it. I have a right to know what you did to me."

Stribog paused, then nodded. "All right. I'll give you your answers." He walked to the desk chair, pulled it to the side of the bed, and sat with a grunt. "The 'him' I speak of is my brother, Perun. The most powerful of we four brothers already, God of Sky—thunder, lightning, some other things—but he became greedy for more. First, he took from my brother Simargl, and now Simargl lives chained and helpless."

"Perun didn't chain him," Morana said, matter-of-factly.

He waved one hand dismissively. "He didn't, but he weakened him, which meant that when others came for him, they could do that thing. Then he took from my brother Radogost, his spear and helmet. With each thing he stole, he became more powerful still. And yet, he wanted more. He wanted to be supreme over us all, stronger even than our father, Svarog, except that for long ages Veles nipped at his heels. For long ages more, Perun licked the wounds Veles gave him and stayed quiet. But, at last, his greed surfaced again, and he came for my winds."

The names Perun and Svarog seemed vaguely familiar from the lists of gods Alex had pulled up earlier tonight, but he remembered nothing specific about them. He doubted his father or grandfather would have recognized most of the names either.

Christianity, when it had come at last to Eastern Europe in the tenth century, had come with the vengeance of a jealous god. All Alex knew of Slavic paganism was that—like in so many places around the world—the idols, along with their history and stories and traditions, had been shattered and burned by Christian missionaries until the communities were left with only shards of their old beliefs. Too little remaining to ever piece them together again. Folktales had survived, but even those had transformed over time as they folded Christian principles into their morals.

"I don't understand," Alex said. "What is this thing you're looking for?"

"My Horn of Winds. I'm a God of Wind and a spreader of things. I move seed, pollen, clouds. I bring symmetry. Each of my grandchildren is one of the eight winds, but I orchestrate them through my horn." Stribog swayed his hands like a conductor. "Without them, I can summon wind, but not the eight winds I need for balance. Perun ambushed me, tried to steal the horn. With it, as a god of storms, he could have terrible power. Too much. No balance. To keep it from him, I heaved it down from me and far away."

"Stupid," Morana said.

"He didn't get the horn." Stribog winked again at Alex.

"And you don't have it either," she retorted. "Winter needs the winds too, old man."

He shrugged. "I know it landed near here. I know Perun watched me when I came to find it. I fooled him into thinking I had it and captured him when he tried to come after me for it. Now he is bound, I look again."

"That's why you were away? You were out looking for this horn?"

"Yes." Stribog pursed his lips, considering his answer. "We had planned to be back, but we were delayed."

"By what?"

He gave the ghost of a shrug. "Our presence here draws others."

"Or Perun's allies sent the others here to hinder us," Morana interjected.

"Or Perun's allies sent them to hinder us," Stribog conceded. "Either way, some are here already and more will come."

"What others?" Alex bit back the rest but avoiding saying the word wouldn't change facts. And hard as all this was to swallow, the healing Morana had done was real. The kite flying in pouring rain had been real. The fight in the field. The kite—no, Perun—shoved inside him. The ancient Slavic gods were real. He forged ahead. "Other gods are coming?"

Stribog shook his head. "No. Not gods. Probably no gods. I speak of lesser entities—different peoples have different names for them—chort, demons, devils, spirits, sprites, fae. No true threat to me or to Morana, but they can be mischievous. Where we tread, they follow. A few are here already. Some aid me. Some try to impede me. One delayed our return." He glanced at Morana.

Alex expected her to say "stupid" again, but she remained silent.

"Why the hell would you want me with you? If supernatural beings are out there, I'm just going to be a liability."

"You will be with us if Perun wakes again. Also, if you encounter one of these lesser beings, we can help you. If you stay here, they may find you while we're gone. They're curious creatures. They'll be drawn to those with whom we associate. Once they find you, they'll be drawn to those you associate with as well."

Alex flashed on the memory of his walk in the woods with his nephews. The shadowy figure in the trees. The air of danger he'd felt.

Stribog drew breath to continue his list of reasons, but Alex cut him off. Alina and Dan. His nephews. He didn't need to hear any more.

"All right. I'll go with you."

Chapter Seven

IT HAD BEEN mutually agreed the night before that Alex would sleep in Stribog's spare bed. The decision left no need for Alex to get a ride home and it gave both parties assurance that one wouldn't leave without the other.

For Alex, the night passed in a fugue of slamming motel doors and disturbing dreams. He woke around four in the morning from a particularly vivid dream that federal prisons were hiring forest rangers as guards. He'd been transferred from Lolo Forest to Pelican Bay Prison due to his familiarity with the facility. About to begin his first day of work, he'd planned to object to the transfer but he couldn't find the driveway to the front entrance of the prison and drove his Forest Service truck up and down a street bordered by a solid stand of trees. He'd grown more anxious with each pass, knowing the odds that his new boss would listen to his objections and allow him to return to Montana dwindled minute by minute in proportion to his tardiness.

He woke with a start and looked around, confused. Parking lot lights bled through the slit in the drapes and cast pale shadows over the empty bed next to him. His gaze slid over the silhouette of Stribog, sitting fully dressed and unmoving in the chair near the desk. Alex rolled onto his side, but sleep was slow to return.

Shortly after dawn, he woke from his deepest sleep of the night. The coffee pot hissed like a steam radiator in counterpoint to Stribog's humming. Alex swung his legs out of bed as Stribog crossed the room and handed him one of two cups of black tea he held.

"We seek adventure today, yes?"

Alex sincerely hoped not. He'd had about all the adventure he could stand. "So, is this a normal-sized horn you're looking for?" He held his cup and other hand about a foot or two apart.

Stribog shrugged. "It depends. Probably."

Alex ignored the enigmatic answer. "How are you looking for it? A street-by-street grid search, or something?"

"It won't be in the town. I suspect it chose this place for the woods. Trees have magic in them."

Alex lowered his cup without drinking. "You're planning to search hundreds of thousands of acres of forest for something the size of one of my work boots? How can you hope to find it?"

"I'll hear it when I'm near. I'll feel it before that. Trees have magic, but ancient trees more so, and there are only a few of the ancient ones left. We looked in your Simpson-Reed and Stout Grove already. Today we try the boy's trail."

"Boy Scout Tree Trail?"

"Yes, that one." Stribog downed the last of his tea. "We'll leave when I get back. I have to pay old witch."

Alex wondered for a moment if Stribog was speaking of some debt to a literal witch until he waved his empty cup in the direction of the motel office, tossed the cup in the trash, and left. He heard Stribog pound on Morana's door and bellow for her to be ready to leave.

Stribog returned a few minutes later and Morana entered behind him. The open door bathed her face in milky morning light, and Alex upped his estimate of her apparent age to early twenties. When Stribog returned, they all loaded into the rental car with Stribog driving, Morana in front, and Alex in the back seat. They were nearly out the east end of town when Alex spoke up.

"Are you planning to stop somewhere for food? Because there's not much in the way of options past that light up there."

"Ah. Yes. Breakfast," Stribog said, obviously considering it for the first time. "What is good?"

"I don't know about good, but the fast-food places are quick. If we'll need lunch too, then the grocery store on the left would be better."

"Okay. The store." At the next block, Stribog pulled into the parking lot. He turned the car off but made no move to get out.

Alex opened his door then paused. "Are you coming in?"

"I trust you," he said, then added, "Bring chocolate. I like your chocolate."

"Morana?" Alex asked. She shook her head.

"Morana doesn't like food," Stribog said, by way of explanation.

"Ever?" Alex asked. She shook her head again. Curious, he asked Stribog, "Do you want food because you need it or like it?"

"I like it."

"Okay, so pretty much I'm shopping for myself?"

"Pretty much," Stribog agreed. "Here." He reached into the pocket of his suit pants and pulled out a roll of cash. Twisting in his seat, he fanned it out for Alex to take what he needed.

Alex plucked two twenties. "We're coming back tonight, right?"

"Of course."

"Of course." Alex grabbed two more twenties before Stribog put the money away. "So how does a Slavic god come by American money these days, anyway?"

"I had a trinket or two with me when I came here."

Alex headed for the store, trying to imagine what pre-

Kievan-Rus jewelry or other "trinkets" might have been worth in the right hands. Or even the wrong ones.

Fortunately, like in Montana, practically every store in Del Norte County—from the dollar stores to feed stores to gas stations—stocked outdoor gear. In addition to power bars, chocolate, and other ready-to-eat foods, Alex scoured the hardware aisle. His clothes were okay: jeans, T-shirt, flannel-lined canvas work shirt and heavy jacket from last night, but a few basic supplies would make him feel better. He grabbed a rain suit in packaging about the size of a manila envelope, a cheap nylon backpack, a Mylar emergency blanket folded to not much bigger than a deck of cards, water purification tablets, an aluminum water bottle, a five-dollar folding knife, and a grill lighter.

Back in the car, they headed out of town on Howland Hill Road. Stribog circumvented a "road closed for the season" barricade without slowing. Alex experienced a jolt of anxiety before remembering that his ankle monitor wouldn't alert unless he left the county. As long as no one specifically looked up his whereabouts, they'd never know he'd been here. Even if they did look up his location, the road was close to town and the odds were low that anyone would put together that he was going a mile or two down a closed road.

They proceeded down the narrow and muddy dirt road into the giant groves of Jedediah Smith State Park. Alex had spent his first twenty years among the towering coastal redwoods, but they never ceased to amaze him. The tallest living thing on the planet, found only along a four-hundred-mile stretch of coast from far Northern California to the very southern tip of Oregon.

He'd grown up on family outings to these ancient groves. And during the years his parents were ill, he'd spent hours in solitude among the old-growth trees north and south of Eureka, sitting with his back to trunks twenty feet in diameter, trying to absorb their strength and peace. Trying to refill his own dry wells before returning to school demands and hospice workers and medication schedules and his sister's tears. These majestic trees had stamped their tranquility and endurance onto his heart and soul, and they were responsible for laying the foundation for his love of the outdoors and his career in the Forest Service.

Alex pressed his forehead to the side window and craned his neck, letting his gaze travel from their immense trunks up to the crowns sailing three hundred feet in the air. It hadn't surprised him to hear Stribog say they had magic in them. Trees, up to two millennia old, that had once thickly covered the entire area. Now, after a mere two hundred years of settlers and civilization, less than five percent remained.

The road was narrow and curving, rutted into jarring potholes by the rain. Stribog's speed concerned him, more so when he rolled down the driver's side window and stuck his head out like a dog. At least the cold wasn't an issue. The blast of cool air swirling from the window into the back seat was less chilly than being closed in the car with Morana.

"So, is this thing metal? Wood? Like a hunting horn or war horn or something?"

"Bone. From the horn of a wisent." The car swerved alarmingly toward the embankment as Stribog indicated the size and shape by sweeping one hand from the right side of his head outward and up. "But we find it by feeling it, by listening for it." He thrust his head out the window once more, elbow braced over the sill.

Alex had no idea what a wisent was, but he cared more about staying on the road than finding out. "Would it be easier if I drove?" he asked. "Or Morana, if you'd rather."

Stribog pulled his head inside again. "Morana is busy. You can drive." He stopped in the middle of the road and traded places with Alex.

As Alex came around to the driver's side, he asked the question that had been niggling at him since last night. "If you could teleport or whatever from Russia to here, why do you drive a car to get around?"

"The fight with Perun weakened us both and being here, in this land, impairs me more. I must conserve my strength until I have my horn back."

Stribog climbed into the back seat and rolled down the window. "Faster," he said when they were moving again.

Wind was a subtle thing among the old-growth trees. The enormous trunks blocked it at ground level but, beneath the rush of air from the open window, Alex thought he heard the breeze sighing in the branches high above. Morana, to his right, sat staring straight ahead, and he noticed for the first time that the worst of the mud and potholes were icing over a few yards in front of the car. He wasn't sure that ice was better than mud at this speed but, as long as they didn't go off the road, at least it should help keep them from getting stuck or bursting a tire.

"Faster," Stribog shouted.

Alex accelerated. His focus intensified as ice crystals appeared on the road ahead like a time-lapse photography of frost forming on glass. He made minute adjustments on the steering wheel, tapped the brakes on the curves, and kept the car centered on the road. For the moment, he controlled Morana and Stribog's destinies, instead of the other way around.

"Stop!" Stribog commanded.

Alex pushed the brake pedal as hard as he dared and guided them to a stop, fishtailing only a little.

"Back there," Stribog said.

"Boy Scout Tree Trail is just ahead," Alex said.

"Did you feel it?" Morana asked.

"No. Something else. Behind us. Go back."

Alex draped his right arm over the seat, twisted his neck, and backed the car around the curve in the road.

"Down there," Stribog said, pointing to the right side of the road.

Alex parked on the shoulder, though there seemed little chance anyone else would come along. The ground banked sharply down past the edge of the road, but Stribog and Morana confidently negotiated the drop-off, deadfall, and thick ferns. The ground grew more level, and less than ten minutes later, Morana stopped and looked to her right. Stribog's gaze focused on the same area. He barked a command Alex couldn't translate from what might have been an ancient dialect.

The ferns ahead parted and a pair of creatures, not quite knee-high, appeared. At that size, Alex expected some kind of animal, but when they emerged, he could only stare. They were clothed in coarse homespun with tall hats and possessed wrinkled human faces over stout human shapes. His muscles burned with adrenaline and the center of his chest grew cold and hollow as they approached.

With great industry, they began stamping the grass and clover and ferns flat. Alex took two quick steps back as they neared, but his brain couldn't shake the impression of animated lawn gnomes. Something larger approached behind the gnomes, still hidden by the huge tree trunks ahead. A man, gauging by the quality of the footsteps and the rhythm of two feet. Or something like a man. Alex snapped his head toward Stribog, weighing his reaction, ready to run if Stribog showed alarm. Both Stribog and Morana waited calmly, ignoring the little gnomes at their feet. Two more of the creatures arrived and began stomping undergrowth as well, as if to make a smooth carpet for the thing behind.

The man emerged maybe fifty feet from them. He wore a robe of midnight blue trimmed in gold, its elegance blunted by the fact that it hung baggy on his emaciated frame and frayed at the hem and cuffs. As he drew closer, Alex saw wrists as thin as a child's poke out from the wide sleeves, and the bony fingers of one hand clutched a walking staff of carved wood. His gaunt face collapsed around high cheekbones and molded to his skull. He had salt-and-pepper-colored hair that grew thick to his shoulders, but an astonishing long beard of shiny metallic strands of copper. Most surprisingly, his upper eyelids drooped in thick folds onto his cheeks, obscuring his eyes and effectively blinding him.

This past week had been a journey down a long and bumpy road for Alex, as he'd slowly moved toward acceptance of the idea that he'd been pulled into the presence of ancient Slavic gods. That road had just ended in a cliff and his brakes had failed.

The last pair of the six little attendants accompanying the strange man tugged at his robe to guide him to a stop in front of Stribog and Morana. The man dipped his head to the two gods. "*Pan. Pani,*" he said. A formal honorific, Alex assumed. He ignored Alex as thoroughly as he ignored the servants at his feet.

"Speak English," Stribog said, giving no show of respect in return. A fact Alex filed away.

"You will excuse me if I sit?" he said in lightly accented English, with an affectation of indifference that made him sound simultaneously self-important and bored.

Without waiting for an answer, he shifted left at the little creatures' urging to an enormous, downed log. The moment he sat, the same two sprang up to his shoulders and, with effort, hauled his heavy eyelids open, hand over hand, grunting with exertion. They struggled to hold the thick folds piled near his eyebrows while the man's sharp blue eyes shifted to regard them all.

"What have you learned while we were away?" Morana asked.

Alex tried to pay attention to the question, but the exponential uptick in weirdness in the past few minutes only allowed him to process fragments. His world suddenly felt as foreign and disorienting as it had the day he'd been arrested out of the blue at his cabin and locked in a unit of the Missoula County jail with forty other inmates.

"Little yet," the man replied, "but my servants have been gathering information, such as it is. Various ones are still arriving, as expected"—he spread his long bony fingers to indicate his gnomes and others of the "lesser beings" Stribog had mentioned last night—"but none of your brethren." He nodded to Stribog and Morana. "None that I know of, anyhow. Those creatures that I trust have been instructed on what to look for and that they should come to me with any information."

"And Likho?"

"I have not seen him since we last spoke. I think you put him in his place quite effectively. The leshy has arrived, though. He may be the most likely to prove helpful."

"Good. I will summon him." Stribog turned to Morana and Alex. "Back to the car now," he said, striding off toward the road.

Safely back in the car, Alex gripped the steering wheel to stifle the tremor in his hands. "Was that Koschei?"

"Yes, Koschei," Stribog answered from the back seat.

Koschei, the Deathless, one of the few characters Alex knew from Russian folklore, also from Ukrainian lore as Viy. Often described as skeletal, which had been a clue, but Alex had guessed the identity from having once heard about the heavy eyelids and beard of copper. He was most often depicted as an antagonist, stealing young brides from the hero.

"Is he the one you said last night was helping you?" He started the car and pulled away from the shoulder back onto the dirt road.

In the rearview mirror, Alex saw Stribog nod yes.

"Do you trust him?"

"I trust no one."

Alex had also heard of leshy, either spirits or deities of the forests, but not the other one Stribog had mentioned. "Who is Likho?"

"Likho is Misfortune, ill fate," Morana said. "He is one you must avoid at all costs. And have a care around Koschei as well. He is more powerful than he appears."

Stribog stuck his head out the open window. "Drive faster." Alex accelerated. Stribog scented the air like a gray-haired basset hound.

In less than half a mile, Alex slowed. "That's the parking pullout for Boy Scout Tree Trail on the left. If you want to keep going, Mill Creek trailhead is just ahead on the right. After that, you hit Hiouchi in about another mile, a little town of a couple hundred people or so. Past Hiouchi is Smith State Park."

"Park here. I want to see boy's trail."

Alex pulled in and turned the engine off. The trail was short, only a couple of miles. He debated leaving the backpack before remembering the Stout Grove trails weren't long either, yet Stribog and Morana had been gone three days. He grabbed the pack.

The three of them started up the trail. Stribog set a quick pace, swiveling his head side to side. Morana looked relaxed, almost distracted. Alex couldn't tell if she was searching as well or just along for backup. Alex trailed behind them, feeling superfluous. He wouldn't find the horn unless he tripped over it. He was only there so they could babysit him.

His thoughts cycled and flashed through a horror montage of the last twenty-four hours: The figure he'd seen when walking with the boys in the woods. Perun trying to claw out of his body last night. A finger emerging from his skin like something from *Alien*. The weird little gnomes this morning. Koschei's eyelids being lifted like velvet theater curtains.

More concerning, with all that afoot, the thing Morana had sounded most concerned about was him running into Likho. Stribog told him last night that where the gods go, these creatures follow, and that they'd be drawn not only to him, but to the people he associated with. He should have called Alina this morning and at least told her to stay away from the woods near the house. Once Stribog broke his silence, he'd see if he could get reception.

Alina would have realized by breakfast that he'd been out all night, but she hadn't checked up on him. She worried, but she never mothered him, never nagged, never intruded on his privacy. He owed her the honesty they'd always shared. Instead, he seemed to be moving further from it day by day. It was Thanksgiving tomorrow, a time of family and sharing, a day important to Alina. He wanted the air cleared between them by then, but that meant figuring out how much he could tell her without her thinking that he'd suffered a psychotic break.

Out of habit, he scanned the trail for tracks. He identified the usual suspects: raccoon, skunk, birds, squirrels. Black bears probably wouldn't be sleeping yet but prints here, where there were tourists so much of the year, would be unlikely. He stopped and bent closer to look, suddenly realizing what he should have noticed before. Stribog and Morana were leaving no footprints in the damp brown earth of the trail. He thought back to what Stribog said last night, about his and Morana's forms being real and yet not real. Like the thing Alex carried inside his body. He put a hand to his belly, his index and middle finger spread to straddle the bulge in his skin.

Stribog stopped, pulling Alex from his thoughts.

"Ah, we are lucky he is near."

"Lucky?" Morana said. "To have Likho near?"

"No, leshy. This way." He pointed into the woods at their left.

"Likho, I think. You'll be chasing shadows. Likho will make himself scarce if he thinks you come for him." Morana followed Stribog through the trees and Alex trailed behind them both.

"The leshy is a forest spirit, right?" he asked.

"Yes," Morana said. "He takes care of the trees."

"Nice there's at least one benevolent spirit out here." A couple of house sprites were nearly the only things from his grandfather's Russian folklore tales that Alex could remember not terrifying him as a child.

"He does what is in his nature. As we all do. To trees, he is benevolent."

Stribog stopped about fifty feet ahead of them and motioned them both to silence. Alex craned to see but perceived nothing but old-growth trees, ferns, and ground cover. Stribog began talking to thin air. Alex understood maybe one word out of ten, not enough to piece together what was being said. Stribog's voice rolled in calm waves, a cadence more suited to song or poetry. Without ceasing or turning, he waved one hand at his hip for Morana to come forward. With Morana's cryptic description of the leshy, Alex figured it prudent to stay put.

A moment later, pine needles crunched behind him. He turned. A boy of perhaps seven or eight stood in profile to him, well back on the trail, left eye studying him. Alarmed, Alex put a finger to his lips then moved toward him, his palms out in a gesture to herd him back to his parents, or class, or anywhere that was away from Stribog and the thing he spoke to. The boy didn't move. Alex listened for others coming down the trail. He heard nothing but Stribog, who paused now and again, as if talking on the phone in a conversation where Alex could only catch one side. He made a more insistent shooing motion. The boy went wide-eyed and trotted ahead and to Alex's left.

"Wait," Alex hissed, and took a few jogging steps to catch him by the arm. His fingers brushed the nylon sleeve of the boy's rain jacket and slid off. The boy ducked behind the bole of one of the giant trees and hid. Alex rounded the tree and stopped. The boy was gone. Not out of sight. Gone.

"Oh, shit."

He'd been an idiot not to have suspected the child to be more than he seemed after encountering multiple supernatural creatures in these woods already. He ran a few steps back the way he'd come and looked to his right. Morana was nowhere in sight. He listened for Stribog and heard nothing. Maybe he'd jogged farther after the apparition than he thought. He walked a few steps more, still seeing neither of them. "Oh, come on," he muttered.

The trees were well spaced with little undergrowth beneath their towering canopy, but the sheer mass of the trunks made it difficult to see clearly more than a hundred feet or so. He turned left and headed for the main trail in case they'd gone back that way looking for him but after a minute or two still saw no sign of the trail ahead where it should have been. He couldn't have missed the trail as well as both of the gods. This was crazy. He didn't get lost in the woods. He certainly didn't get lost in a matter of steps. The logical part of his brain told Alex that he was the one no longer in the right place, not Stribog and Morana.

There was no indication of having been transported to any mystical place or having moved any great distance. He saw no change in weather or terrain, landscape, flora, or fauna. Everything pointed to him still being somewhere in Jedediah Smith State Park. Just not in the same location he'd been a minute ago, and with no idea where he was in relation to the trail they'd been on.

The hell with his pride and the hell with disturbing Stribog's negotiations.

"Stribog," he yelled. "Morana."

There was no answer.

Chapter Eight

"S<small>IT DOWN</small>, J<small>AKE</small>," Alina said.

Jake continued to stand bent over to "drive" the car-shaped grocery cart down the condiment aisle.

"Jake." No response. She tapped him on the shoulder.

Jake turned with a grin on his face, the yellow plastic steering wheel gripped in both hands. She motioned for him to sit, guiltily realizing after she'd done it that she'd used the same hand signal she used for Bonkers. He plunked into the seat making acceleration noises while she clipped him in with the strap she'd neglected in her hurry, then looked for spare hearing aid batteries in her purse. A woman pushed a metal cart between the shelves and the car-cart with exaggerated maneuvering to demonstrate her annoyance at the narrow gap.

Alina gave up on the spare batteries and barreled on through the store, guiding the cart with one hand and reading her shopping list on the phone in her other. Thumbing the screen to the clock she muttered "Damn," pretty sure Jake couldn't hear her. Time constraints were nothing new. She could shop faster without Jake, but it would mean stopping work earlier to get the shopping done before picking him up from preschool. Thinking of her work schedule led her to wonder again how Alex had gotten to work this morning. His motorcycle had still been parked in the drive when she got home from taking David to school, but he hadn't been at breakfast and wasn't in his cottage. He must have stayed out overnight, maybe with the person in the Trans Am she'd seen pulling away from the driveway last night. She hoped he'd been out having fun for once. It would be good to see him remember joy and laughter again.

The wait at the checkout seemed interminable and she reminded herself that three people in front of her wouldn't even count as a line in larger towns. Once outside, she strapped Jake into the back seat and drove through the school zone, alternately accelerating too hard then braking for traffic. In the end, she made it to David's grade school in time to sit in the queue with all the other parents inching forward into the pickup zone.

Once David had been safely buckled into the front seat, she relaxed, pulled out of the school driveway, and turned south. The same woods that bordered their home ran widthwise almost to the west side of the school grounds, forcing Alina to drive more than a mile out of her way to get around them when the actual distance would only have been a few blocks as the crow flies.

"Did you get your class pictures back today?"

"Uh huh." David opened his Spiderman backpack, pulled out his math book and removed a white paperboard envelope from beneath the front cover. One tab tore as he pulled the envelope open.

"Oh, honey, wait. I'm driving, and you'll get them smudgy."

Too late. He'd already reached inside and now held out the strips of photo proofs to her, one thumb pressed to his smiling face in the middle print.

She glanced at one of the photos so she could tell him it was nice, then looked again. "Did Mrs Schumacher make a face?"

He'd told her on the day the photos were taken how one of the teachers had made some of the children smile by making funny faces.

"No. The photo guy told her to stop."

"I want to see," Jake said from the back seat.

"I'll show them to you when we're home, Jake," she said loudly, looking in the rearview mirror. "It's a very nice photo," she told David. "You look kind of surprised, so I thought maybe she did something funny."

"The picture guy told me to open my eyes big." David repacked his book.

She composed her face into what she felt sure was a convincing smile rather than the seething snake pit of anger that flashed through her. "Well, it's very nice."

She'd tried to be understanding when most of the teachers continued to mispronounce the boys' four-syllable surname of Inoue, despite repeated corrections. She'd fielded the occasional questions about Dan's heritage for years by stating his birthplace, "Eugene," without batting an eye. She'd fielded the "What kind of Asian is he?" follow-up from the persistent, usually by giving them what they wanted and saying his parents had moved to Oregon from Japan, without bothering to explain that he was adopted. But now the school photographer stood as a new reminder that it was time to teach her children how to deal with ignorance. She placed the photos in a cubby within the dash.

"What else did you do today?"

"Tamelin grabbed my wand from me at recess, but Mr Tensmore made her give it back."

"Your wand?"

David nodded. "It was a good one. That long"—he held his hands apart—"and bent a little at the end." He crooked his index finger. A stick, Alina assumed. "We used the wand to make the forest monster go away."

"Forest monster, huh?"

"I want to see a monster," Jake said, his batteries apparently working just fine after all.

"It had a house that followed it around like Bonkers follows us in the backyard." David tented his hands together like a sharply peaked roof and bounced them along.

"Well, any monster that has a house that follows it around sounds pretty neat to me," Alina said.

She took her eyes from the road for a moment to smile at David and check his mood to see if she'd be up during the night with a nightmare, or if the "monster" had been a fun game of invent-and-conquer. What she saw instead was neither fear nor play. His face held the same matter-of-factness Dan had shown when he told her four years ago about a man who'd walked into his bank in Eugene. With no proof, no action or word to back up the suspicion, Dan had been certain the man's intent had been to rob the bank. In the end, the guy had fiddled with a form at the center counter and then left. Two days later, someone with the same description had robbed a bank at the north end of town. And today, David had seen something unusual, she felt sure, and he and his friend had woven the strangeness of it into their recess game.

There were a lot of different monsters in the world. Some were disguised as cancer, some as genetic landmines that detonated without warning. Some were human and walked the streets of every town, large and small. They might live in trailer courts or McMansions, smoke crack pipes or preach Sunday sermons. Some watched school playgrounds through binoculars from the woods.

A familiar wave of helpless anxiety tightened her stomach. Her need to be vigilant and to keep the monsters away from her family wound her like an old clock, twisting her muscles tight. But her vigilance and her will and her anger had never been enough. Counting pills, holding hands through chemo, and hospice meals with smiley faces in jellybeans hadn't been enough. Pre-natal care and good food and regular pediatric visits hadn't been enough. She had failed each time. The monsters always won.

*   *   *

MIKE MURPHY ELBOWED his back door open and hauled a bucket, pump, net, filters, and chemicals to his bathtub-sized koi pond. He'd never asked permission to put the pond in, but he'd erected a wooden backyard fence that kept it out of sight and neighborhood kids out of the pond. Besides, he only had one neighbor, being in the first trailer of the row at the outer edge of the trailer park with his backyard bordering open land. On top of that, he didn't care much if the trailer court manager found out or not. He'd managed to keep his fish alive through the winter last year and he planned to do the same again.

A door banged open on the other side of his street. The exuberant sounds of his neighbor's two children tumbled out with them onto their front lawn. The boys' shouts snuck around the sides of his pink-trimmed single-wide while Mike checked the temperature and pH of the pond. Their play and their arguments—conducted at equal volume—bounced off the hill directly behind his fringe of backyard. The sounds cavorted around him, as if the detached spirits of the two children capered in his own yard.

A new sound intruded, and the flutter of wings drew his gaze a little way up the short hill to a scraggly pine tree. There, near the top of the tree, an owl swayed on a thin branch. He'd seen it yesterday evening too. Barn owls were common in the area, but this one was larger. It looked as rough as the tree it had chosen to perch in: thin, with its beak slightly crooked and its head and body feathered sparsely, like a molting chicken. Or roadkill. The owl's large eyes seemed to be trained not on the fish, but on him, the same as they had been the night before. Mike stared back, challenging it to try something. It didn't. He flung a rock at it, but the stone fell far short and the owl didn't budge. He wondered if owls could catch rabies.

He plugged the water pump into his extension cord and lowered it into the pond. The fish spooked at the motor and swam in jerky circles. "Easy there," he said. "A little of the old out and new in. Same as always."

Mike pulled his solitary lawn chair over to the edge of the pond while the pump ran, careful to sit with his weight to the right of the frayed webbing. He removed the last item from the bucket, and the beer can gave a hearty hiss when he opened the tab. He held it aloft in salute before taking a sip. "Happy birthday, kiddo."

The voices of the neighbor's boys still ricocheted around him as the children acted out a new day of social development on their fitful path to maturation. Sometimes they cried over wounds—perceived or actual, physical or emotional. A distress call like any young, wild animal makes. Today, more than most days, the sounds of the play and the fights and the hurts embodied Mike's missed opportunities. Today marked twenty years to the day since he'd come home on leave for Jimmy's eleventh birthday and had been handed divorce papers to sign while another man attended his son's party.

The breakup of his marriage could have been repeated in one form or another by a third of the career Navy guys he'd known. Still, over the years he'd questioned if he should have fought harder to stay home, or at least tried harder to remain connected to the kids, whether they'd wanted him to or not. His oldest, Jimmy—Jim now, according to his siblings—had taken the split the hardest. He remained the only one of his four who'd never acknowledged the money Mike sent. Thirty-one today. Only a year younger than Alex Orlov, he realized.

Mike turned off the pump, rinsed the filters, and turned on the hose to refill the pond. With the same practical approach and finality of closing a valve, he shut down the melancholic drift of his thoughts and wondered, instead, how Alex was faring.

When Alex hadn't shown up for work this morning, he'd told Frank the hernia story and said he might be out for a while, but that he'd probably call soon with an update. He was pretty sure Alex hadn't called, though. He felt certain Frank would have mentioned it to him. It seemed out of character for Alex not to call in himself and, worse, it probably meant a breach of his parole conditions.

The sun set somewhere behind his hill. He turned off the hose and gathered up his equipment as dusk settled. There was no evening star, as usual, none he could see behind the fog and cloud, anyway, but still enough light that he could make out the owl in the tree. Its golden eyes seemed to have grown brighter in the early twilight.

Mike finished off his beer and gave the owl a contemptuous burp. The owl opened its crooked mouth wide. Impossible to see at this distance, he knew, but in the half-light, Mike could have sworn he saw the shimmer of small teeth.

He kept his pace unhurried and his movements natural. Turning his back on the raptor, he forced his muscles to relax and climbed the rickety steps, resisting the urge to look over his shoulder. Once inside, he set the bucket down and reached out to pull the aluminum door closed. He and the owl watched each other for a few seconds more, and then it launched into the air. It flew silently over his trailer and away.

Chapter Nine

ALEX CALLED OUT again for Stribog and Morana. Still no answer.

Without moving, he studied his surroundings in all directions while a barely controlled panic tugged at his breath. Being lost when he had supplies, skills, and a phone didn't spook him. Being lost when the embodiment of misfortune was fucking with him, while Koschei and some forest spirit out of folklore lurked nearby, terrified him.

He saw no tracks, not even ones leading to where he stood now, which implied that something was either screwing with his perception or teleporting him somehow rather than leading him in circles. The sun was little help, lost in the treetops and clouds overhead. He closed his eyes and reviewed his movements from the time he'd first seen the boy to this point, then turned in the direction where the trail ought to lie.

Opening his eyes again, he walked forward, taking careful note of the texture of the ground beneath his boots in case his sense of touch perceived things his eyes didn't. After walking what felt an appropriate distance, he stopped. He saw no sign of the trail and had felt no smoothness of ground. More disturbing, the slope of the terrain and subtle individual characteristics of the trees had changed as if he'd shifted to an entirely new location in the forest.

He yelled one more time for Stribog and Morana. Slipping out of his backpack, he found and unwrapped the emergency Mylar blanket, spread it over the damp ground where no sticks or branches would puncture it, and sat down cross-legged. He determined not to move farther than he could reach in any direction from this position in case it radically changed his location yet again. Lost hikers usually made the mistake of getting themselves more lost by trying to find their way out. If the rules of physics no longer applied and he shifted location—perceived or literally—with each step, then his situation was exponentially worse than the average lost hiker.

If something was messing with his perception, then Stribog and Morana should still be close and the best thing he could do was wait. And if something was moving him around the forest, well, he hoped it wouldn't take two gods long to break a spell cast by some evil spirit.

The clock on his phone showed the time to be not quite half past ten and he had food, water, fire starters, weather protection, even a spy thriller on his phone that he'd downloaded from the library. And if Likho watched him from some nearby hiding place, waiting for him to panic, then he hoped the thing choked on its own bile.

He opened his book and began reading to keep himself still. An hour later, he'd lost count of how often he'd checked the time. He hadn't been able to charge his phone last night and reading had dropped the battery in his cheap, off-brand phone from fifty-four to thirty-six percent. He turned the phone off and fought down his renewed impulse to go searching for the trail. Hopefully, he wouldn't be here another ten minutes, but in a worst-case scenario, the supplies he'd brought along could keep him comfortable enough for two or three days.

Two hours later, he opened a pack of rice cakes and one of the squeeze packets of peanut butter. He studied the woods around him and imagined walking a hundred feet and popping out of this spell like escaping a giant soap bubble. Lost hikers doing dumb things didn't seem quite as dumb as it used to. He lay back, closed his eyes, and woke sometime later from dreams he couldn't remember. Alarmed, he studied the woods for any change but saw no indications he'd moved anywhere. A quick look at his phone showed it was ten past two, same day, same year—so he hadn't been Rip Van Winkled either. His battery was at thirty-four percent. Alina would be picking David up soon. If his situation hadn't changed by four, he'd need to call her before his phone died. He turned the phone off again and tried to return to his nap, but sleep eluded him.

Four o'clock arrived, and his sister answered on the third ring.

"Hey, it's me," he said, keeping his tone casual.

"I keep telling you I don't want to extend my car warranty."

"Yeah, that's what you always say, but I sense you weakening."

She snorted.

"Hey, look, my phone battery's running low and I'm not sure if I'm going to be back tonight. I didn't want you to worry if I'm not there for dinner and you can't reach me."

"Stray cat strutting somewhere?"

"Yeah, no," he said deadpan. "I'm in Jedediah Smith Park right now with a couple people I met recently. We're on Boy Scout Tree Trail, but I don't know how long we'll be here. I wanted to give you a heads-up about dinner, but I was also calling to tell you not to let the boys play in the woods by the house. When I took them on that walk yesterday, I saw a stranger out there. Nothing happened. The person didn't come close, and I don't think the boys even saw them. Something about it just felt off, and I haven't seen you since then to tell you. It's probably nothing, but watch for anyone you don't know around there, okay? Even other kids."

"Okay." He felt her pause, as if about to say more, but then only said, "Thanks."

"So, you know there's been stuff going on I haven't told you about, right?"

"I figured. You've seemed... I don't know, not yourself. It's all right, though. Don't ever feel you have to tell me everything. We all need a little privacy sometimes, especially living so close."

"Thanks, but this isn't that sort of thing. I just haven't been sure where to start. Remember the old man I told you about? The one flying a kite in the rain last week?"

"I remember."

"Well, I keep running into him. He and a woman are visiting from Russia. I ended up staying at his motel last night, and I drove them out here this morning."

"Oh. Uh huh." He could imagine the questions that marched through her mind, especially why he'd stayed at their motel. "Do you want to invite them over for Thanksgiving tomorrow? I'm sure we have plenty." She was sincere, he was sure, but sounded more hesitant and curious than anything.

"No," he said, a bit abruptly. "Thanks, but no. I just wanted to let you know where I've been so you wouldn't worry. And to tell you about keeping an eye on the boys."

"You know I will anyway, but I appreciate the warning."

"Sorry I didn't mention it yesterday."

"Are you sure you're okay? You sound... I don't know, weird."

"No weirder than usual," he said. He could hear himself trying too hard.

"Yeah, well, that's enough. Don't want too much of a good thing."

"Right. Anyway, I hope I'll be back tonight, but if I'm not, don't worry."

"Got it."

They signed off and the woods around him felt somehow quieter than before the call.

He shoved his phone into his backpack so he wouldn't be tempted to constantly check the time. Careful not to take more than a step in any direction, he slipped into the backpack straps just in case, and gathered what rocks, dry leaves, and pine needles he could reach. Fifteen feet back and he would've had the resources of an enormous, downed tree. Twice that in any direction, and he could've sheltered against a living tree. He sighed, sat again, and built his tiny, triangular fire base, though he held off starting it. His fuel was limited, and if Stribog and Morana hadn't been able to see him there was no reason to believe they'd see smoke.

There were a whole lot of things he felt uncertain about right now, but if he was sure of one thing, it was that Stribog and Morana were looking for him. As long as he imprisoned Perun, they'd be as heavily invested in getting him out of this predicament as he was. He lay back on the Mylar blanket and closed his eyes.

"It'll be dark soon," someone said.

Alex sprang to his feet. The boy sat on a deadfall trunk a hefty stone's throw from him. The light had waned to gloom under the tree canopy, but it was still strong enough that he finally had a good look at the boy. He was pale and thin, and dressed like any other eight-year-old, down to the windbreaker he'd been wearing earlier. But one feature drew Alex's gaze and held it. The boy had only one eye. Where the right should've been, there was nothing, just skin from forehead to cheek. He tried to remember if he'd been missing the eye earlier and recalled the boy had stood with his right side turned away from him.

"The dark doesn't bother me," Alex responded truthfully and in a mostly steady voice. He spoke in English, though the boy's words had been in Russian.

"We'll see soon enough," he said.

"Are you Likho?"

The boy smiled with pompous satisfaction but didn't answer.

"What do you want?"

The boy's shape shimmered into something like a one-eyed hairless orangutan, then back again. "You are two." His gaze lowered to Alex's midsection.

"I am. And you don't want to mess with either one of us." His knife lay inside his pack but the fire ring at his feet contained a few fist-sized rocks. He bent and picked one up as nonchalantly as he could and held it at his side. "If you take me back to my friends, they'll reward you."

"Your friend rewarded me already." The boy tapped the place where his other eye should have been.

"Stribog? You're the one Koschei said he put in his place? So, you're keeping me as revenge against him."

"Tell me what Stribog seeks in this place, and I'll let you go."

"Morana told me that you sow misfortune... are misfortune... whatever. So I'm guessing if I tell you what he wants, you'll try to prevent it."

Likho shrugged.

"Maybe you'll lose your other eye for trying."

"It'll be dark soon," Likho said again.

"I'm not afraid of the dark," he repeated.

"You'll be alone."

"I'm not afraid of being alone either."

"We'll see."

Likho vanished.

ALEX FINISHED HIS dinner of peanut butter, rice cake, and power bar. He'd just started a tiny campfire when Likho came back, appearing in his hairless orangutan

111

form. Still one-eyed, but larger than the boy. More goblin than orangutan, really. Bony skull, sparse hair, long teeth. Alex stayed seated but furtively opened the folding knife he'd had ready at his side.

"You'll never find your way home without my help," the goblin growled.

"I don't need your help. I have friends who'll help me. Friends who are more powerful than you."

"Then why haven't they helped you already?"

Alex wished to hell he knew.

"What is the other you?" Likho asked, pointing a long, yellow finger at him and peering as if he could see inside. He took two shambling steps closer, perhaps twenty-five feet from him now.

Alex didn't respond.

"I can make bad things happen to you."

"You must be so proud."

The thing shifted back into a one-eyed boy, his head cocked, trying to puzzle out Alex's meaning. "Why is Stribog here?"

"You'll have to ask him."

Likho took another step. Alex gripped the knife handle, keeping the blade out of sight by his leg.

"The other one, it isn't you, is it?"

"Release me and I'll tell you."

"You'll tell me anyway."

Alex heard the patter of rain in the trees before he felt it. It strengthened to a shower by the time he'd unpacked his rain gear. He tried to hurry by pulling the wide-legged pants over his boots and slowed the process more than if he'd stopped to remove them. The rain turned to a cloudburst before he got his arms into the jacket and the hood pulled up. He cursed. Wet hair and damp clothing would sap his heat quickly.

He looked around, but Likho had either moved beyond

his firelight or vanished entirely. Tenting his foil blanket as high above the firepit as possible, he tried unsuccessfully to breathe life back into the embers while wondering if Likho had caused the rain, timed his appearance to it, or if the two occurring together had been a coincidence.

He rummaged in his pack, found his phone, and turned it on for the first time since he'd called Alina. The home screen showed a time of almost quarter to nine and a battery at fourteen percent. He had nearly the entire night still in front of him to endure. He speed-dialed Alina before he could chicken out, still not sure how to tell someone the impossible.

"Hey," she answered. "Are you on your way?"

"I have a feeling I'm not going to make it back tonight."

"Oh. Okay. Are you at the motel again?"

"No. I'm still out at Jedediah Smith."

"What are you doing out there in the dark? And isn't the park closed for the season anyway? I didn't think of that until after we hung up."

"Yeah, it is, but I'm stuck out here for now. Look, my phone's gonna die and I have some things I need to tell you." He could feel the worry in her silence, but she allowed him to continue uninterrupted. "I didn't tell you about the Russians before today because I know this is going to sound pretty crazy."

He started with the kite-flying incident and told her everything: the second man in the field, the kite vanishing, all of it. Concerned about his battery, he quickly summarized the rest of his week—lowering his voice and glancing around to see if Likho was eavesdropping when he mentioned Perun and the horn. When he finished, the silence was so profound he took his phone away from his ear to see if it had powered off. It hadn't, but seven percent glared at him in red from the upper right corner.

"You know how this sounds, right?" she said.

"I do. It's not a meltdown, I promise. Trust me, I questioned my sanity for a while too. But today... if you'd seen the things I've seen today... I feel like I fell down Alice's rabbit hole." He picked up a twig at his crossed feet and snapped it into small pieces with the thumb of one hand. "I'm pretty sure I'll be home soon, but I wanted you to know where I am and what's happening. Stribog told me that these 'lesser' creatures might find their way to people I associate with. I need you to know all this so you can keep an eye out and know what you're watching for."

"Okay, well, first things first." He heard keys rattling in the background. "You're still parked at Boy Scout Tree Trail, right? I'm on my way out there, so you listen for me calling for you."

"No," he said, more sharply than he intended. "Alina, no. Don't come out here. Not under any circumstances. Stribog and Morana will find me sooner than you ever could, and I'll head home as soon as they do. I'm okay. You know I'm fine in the woods and I've got everything I need with me. *Don't* come out here." He paused to make certain she wasn't going to push back.

"And, please, whatever you do, don't report this. I'm here at night, off-season, with nothing but a crazy-ass story. The last thing I need is law enforcement responding and this getting back to my parole officer." It was all true, but at this point he would have said anything to keep her from coming into woods riddled with evil fairy tale characters. "Promise me, okay?"

She hesitated, which was good. If she made a promise, she'd keep it.

"I promise," she said at last. "On one condition. This deal expires in twenty-four hours. Less than twenty-four. I'll push Thanksgiving dinner as late as six and if you aren't back, I'll come out there looking. If I can't find you, I'm reporting it to the police. Understand?"

It was the best he'd get.

"I understand. But try not to worry. And hold off on the heroics if you can. Trust me, I'm fine out here and I'm certain I'll meet up with Stribog and Morana again soon. I just called because I wanted to fill you in on everything." Everything except Likho continuing to torment him and his mounting fear of what-ifs.

"Yeah, well, you know that doing it at night, right before your battery dies, makes it sound like you think this might be your last chance to tell me."

She knew him too well.

"It's not that," he said in half-truth. "I knew you'd be trying to reach me if you didn't see me for a couple of days and you'd worry if you couldn't get through."

She gave a resigned sigh. "What am I supposed to do with all of this, Alex? This is a hell of a story to dump on me and then tell me not to worry."

"I know. And I can guess what you're worried about. It's okay if you don't believe it all, but I promise you I haven't lost my shit. I'll be home soon, and I'll give you what proof I can then." He ran his fingers lightly over the bulge in his abdomen. "In the meantime, at least you know where I am and what's been going on and to keep an extra eye on the boys."

He waited for some acknowledgment but there was none. His phone's screen had gone as dark as the night.

LIKHO CAME BACK in goblin form twice more during the night, but he didn't speak so neither did Alex. He'd been unable to restart his fire and slept as best he could, curled in his foil blanket against the off-and-on drizzle and cold.

An hour or two after sunrise, he heard Likho approaching again. The creature had done him no physical harm so far, and he was starting to get the cocky idea it had constraints on how directly it could accost him. He was lying on his side, cold and miserable despite his layers. The large bare feet of the goblin came close. Much closer than the previous times. Alex's discomfort and lack of sleep added annoyance on top of his fear.

"Don't you have any other friends to talk to?" he sniped, still lying on his side.

"He sleeps," the thing said, and Alex wondered why Likho would say that when he was obviously awake. He wondered if he'd translated the words incorrectly until he looked up to see Likho pointing at his belly. "I recognize him now."

"Then you know he's no one to be messed with."

"He tries to wake, but like a drunkard, he can't."

Alex said nothing, unsure if this turn of events would work for or against him. Likho squatted. Bracing on one arm, it leaned forward, one yellowed, ugly hand reaching for Alex's midsection.

"Hey," Alex croaked in surprise. He pushed quickly into a sitting position and crabbed backward a few inches. He left one heel planted, concerned that if he moved from his spot, he'd shift to another part of the forest. Farther from where Morana and Stribog might be homing in on him.

"I can wake him," the Likho-goblin rumbled.

Alex's belly cramped. "Leave me alone."

Likho's gaze snapped to his face at the hint of panic in his voice. "You could run from me."

"I could, but I won't." Prison had taught him well. If you see a cat, don't be a mouse. He tested his theory of Likho's limitations. "You can keep getting me more lost if I move around, but you can't touch me, can you?"

"Maybe I can't. But *he* could." The heavy arm pointed to his midsection again.

Alex's cramp worsened. He started to draw his leg in, instinctively going fetal, before realizing his heel had inched to the edge of his perceived circle of safety. Having crabbed backward already, pulling his legs in might be the equivalent of taking a step. He forced the leg straight. Despite the chilly dawn air, he wiped a bead of fear-sweat from his upper lip. He did the math to reassure himself; it had been less than thirty-six hours since Morana worked her magic on Perun, meaning he should still have a minimum twelve-hour safety margin.

The goblin walked a full circle around him, bare feet slapping the soft earth. The amorphous representation of Perun inside Alex shifted to follow. Left rib pressure, left kidney, spine, right kidney, right ribs, belly just below the sternum. Likho smiled. He dropped to sit cross-legged in front of Alex. With a large, gnarled finger, he began sketching symbols over dirt, ferns, and grass, moving intricately and ceaselessly, not seeming to notice the obstacles in the way.

Alex jerked forward as a strong impact struck his abdominal wall, pushing the flesh-covered nail into the last barrier, the layers of his skin. He folded over his outstretched leg and fought to catch his breath.

"Stribog," he yelled. "Morana."

The wave of pain subsided, and he forced himself to scoot forward, toward the goblin, so they sat nearly knee to knee. Likho continued to draw runes with his right hand, reaching out toward Alex's midsection with his other. There was another strong punch from inside. Alex felt a sudden yielding, like the skin of a firm tomato giving way under a dull knife. A wave of pain unlike any he'd experienced this past week rolled over him. He cried out and pressed both hands hard against his belly, pushing against the foreign digit beneath his layers of clothes. He no longer felt the sensation of flesh between his hand and the digit moving under his shirt. He reached beneath his jacket and shirts. Warm wetness coated his hand in red. Alex groaned in fear.

Like birthing a child, the slow and agonizing crowning ended with a sudden terrible tearing and the sense of emptying, an emergence from him carried out on a gush of pain and gore. Warm blood flowed through his hands, too much to hold. It smelled of copper and steamed in the chilly, damp air. Alex collapsed onto his side, hands held tightly to the bloody mess of his abdomen.

The pair of brown boots that stood in front of his face were dry and clean. As were the white leggings and tunic. And above them, the stern face of Perun.

Chapter Ten

LIKHO FLICKERED BACK into his goblin form and looked to Perun, awaiting instructions.

Alex wished *he* had a different body to shift into, one more imposing, less dying. Blood soaked his shirt, and his exposed skin looked pale as ivory paper. Nausea made him sweat even though he felt as cold as a Montana stream. As cold as if Morana held her hands on him.

If only she did.

Perun squatted in front of Alex. His outward age seemed indeterminate, anything from thirty to fifty, but strength radiated from his lean body and his eyes flashed gold within the blue.

"He hasn't found it yet, has he?" he said.

Alex knew which "he" and "it" Perun meant. He shook his head no. He couldn't remember if Perun had spoken to him in Russian or English. He couldn't focus on much of anything except pain and horror.

Perun stood again and addressed Likho in Russian. "I want to know who else has arrived here." He looked about the forest as if gauging where "here" was.

"The leshy is closest," Likho said.

"Good. Take me there."

"And him?" Likho nodded to Alex.

Perun looked down with the utter disinterest he might show a beetle dying at his feet. "What of him?"

Perun took a single step forward, Likho at his side, and both vanished.

Alex should have felt relief at their leaving, but discarded by them, injured and possibly dying, he felt only cold emptiness. He dragged his pack close and reached into it with one bloody hand. He held his other tight against his belly but couldn't feel the extent of the injury beneath his clothing. Pulling his phone out, he pressed the power button as hard as he could, hoping the battery held some untapped vestige of charge after resting overnight. The screen remained black.

Alone and lost, he was too afraid to look at his wound. He'd seen animals that had bled out from trauma inflicted by antlers or claws. Direct pressure wouldn't be enough to save him from bad internal damage, but it was better than doing nothing. With sticky fingers, he dropped the phone back into his pack. Opening his rain jacket and the coat beneath, he wrapped his thin, crinkly Mylar blanket tightly around his middle over his flannel-lined work shirt and T-shirt. Shock made his fingers clumsy, and his brain ran on half its cylinders while blood rushed to his core. The damp scent of pine seemed to intensify around him as his ability to concentrate diminished.

He struggled through foggy memories of two nights ago in the motel, Stribog saying that if Perun forced his way out it would hurt like hell—and it had—but he'd also said the physical manifestations were only *representations* of the metaphysical. If that were true, though, why was his body in shock and why were his hands and shirt covered in very real blood? And even more compelling: Why trust anything Stribog said? Both Morana and Stribog had deceived him and used him for their own ends.

Mortally wounded or not, he wanted to get out of this area. Koschei might wander over for a look, or the leshy could take an interest in him, or Perun and Likho might decide he was worth keeping around after all. And if the wound *was* mortal... well, he'd rather die doing something than doing nothing.

He shifted to his hands and knees and felt for the first time the disturbing sensation of the gash in his skin puckering with his movement. Slipping his daypack straps over one wrist, he crawled a few feet clear of his circle of safety then stopped and craned around to see if his location had radically shifted. It hadn't. As he'd hoped, Likho's spell seemed to have ended when he left with Perun.

He could tell the relative position of the sun behind the clouds and guess the approximate time of day. If he was still somewhere in the vicinity of Boy Scout Tree Trail, the road should lie roughly to the south. And if he made it to the road, he'd eventually find the parking lot.

Weak and dizzy, he moved forward, hand and knee, hand and knee. Sticks and small rocks bruised his kneecaps, and the scent of wet, loamy earth filled his nostrils. His daypack caught repeatedly on the undergrowth. He thought of home, of safety, of family.

Within a few yards, the effort began to warm him, spreading heat from his core outward to his fingers, his knees, his toes. In a few more yards, he felt a surge of strength. His arms trembled with jittery, adrenaline-laced energy, as if he'd drunk back-to-back espressos. He knew it wouldn't last long and used the adrenaline boost to crawl faster while he could, tipping his head every couple of minutes to check his direction.

The heat in his belly became a small sun. It seemed to burn a map of the dimensions of his wound; from the gaping internal cavern he imagined below his stomach to the gash through skin and muscle, which no longer seemed to pucker and shift with his movement. The heat seared him, made him sweat and gasp. He remembered the dangerous peace and warmth that had stolen over him when he'd nearly died of hypothermia. People who died of hypothermia were sometimes found undressed, as if they'd felt too hot. Perhaps this was some equally dangerous illusion.

His daypack caught yet again. Irritated, he jerked it free forcefully with a surge of strength that made him wonder if he could stand. He pushed upright onto his knees, then to his feet, dragging the daypack up to his shoulder. His eyesight took on a sheen, a pale golden glow at the edge of his vision; maybe low blood pressure from standing. He walked unsteadily through the forest, checking his direction of travel frequently against the sun.

The undergrowth rustled behind him. Like any prey animal, he froze, standing as still as one of the great trunks around him, holding his breath and listening. His patience finally broke. It could be anything from a chipmunk to the leshy. Whether fairy tale monsters followed him or not, he wouldn't get home if he didn't move.

Coming upon a downed tree at least two hundred feet long, he circumvented it by angling to his left. Skirting the crown branches, he looked up and stopped in surprise. The wide, pale dirt of a trail cut a swath through the forest floor just in front of him. Exhilarated, he stumbled onto the path and turned left, hoping it was the same trail they'd started out on yesterday morning. His pace increased on the level ground and his weaving steps steadied. It had rained last night, possibly washing some of his footprints from yesterday away, but if he ran across them, he'd know he was close to the road.

He heard footsteps and someone speaking Russian from just out of sight down the path ahead. Throwing himself back into the woods, he struggled to move silently and hide the neon orange daypack under his jacket.

"Alex Orlov," Stribog's voice called out. "Why do you hide?"

Alex emerged again onto the path, looking about carefully until he saw Stribog and Morana coming toward him, only about a hundred feet away.

He'd focused on receiving salvation from these two for nearly twenty-four hours. Now he had it, he was no longer sure he needed it. He pulled his rain jacket aside, untied the space blanket, and pulled his shirts up for Morana to see.

"He tore out of me," he croaked.

Stribog flung his hands out and up, a universal "So what?" gesture. "Yes. He has escaped. This makes things much worse."

Alex finally dared to look as well. Dried blood coated his abdomen and clothing, but he saw no fresh blood and no sign of an open wound beneath the crust, not even a scab or scar. A Schrodinger's wound; simultaneously real and unreal. Just as Stribog had said, he'd suffered pain, bleeding, and physiological shock without actually sustaining an injury. Hopefully not, anyway. He probed the skin with his fingers.

"Makes things worse for me," Stribog continued, "not for you. You'll feel back to normal soon."

"What now, old man?" Morana asked.

He shrugged. "Same as before, we look for the horn. Only now, we are in a race to find it before Perun does. He can't be allowed to become so powerful. And I will never leave here without it. I'll fight him to the death before I give up my winds." He looked at Alex. "Where is Perun now? Did he say what he planned?"

Alex checked once more for any wound under the blood then let his shirt fall back in place and tried to focus through his haze of relief and conflicting body signals. "He asked Likho to find out who else was here, then take him to the leshy."

"Hmph." Stribog grunted. "So they're close."

"Let Perun and Likho have this wood," Morana said. "We covered it twice over looking for him." She flicked a finger in Alex's direction. "You felt nothing of the horn. We should try something new. Time is against us, and we both grow weaker each day here."

Stribog stared in the direction of the leshy. His face darkened and his jaw clenched. He turned purposefully to Morana. "I defeated him once already. You and me together, we could beat Perun again."

"You defeated him by tricking him as he arrived. Now he's prepared for battle."

"I didn't have you with me, though. I'm sure we could do it. Me to imprison him, you to control, Alex to hold—"

Alex cut him off. "No way in hell," he said through his teeth. "Don't you *dare* try to use me again. I'll fight you with everything I have. And if you try to force me, I'll cut him out myself." He shouldered past the gods and started walking. "I swear to you I will."

"You feel strong enough to walk all the way home?" Stribog said it like a challenge.

Alex reached into the pocket of his jeans, pulled out the car keys, and dangled them from one finger for them to see. He heard Stribog sigh, and a moment later the tread of footsteps behind him.

"It was only thought," Stribog muttered, lapsing into imperfect English.

The burning glow in Alex's middle remained hot, fueling him, invigorating him. Anger burned away the fear and despair that had gripped him for the past day and night. Put a mountain in front of him, he'd hike it. Let Stribog try to imprison Perun inside him again, he'd knock the old man into next week. Alex marched down the trail toward the car with Stribog and Morana following silently behind.

They reached the parking lot and Alex took the driver's

seat without asking. He drove out of Jedediah Smith Park nearly as fast and recklessly as they'd driven in. Less than twenty minutes later, ten past ten according to the rental car's clock, they entered the town limits. The furnace in his abdomen had banked to a warm glow and his anger had settled to a low simmer, but his thoughts exploded in a hundred directions a minute trying to process recent events. Half a mile from the house he stopped the car and got out, because like hell he would take Stribog and Morana to where Alina and Dan and the boys lived.

He paused to grab his daypack from the back, not only because his phone was in there, but to keep Stribog and Morana from having anything personal of his in case they could use it to locate him or conjure him or who knew what. He could make sure to avoid Lower Lake Road and the Whale's Tail and the forests for as long as it took to feel sure they had what they'd come for and had left the area.

He drew a breath to sarcastically wish them good luck finding their damn horn, then thought of wishing them luck without the sarcasm. In the end, he just closed the back door. He slung one strap of the pack over his shoulder and started walking down the road. Behind him, he heard the heavy crunch of Stribog on the dirt road coming around to the driver's side, the car door closing, and the tires slowly making a U-turn then picking up speed as they drove away.

ARRIVING AT THE farmhouse, Alex felt like Dorothy waking up from Oz. Alina emerged from the kitchen, worry sketched on every angle of her face. Bonkers burst through the open door, joyous as always. The boys tumbled out behind the dog, wondering what was happening, and Dan stood framed in the doorway. The smell of food cooking hit him as he approached the stoop. Roast turkey overwhelmed the underlying scents of onion stuffing, allspice and cloves, baked apples, and pumpkin pie. He'd forgotten until this moment that today was Thanksgiving.

"Are you all right?" Alina asked, low enough that Dan and the boys wouldn't hear. She scanned him head to toe and gasped at the spots of blood on his jeans and backpack, though he'd rinsed the dried blood off his hands with his water bottle and zipped his jacket over the worst of the bloodstains on his shirts.

"Yeah. Fine. Hey, Dan," he said, not slowing as he pushed through the door.

Dan stepped back to avoid being bumped. His lips held an uncertain smile and half-formed greeting. Alex guessed Alina hadn't shared what he'd told her yesterday but there would've been no way Dan would miss Alina's concern last night.

Alex stopped in the middle of the kitchen with his back to them and let the daypack slide off his shoulder to the floor. He'd forgotten to take his shoes off outside. Making it to this point, inside the house with all his family healthy and surrounding him, had been the goalpost he'd focused on since Likho first got him lost in the forest. Only now could he take a full breath and allow himself to believe the insanity of the past week was behind him. They were all going to be okay.

"Robot walk! Robot walk!" Jake yelled, jumping on Alex's foot.

"No," Dan said, picking up on the emotions in the room as perceptively as always. "That's for us. We don't need to make Uncle Alex play too."

"Rawr!" Alex said, making his hands into claws over Jake's head. "I'm no robot. I'm a T. Rex and I stomp through the jungles."

David came at a run, ramming into his leg and jumping on his other foot. Alex clomped through the kitchen with exaggerated, high-knee steps, finding one small outlet for the nervous energy still coursing through him.

"Great," Dan said with a smile. "Just when the robot game was finally starting to lose steam."

Alex stopped at the end of the table. With one hand on each boy's shoulder, he gave a gentle push and they both jumped off. They tore into the living room roaring dinosaur roars, David first, then Jake imitating his older brother.

"Dan," Alina said, "would you mind keeping an eye on them so they don't pull the house down?"

"Sure," he replied, with no hint that he'd obviously grasped that she wanted to talk to Alex alone. A moment later, the TV turned on and clicked to a loud East Coast college football game just starting.

Alina turned on a hand mixer and spent ten seconds blending already mashed potatoes. She turned the mixer off. "So," she said casually, "everything worked out okay, I guess?" She grabbed a towel and wiped her hands excessively, glancing at him over one shoulder.

"Do you believe me, or do you think I'm crazy?"

She folded the towel, set it down, and finally turned, bracing both hands on the counter edge behind her. "A little bit of both, I guess."

He shrugged. "I get it. I'd probably think the same." He slid his rain jacket and coat off and let them drop on the floor. She clasped one hand over her mouth, though the blood on his flannel-lined work shirt had darkened to blend with the deep green material and brown dirt from the forest. He lifted the work shirt and the more heavily soaked T-shirt with no idea what either of them might see now on his belly. Dried blood still crusted his abdomen. Wide swaths where the skin had rubbed or folded held only a light reddish stain. The skin beneath was pale and whole.

"Alex," she said, alarmed. She moved to him in two quick steps and touched the carmine-colored flakes. Fingertip-sized chunks crumbled to dust and drifted to the floor. She brushed at the rest and it flaked and disintegrated, showing clearly that no injury lay beneath. Her fingers rested near his navel. He lifted his shirts higher, showing her pale, unstained, unmarred skin above to prove there was no other wound. She stared up into his face, her brows knit in confusion.

"I know. Let's sit down."

He let the shirts fall back in place and pulled a chair out at the table. Alina took one next to him. He filled her in on everything that had happened since his phone went dead. She didn't interrupt him. He hoped that being here with her, where she could look him in the eye, would help her believe his story. She'd already heard the weirdest and hardest to believe parts and they'd had a little time to sink in. When he told her about Perun breaking free, she kept glancing to his stomach, though disbelief still creased her brow and tightened her eyes.

"I thought I was going to die. I really did." He looked away and rubbed at a rough fabric leaf on the plastic pumpkin and ivy centerpiece. "And then I got this weird energy boost and I thought it was shock. And then I just kept feeling better." He made himself let go of the leaf. "I met up with Stribog and Morana on the trail. They were looking for me. Well, they were looking for Perun, anyway. We drove back here together."

"I didn't hear you drive up," she said, still unsure.

"I know. I got out near the airport."

She looked at a corner of the orange holiday tablecloth for two full breaths. "Okay," she said. "I believe you."

She met his eyes, and he could see the conflict there.

The story was unbelievable, but her faith in him was absolute. Just like when he'd told her at their mother's funeral that they'd be okay. Just like when he told her he was innocent of the crime he'd been charged with. If she said she believed him, she did, no matter the evidence to the contrary. He wrapped an arm around her shoulders and pulled her into an awkward embrace. She hugged him back, then pushed away and stood.

"So, it's over now?"

"It's over," he said.

She let out a long breath. "Well, okay then." She turned and braced one hand on the archway, speaking up to be heard over the game. "The Thanksgiving meal will be at two, like usual, not six. Let's get cracking."

Alex showered and changed, then jumped in to help out as well. The residual tension evaporated over the rest of the morning as the three of them cooked and spilled and had one almost-food-fight. At quarter past two, they were all seated at the table and passing around plates of food that could've fed four times their number. He dug into the feast with abandon.

The family time and the meal, the wine and coffee that followed, all left him satiated in more ways than he could count. A game of pin the tail on the turkey ensued, followed by pie and the family edition of Trivial Pursuit. The comfort of the festivities somehow managed to cushion all the awful events that Alex had endured over the past few days. It was his first Thanksgiving with his sister in years, and the perfect holiday to fold him back into home and happiness and normalcy.

Around sunset, Alex and Dan tackled the mountain of dishes while Alina played outside with Bonkers and the boys. She came in before they were halfway through the pile and tried to help, but they shooed her out to the living room.

"Hey, Dan," she said a few minutes later, "do you know that boy they're playing with?"

She was kneeling on the couch, keeping an eye on David and Jake from the living room. Dan leaned into Alex to see the yard from the small kitchen window.

"No, I don't think so. Probably someone visiting family for the holiday."

"Probably," she said. "I just couldn't think of anyone with family the right age for a young boy."

Goosebumps ran up Alex's arms despite the hot water flowing over his hands. Panic bloomed in his chest and circled his ribs like a tight band.

"Sorry, hon," Dan said. "I'm gonna bet that even you don't know all the neighbors around here that well."

Alex turned the water off and looked out the window, then stepped back to see Alina through the archway.

"I don't see them. Where are they?" He tried to remember if he'd mentioned Likho in his boy form or only as a goblin.

"Yeah, like you'd know a neighbor's boy when Alina doesn't," Dan quipped.

Alina had picked up on Alex's tone, though, and knelt frozen in place, her worried eyes locked on his.

"Seriously, Alina. Where are they?" He got to the living room in four long strides and leaned over the sofa, hands braced on the back.

Dan followed Alex out of the kitchen, the dishtowel still in his hand. "What's going on?" he said, in a tone that meant somebody better tell him.

Alina was on her feet. "They're there," Alina said. "Right by the porch." She pointed, but she was already moving to the door at the end of the couch that led to the back porch steps, Alex right behind her. She wrenched the door open and hurried down the stairs, snapping at David and Jake to get inside. She grabbed the boys by one arm each and hauled the protesting and alarmed children up the steps.

Alex leaned against the porch railing, scanning for the child Alina had seen. At the end of the driveway, walking away from them all into the encroaching dusk, was a thin boy of seven or eight. He was about to disappear around the hedges bordering the property.

"Likho," Alex yelled like a command.

The boy turned.

Smooth skin covered the boy's face from eyebrow to cheek where his right eye should have been.

PART TWO

Chapter Eleven

ALEX RAN.

Leaping the last of the porch steps, he bolted down the lawn. *Stupid*, one corner of his brain insisted, chasing a supernatural being, but two days of repressed anger burned like a furnace in his chest.

Likho turned left at the road, trotting toward the woods. Alex, only steps behind him now, cornered without slowing. One foot slipped on the gravel. He touched his hand to the road like a speed skater on a tight turn, and levered forward, barely missing a step.

Likho was nowhere in sight. Alex stopped and scanned in all directions, then continued running down the block to the edge of the woods. He stopped again and listened but heard nothing except distant traffic somewhere to the east of the swath of trees ahead and a slight hiss of surf at his back. His breath came hard, as much from fury as from the sprint. Adrenaline pumped through him, urging him to chase the little shit who'd tormented him and, worse, now threatened his family.

His family... *Fuck*.

Alex knew too well how Likho could jump about. He turned and ran back to the house, anxiety squeezing his heart like a fist. The driveway and back porch were empty. He bolted up the three steps to the kitchen door and burst inside. Through the arch into the living room, he saw Alina and Dan on the couch with the two confused boys between them. The look on Alina's face when she glanced up shattered him.

Dan's expression was hard. Uncertainty manifesting as anger.

"Alina says she doesn't know who that was, but it looked like you did," he said as Alex entered the living room.

Alex glanced from Dan to Alina, unsure what he should say.

Dan gave Alina space to explain but she mumbled to Jake instead, speaking slowly near his hearing aid. "We're not mad, sweetie. I didn't mean to scare you. It's just that's not a nice boy and I didn't know you were playing with him. We want you to play with your regular friends, okay? The ones we know."

Jake held one of his toy cars, rolling it up and down his leg, his recent upset already fading. David, older, had the wide-eyed uncertainty of a child who understands something important just passed but doesn't know what. He sat wrapped in stillness, as silent and unmoving as any young creature when a mother alerts to danger.

Alex took a chair opposite the four of them. Dan's silence asked the questions as loud as words.

"What has Alina told you about the last couple of days that I've been gone?" Alex asked him.

"Not much. She said you were with some friends." Dan glanced at his wife, his look more hurt than frustrated.

"None of this is her fault. I wanted the things I told her to stay between us. Not that I don't trust you," he added quickly. "It's nothing like that. It's just... this isn't an easy thing to believe. I didn't want it to cause any strain between the two of you." That had clearly backfired, but he left the obvious unsaid.

"I thought it was something that only involved him," Alina said. She addressed Dan, though her eyes were on Alex. "I didn't feel I had the right to share it with you. I was wrong. I'm sorry."

"Okay. Whatever. Somebody tell me now."

Alina's gaze stayed locked on Alex.

"I'm not jacking around," Dan said.

"David, can you show me the new racetrack you've been building?" Alina took the boys by one hand each and stood from the couch.

"I put my blue car on it, but it fell off," Jake said, spearing the red car in his hand toward the ground. He made a loud crashing noise.

David finally spoke. "Why isn't the boy nice?" he asked his mom.

"He just isn't." She led her sons to the staircase without looking back, leaving Alex to figure out how to tell his own tale.

He took a deep breath and dragged a hand down his chin, wondering how best to approach this.

"Are you at all religious?" he asked. He'd never seen Alina or Dan attend church.

"Not especially." Dan's tone was cautious. "My dad was Buddhist and my mom Protestant. I went to a Protestant grade school. Why?"

Because it might have made this slightly easier, Alex wanted to say.

"Okay, think of anything you unequivocally believe in that you can't see. Life after death. An infinite universe. Free will or fate. Whatever."

Dan's tone was soft and level. "Yeah. No. I'd rather you just tell me what the fuck's going on."

Alex paused again. "I came home today with my clothes covered in blood. A lot of it, all of it mine. But there's no wound. It's already gone. No trace of it left. Alina can back this up. She saw me before I washed up and put my clothes in the laundry."

"If you're trying to tell me you're Jesus come again or something, I'm going to stop you right now."

"No. No, this isn't about me. It's about a group of strangers I ran into last week. They started to fuck with me as soon as I met them, and they still are. Hard. I have no proof they are who... what... they say they are, and I sure as hell didn't believe them at first, either. But I believe them now." He picked for a moment at a broken callus on his hand, then looked up to meet Dan's eyes.

Dan remained silent, not in a good way. The Peanuts Thanksgiving cartoon played in the background, with Peppermint Patty complaining to Charlie Brown about his impromptu holiday meal. Upstairs, the boys argued over future racetrack construction.

Alex forged on and summarized the events around the kite that led to the finger sticking out of his belly, which Mike had seen. Then about Likho trapping him in the woods and the phone calls he'd made to Alina from there. They were the only semi-corroborated things he could come up with, but here—safe at home, full of Thanksgiving dinner—it sounded even crazier than when he'd told Alina. He didn't even have the sliver of proof he'd given his sister.

Disbelief bordering on derision colored each of Dan's words when he finally spoke. "So you chased a second grader down the road because you think he's some monster out of Russian folklore?"

"The boy in the forest had no right eye. No eye socket. No scar. He said Stribog had done it to him. The boy in the driveway had smooth skin where a right eye should have been."

"Did Alina see that too?"

"I don't know. The first time I saw Likho, he kept his right side turned away from me."

The silence filled the space between them with a weight that felt almost palpable.

"You know I'm adopted, right?" Dan said.

Alex tried to follow the whiplash change of topic. "I do."

"You know how old I was when I found out?"

"I think Alina said you were a teenager."

Dan nodded. "Fifteen. I learned it from friends of my parents when they were visiting. They didn't realize I'd never been told." That part, Alex hadn't known. "Do you know how many lies my parents told me over the years?" His voice was low and tight with suppressed emotion, past and present. "Lies to explain how I was born in Portland when they'd always lived in Eugene. Lies to explain why I was an only child." He laced his fingers and sat forward. "Honesty is important to me, Alex. And nothing is more important to me than my children."

They were the qualities that made Dan and Alina's marriage so strong. Alina was one of the most honest people Alex knew, and her devotion to her children was fierce.

"All I understand right now," Dan continued, his words quiet, his jaw tight, "is that you're saying you've brought danger near my family. If you're lying, stop. If you're not, then I don't know if this has anything to do with your prison time, but whatever it is, wherever it came from, I want it gone."

Dan's fingers were laced in a knot on his knees. Anger and confusion and the lifelong hatred of confrontation Alina had told Alex about added a slight tremor to his words. His warning expression and careful control struck Alex harder than a fist. Dan waited for Alex to nod.

"I'll take care of it," Alex said. His brother-in-law stood and headed for the stairs. "I promise," he said to Dan's rigid back.

Alex sat alone in the living room, listening to his sister and her husband talking in low voices above, and to the kids drowning them out with their play that had returned to full volume. This morning, he'd never wanted to see

Stribog again; now, getting his help was all he could think about. He needed an ally strong enough to confront Likho or, at the least, someone to teach him how to fight the thing himself.

A text alert pinged on his phone. He slipped the chain over his head and saw the text was from Fen.

Happy Thanksgiving, Turkey, accompanied by an emoji of a cartoon turkey.

Alex thought about giving him a call to say Happy Thanksgiving back and update Fen on what his lawyer had told him, but he didn't have the energy for it tonight. It wasn't like he could share any of the crazy from the past few days, and the last thing he wanted was to be evasive when he and Fen were only a few days back into being on good terms.

You too, he texted. *I'll give you a call next week.*

He sighed and stood to leave. Glancing into the kitchen, he saw the last few items still on the table. On impulse, he crossed beneath the arch and set an empty wine bottle from dinner on the floor under the table for luck; a Russian superstition his grandfather had observed. If fairy tale characters were walking around in the woods and he was having conversations with Slavic gods, then maybe superstitious nonsense wasn't nonsense at all.

Leaving Alina and Dan to their privacy, he headed for his cottage. Since he still had his phone out, he pulled up the number for the Four Winds from his frequent calls there two nights ago and dialed as he walked. Neither Stribog nor Morana answered.

Once inside, he thought again of the wine bottle he'd placed under the table. For the first time in years, he remembered the amulet his grandfather had given him before pitching a championship baseball game in junior high; a small horseshoe for luck with a fish to grant wishes jumping across the middle. It couldn't hurt to find it. The only thing he could think of that might counter Misfortune would be a whole lot of luck.

On hands and knees, he started pulling out the small boxes and bags of personal items he kept stored beneath the bed. Reaching for one at the end of his grasp, he bumped it away with his fingers. Stretching out flat on the floor, he spun the corner of the box toward him, and again once more. As the box came nearer, his view under the bed changed. He found himself staring past the end of the mattress to the floor under his small desk against the front wall. Something squatted there in the shadowed corner. He tried to de-anthropomorphize the thing, picturing it as a shoe propped half against the wall with laces on the floor instead of legs, or one of Bonkers' toys with fuzzy protrusions. A minute movement occurred near the top of the shape, hidden in the deepest shadows. Eyes had blinked.

"*Eto plohoy dom,*" it said. "*U tebya net ochaga.*"

Alex scrambled backward, scraping his back and cracking his head on the frame of the bed.

"What the fuck!" he shouted at the room in general, one hand checking for blood on his scalp and finding none.

The thing stomped out from under the desk. He lost sight of it for a second until it came around the bottom of the bed and stopped, blocking his path to the door. Alex backed slowly into the corner between the kitchen counter and bed, glancing to see if a knife lay in reach. One didn't, of course.

Less than half the size of Koschei's attendants, it wore a peaked hat of thick fabric, trimmed at the brim in fur. The rest of the clothing was equally archaic: a dark-gray tunic over worn, black leggings, and old-style bast shoes of woven fiber. His thick gray-white beard—yellowed below his mouth—hid all his lower face except for full lips. His nose was large and scabbed, his hands gnarled. His eyes were dark and menacing, but the deep wrinkles around them were stretched into an expression of frustration rather than threat.

Alex's brain replayed what he'd heard and translated the Russian. *This house is bad. There's no hearth.*

His fists relaxed slightly but his mind raced. Likho in some new form? Not likely. The attitude and comment didn't fit. It wanted him to have a fireplace. Or maybe a stove. Maybe so it could live at the back, in the ashes. One of the lesser beings Stribog spoke of, and if Alex's guess was right, one of the very few benevolent ones. At least, benevolent as long as it was treated well.

"I'm honored you traveled here to"—he searched for the right word in Russian—"to protect my home for me. I'm sorry I don't have a stove for you." He nearly said it was in the other house before catching himself. He didn't want this thing going anywhere near Alina's family.

Facing off this way, it would have been easy for Alex to see the creature as some act-two, Disney-esque comic relief at the end of his insane week. It was a mistake he wouldn't make. This thing had no more in common with the Scottish house fairies known as brownies than Koschei's attendants had with lawn-ornament gnomes. They were ancient creatures filled with magic, all of them, and you underestimated them at your peril. His grandfather had spoken with respect of the domovoi guarding the home, and the other protectors of the homestead—livestock guardians, yard spirits, barn spirits, bathhouse ones—but also with caution. Disrespected, a domovoi might set the house ablaze in the night and stand outside to watch the family burn.

Moving cautiously, he said, "I think I have some bread."

He usually kept basic groceries in the cottage to make his work lunches. He pulled a loaf of generic wheat bread from a cabinet and tossed a slice on the floor, not wanting to get close.

The little man picked up the offering and shoved large chunks into his small mouth. Long, uneven, yellowed teeth showed when he opened wide. Narrow teeth, like needles. He gnashed at his food more than chewed it. The rending sounds were disturbing. An unpleasant image formed when Alex pictured the domovoi dealing with cockroaches or house mice.

The domovoi swallowed the last of the bread and nodded in satisfaction. "I clean under the bed?" It nodded to the boxes and bags piled on the bedspread.

"No, that's okay. I was just looking for something."

He unfolded the flaps of a cardboard box while trying to think of a way to get rid of the thing without causing offense. The domovoi grabbed the bottom of the duvet and climbed hand over hand onto the bed, then stood peering into the box, fists on hips.

"My grandfather gave me an amulet on a chain a long time ago." It was what Alex tried to say in Russian, anyway. "He told me it was for good luck. I feel like I could use some."

The little man stomped across the bed to a shoebox and tapped the top. Alex opened it and pulled out a bundle of letters sent by his parents when he'd been away at camp one summer. Below, tangled with soccer, track, and baseball medals, he found the amulet.

Lifting it out, it lay heavy in his palm, the sturdy chain dangling down. It gleamed in the light of his lamp, the horseshoe in gold paint and the jumping fish in silver. It had tarnished only slightly over the years. His grandfather had given it to him when he was fourteen. He'd worn it day and night for the next year. When his father's death coincided with his mother's diagnosis for the same cancer, he'd taken it off and never touched it again. At thirty-two, he knew cancer had nothing to do with luck. He slipped the chain over his head.

"I need a broom," the domovoi proclaimed.

"I'll see if I can get you one tomorrow." Maybe he could find it a toy one. "You can rest for now, Master Domovoi."

The thing looked around his small room and harrumphed, then climbed down the bedspread and disappeared back under the desk. He watched as it flopped onto its side and appeared to sleep.

His forearms pebbled with gooseflesh at another thought. He'd seen the truth of Stribog's words, that the creatures arriving here were drawn to him for associating with the gods, and to the people he associated with. He wondered now if that threat extended beyond his family. Mike Murphy had spent more time with him lately than anyone outside Alina, Dan, and the kids. He'd also interacted with Stribog and Morana directly. Alex hadn't spoken to him since Tuesday evening, when Mike had literally handed him, out of his mind with pain, into Stribog's arms. He owed the man a call to let him know he was okay and to make sure nothing unusual was happening.

"Hey, Mike," he said when the call picked up.

Despite the holiday, he wasn't surprised to reach him, knowing that he had no family nearby. Guilt struck along with the realization that it had never occurred to him to invite Mike to Thanksgiving dinner. On the heels of the thought, though, practicality overrode the sentiment. Best Mike hadn't been here, or he might have been sucked into the drama of Likho's appearance.

"Am I interrupting anything?" he asked.

"No. You're fine. About to turn on the game, is all. What's up?"

There was no hesitation in Mike's voice, no strains of concern that he might be called out for another favor, dragged into another weird scenario.

"Just thought I should let you know that things turned out okay the other night. Sorry I didn't call you earlier, but it was rough for a bit. I only really started feeling like myself again today."

"Glad to hear you're all right."

"Who's playing tonight?" he asked, stalling while he debated if he should warn Mike about Likho and Koschei and all the other things afoot in the county.

"Saints and Bills. I was stationed in New Orleans for a bit. I still try to catch the Saints' games when I can."

Alex couldn't see any way to start. His experience with Dan was still fresh; the anger, the disbelief bordering on derision. And that from family, someone who'd known him nearly ten years. Warning a coworker about fairy tales come to life—worse, someone who probably already doubted his mental stability—felt insurmountable.

"Well, I won't keep you from the game. I just wanted to say thanks again. Enjoy your long weekend. I'll see you on Monday."

They hung up and Alex tossed the phone on the bed in frustration. He rubbed a hand through his hair, wondering if he'd done the right thing. Replaying the conversation, he sifted it for ways he might have broached the topic, or at least given some vague warning.

Like what? *Watch out for one-eyed seven-year-old kids?*

Last time Alex called the motel he'd asked the front desk if Stribog and Morana had checked out, but the man said he wasn't allowed to give information about guests. He planned to call again later, maybe around ten, but he wasn't leaving his family tonight, not even for a short time. He lay back and the amulet under his shirt slid to one side. He laid a hand over it, tracing the patterns beneath his shirt.

If Stribog and Morana weren't back by morning, then he needed a plan of his own. And he thought he might just be forming one. He had plenty of time to review and improve it; with a domovoi snoring under his desk, he wasn't about to sleep anytime soon.

Chapter Twelve

MIKE HUNG UP with Alex, set his phone down, and scraped the bottom of the can. The last of the beef and bean chili plopped into the saucepan, leaving a tiny spray of red polka dots on the chipped white enamel of the stovetop. He wiped the stove, turned down the heat, and left dinner simmering while he checked his phone for missed texts or messages.

His lack of expectations buffered the slight disappointment at finding none. His youngest had called this morning, as he did every holiday and birthday, and that was good enough. They had a connection, however awkward, and through him, he kept up on news of the rest of the family. He stirred the chili and walked to the back door. Still enough light to scan the branches of the tree on the hill, but there was no sign of the strange owl he'd seen last night.

Whistling a bar from an old '70s Styx tune that had been stuck in his head all day, he returned to the kitchen, poured the chili into a bowl, dropped a spoon in it, grabbed a sleeve of Saltines, and carried his dinner to the sofa. Hooking a foot around one of the hacksaw-shortened legs of the TV tray at the side of the couch, he dragged it over and set his food down. He settled on the sofa with a grunt and pulled the tray in close, where the height perfectly matched his low couch and sway-backed cushions.

Someday, if one of his kids came by for the holiday, he'd make a turkey, maybe one of those deep-fried ones, with mashed potatoes and yams. Cranberry and stuffing, and pie. Otherwise, this did just fine, but traditional dinner or not, there'd never been a year that he'd missed giving thanks. He folded his hands in prayer on the edge of the TV tray.

"Thank you for my boys, for my parents, for good health, for food on my table and a roof over my head." He ended with the same as he had since high school. "And thank you for strong hands."

He clicked the TV remote. As the picture and volume snapped on, he heard a squeal of brakes somewhere near the entrance to the trailer park followed by a sharp, yelping whine. He opened his front door and scanned the intersection near his trailer and the stop sign at the main road into the trailer park, seeing nothing. No cars. No dogs. He closed the door and settled again.

A few minutes later, finished with his dinner and dozing with the remote in his hand, he woke to a metallic scratching and soft whine. He opened the door to find a long-haired German shepherd on his doorstep. The animal's coat was mangy and patchy but where it remained thick, the colors were rich shades of burnt orange and black. Highlights of cream painted the toes, the feathered fur at the backs of the legs, and the underside of a tail that wagged tentatively, barely twitching.

They studied each other. The dog didn't pant, just stared up at him, looking intently into his eyes. He assumed this to be the source of the squealing brakes and yelp earlier. He pulled the door wider.

"Trial basis till we see if you're hurt."

The dog understood the words or the gesture and cautiously picked its way inside, sniffing the unfamiliar air and snuffling along the floor.

There hadn't been much opportunity to own animals between his Navy years and the places he'd lived since. He'd always liked dogs, though, and knew food would help him win trust. He opened the fridge and found a value pack of liverwurst lunch meat behind the condiments and Tupperware containers of leftovers. Peeling two slices off the top, he dropped them on the floor and the dog wolfed them down. He filled an empty plastic bowl with water and set it below the camper-sized table opposite the stove. It drank, sending splashes of water in all directions. He patted its shoulder, and the tail wagged a little more vigorously.

He'd never seen the scruffy animal before. If it had been hit, it must have been a fairly light impact. It had no obvious injuries and didn't appear to limp. Settling back on the couch, he ate dinner while the dog watched every dip and lift of the spoon. Finished, he set the dinner bowl on the floor and let the dog lick it clean.

The dog didn't seem aggressive, and he hoped a little trust had been established. Hopefully enough that he wouldn't get bitten in the face trying to examine it for injuries. He knelt cautiously on one knee, face level with its muzzle.

"Okay, everybody stay nice and calm. I'm just going to check you."

Mike began at the head and felt down the neck and body, careful around the ribs in case he elicited a reactive bite. The dog whimpered slightly at pressure just forward of the hip but appeared to have no serious injury. She also turned out to be female. He stood, scrubbing her head with his fingertips, hoping the scruffy coat didn't indicate mange. He checked the neck again, finding no collar buried under the ruff of fur. "Yeah, I think you're going to be okay."

Shelters wouldn't be open until morning at the earliest and, at worst, might be closed for the entire holiday weekend. He sat on the couch again and the dog leaned against his legs. He rubbed her head between her large, black ears.

"Maybe a weekend wouldn't be so bad."

She stared into his eyes—not in a soulful golden retriever manner, like a friend's dog had always done when he petted it—but with an intensity he found slightly disconcerting. A delving scrutiny, an aspect of wanting that went beyond food. Maybe it was a shepherd thing. The only ones he'd known were military dogs with almost human smarts. He scratched her head again and she licked his forearm, instantly dog-like again.

Mike stayed up late, as usual, but let the dog out in the backyard before bed. She checked out the yard, did her business, stared intently at the swimming koi, then drank out of the pond. Back inside, she followed him into the bedroom and sniffed at the framed Polaroid of his kids on his low dresser, knocking it over. He picked it up and wiped the wet nose print from the face of his second-to-youngest boy. All four boys stood in a line, all grinning except the three-year-old, who was picking his nose. His wife had sent the photo to him four months before she'd filed divorce papers. It was the only photo he had of all four kids together, grainy, yellowing, and bleaching with age. He wondered if any of his kids owned a dog now, like they'd wanted back then. Maybe so. They weren't kids anymore. Hell, two of them had bought their own homes. He set the photo back in its place, stripped off his sweatpants and flannel shirt, and climbed into bed.

MIKE WOKE WITH a nagging feeling something was wrong. More than wrong.

A few years after his divorce, his ship had put in at Comalapa in El Salvador. He'd gone to a dance and left with a local woman and had woken in the middle of the night to a man near the bed holding a baseball bat, thumping it rhythmically on the doorframe. Mike had always been big, and back then he'd been in his prime. The two of them had faced off for a long, tense moment before Mike eased past the man and out the front door.

Like that night, he woke now, tense and alert. He faced the doorway to the kitchen, his only movement to open his eyes. The bedroom window of his trailer was high and small, but the moon stared in, at just the right angle to shine across his covers and onto the floor. The dog stood silent in the small pool of light, her face inches from his own, the intensity back in her stare; her lips curled, muscles bunched.

She panted slightly, as she never had earlier in the evening, even when lying near the space heater. A mouthful of teeth shone wetly in the moonlight, white and gleaming; a double set of teeth, upper and lower. Mike's heart pounded at the sight. A mirror image to his own double set of teeth… except that the dog's were straight and long as a wolf's and set in a jaw strong enough to break bones. Like facing off with the man in El Salvador, he maintained eye contact with his adversary, his body coiled but motionless. Out of sight, he curled his right hand to grip the underside of his pillow.

In one swift movement, he sat up with a yell and flung his pillow into the dog's face. It had the impact of a marshmallow, but it forced her back a step and obstructed her vision for a heartbeat while he grabbed a small bowling trophy off his dresser as he jumped out of bed. A Greek column of junky plastic, covered in metallic gold paint, but filled with a resin or plaster that gave it heft.

"Go ahead. Try it." The man in El Salvador had decided not to try him, but over the years a couple of back-alley characters had.

He swung the trophy at the dog's head, but the animal shied back so that the tip glanced off its nose in an ineffectual blow. The dog made an incongruously bird-like screech, snapped once at his forearm, tearing the skin but not finding purchase to bite down, and backed out of the bedroom. Mike followed. She lunged for his arm again, then backed some more. Like a mountain lion— or a shark—it seemed it had been looking for easy prey rather than a fight.

Mike needed room to move. The kitchen was narrower than the bedroom, no more than a walkway. The dog backed, feinting and snapping at him again. If she'd grabbed his hand or arm hard enough, she might've gotten the better of him, but she seemed focused on his chest. He clubbed her another glancing blow from the trophy and grabbed the dinner saucepan off the stove. He threw the trophy at her, then swung the pan in a full-arm swipe, putting his back and hips into it.

The dog sprang away like no dog he'd ever seen, rearing up onto its hind legs and arching back to avoid his swing. It should have fallen over backward. Instead, it continued to move back and, inconceivably, up. The muzzle shrank and curved into a sharp beak; the front legs spread wide and sprouted scraggly gray-brown feathers. The torso shortened and the hind end tucked up into thin legs with hooked talons for feet.

The owl flapped hard twice, hovering near the ceiling of the low trailer. With a sharp cry that showed its teeth— yes, he hadn't imagined it, the bird had teeth, and not one set, but two—it dove for his face.

He clutched the pan in a two-handed grip. Swinging with all his might, he caught the bird under one wing and sent it hurtling into a cabinet. It dropped to the counter but sprang immediately back into the air, this time flying to the living room and aiming for the front door. It hit the door feet first, as if attacking it. Mike ran the other way, to the back door, threw it open, and pitched down the stairs, landing on his left shoulder, his right hand still clutching the pan. Before he could stand, the owl streaked out the open door. He crossed his forearms protectively over his face, but the bird flapped away and over the hill.

Mike lay on the cold, damp ground in his T-shirt and boxers, his breath coming short and fast, his pulse pounding in his ears, his mind foggy with adrenaline and disbelief.

Chapter Thirteen

FIRST THING IN the morning, Alex checked the main house. Bonkers lumbered to his feet and greeted him with his customary tail wagging and slobber. The sounds of someone brushing their teeth in the upstairs bathroom assured him all was well. Probably Dan getting ready for work as federal regulations didn't allow banks to close four days in a row.

Back in his cottage, Alex pulled his riding leathers over his clothes, grabbed his wallet and keys, and drove straight to the Four Winds. Stribog and Morana weren't there, so he went to the diner across the street for breakfast. Thankfully, the morning crew looked to be entirely different from the staff the other evening when he'd been there with Mike.

Over a meal of bacon, eggs, toast, and coffee, he analyzed the problems he faced. Before yesterday, he could have counted on the two Slavic gods staying close to him, but that arrangement had ended once Perun was free. Perun was Stribog's enemy and his problem now. Likho was Alex's, and he didn't know how to fight him without Stribog and Morana's help. He considered going back to the woods to leave a message for them with Koschei, then shook his head at the notion. How had his life reached the level of insanity where a plan like that seemed a rational option?

Worse, what if he couldn't reach the two gods, or if he got a message to them and they didn't care? How did one go about finding a being that could appear and disappear at will? More than that, even if he did manage to find

Likho, how could he capture or fight him? In the flush of anger yesterday, while chasing him, he'd felt capable of taking the creature apart with his bare hands. But in reality, even if he found him and managed to grab him, Likho would likely just disappear—that or transform into the goblin, or worse. As a last-ditch option, he tried summoning Stribog or Morana by tossing his wish to find them out to the universe as a silent prayer, if a not very reverent one.

By half past nine he'd finished his meal and Stribog's rental car was still nowhere to be seen. Time to take matters into his own hands. Over breakfast, he'd fleshed out the germ of his idea from last night and developed it into a plan—of sorts, anyway. One moment, it felt feasible, like it might have teeth; the next, it felt foolishly naive. Either way, it was the only plan he had, and he couldn't sit around, maybe waiting days for Stribog, while Likho came after his family.

He left the diner but drove across the street anyway and knocked on both doors to be sure. As expected, the rooms were dark and there was no answer. He went to the main office. This morning's clerk had no issue with looking up their information or sharing that they'd checked out yesterday afternoon. Alex would be shouting from a mountaintop in celebration if they'd found the horn and gotten out of Dodge, but he'd seen Likho last night. If Stribog and Morana had gone back to wherever they'd come from, the lesser creatures should have followed. All this meant now was that he was left with no allies—such as they had been—and a half-assed plan.

He got back on his bike, then decided to call his parole officer before setting his plan in motion. The likelihood of things going sideways today seemed high. If Likho killed him, then his legal troubles were irrelevant. But if he got swept away somewhere again and missed his biweekly check-in today, the ramifications for him could be long-term. He hit speed dial for Jim Davenport's direct number.

In place of a greeting, Davenport answered the phone with "This is an unusual time of day for us to call, isn't it, Mr Orlov?" For some reason the man always spoke in the royal "we." "Are we working today?"

"No. Frank let the whole crew off for the long weekend." *Better than you got*, he thought.

"And why are we calling from a motel?"

Davenport must have pulled up Alex's GPS data on the computer. Damn, that technology was accurate.

"Just pulled over to make the call."

"All right. Mr Orlov, are you still working?"

They'd covered this already, but these were the official questions now. Like a biweekly unemployment application, the same set of questions had to be asked and answered each time.

"Yes."

"Any change in employment?"

"No." Though it reminded him that he really did need to call Frank. Thankfully, due to the holiday, he'd only missed the one day that Mike had made excuses for him.

"Have you been outside Del Norte County in the past fourteen days?"

"No."

"Have you engaged in any illegal activity or fraternized with any known felons in the past fourteen days?"

"No." But Alex thought wryly that the man's jaw would drop at the company he *had* been keeping.

"Do you have any plans to travel in the next fourteen days?"

"No." Providing he wasn't swept into some supernatural realm.

"All right, Mr Orlov. Any difficulties or challenges I can help you with?" Under the annoying royal "we" and mild condescension, Davenport seemed a passably okay guy. Cynical, but Alex had the feeling he'd be genuinely willing to help someone succeed if they put in the effort.

"No. Things are going fine, thanks."

"Well then, we'll be talking to you again two weeks from today."

That bit of business out of the way, Alex put his phone away and started his bike, committed to setting his Scooby-Doo-level plan into action.

The weather was clear, which in Crescent City meant completely overcast but with high fog and no precipitation. The traffic today looked to be light on commuters and heavy on shoppers. He turned right out of the parking lot and joined the flow, headed for a series of stores that might have opened as early as six o'clock for Black Friday sales or not at all for some of the smaller shops. Driving a crisscross pattern around the city, he followed the list he'd made last night of pawn shops, antique shops, discount stores, a Christian gift store, and a shop that billed itself in the yellow pages as specializing in the metaphysical.

An hour and a half later, he had one pocket of his jacket filled with a rabbit's foot on a cheap ball and bead chain, a four-leaf clover in acrylic, a piece of jade, a bag of "lucky" herbs, a Japanese *omamori* charm, and a small lucky cat. In his other pocket: carp scales, desiccated scarab beetles, a bag of acorns, a small cross, a dreamcatcher, a Turkish *nazar boncuğu*, and a small red Buddha. And in the back pocket of his jeans, the foremost item: a railroad spike.

His last stop took him to a dollar store where he hunted the makeup aisle until he found a cheap kit with powdered foundation on one side and a round mirror on the other. Back out in the parking lot, he opened the case and took a deep breath. If any of this harebrained scheme worked, this should be the "GO" button. He dropped the case on the pavement and smashed his boot heel into the mirror, shattering it. Hopefully, it would help him find Likho today, but if a broken mirror bound misfortune to him for the next seven years, so be it. The last three had been shit anyway. He could deal with a few more to save his family.

The next step was a bit hazier. If the broken mirror didn't draw Likho to him, then he'd have to go seek out bad luck and try his best not to get killed in the process. He knew of a local trail fraught with multiple hazards: steep drop-offs, mountain lions in the area. Maybe being alone and away from help would attract the creature, like it had on Boy Scout Tree Trail. And if so, he'd hope that Likho would continue to keep getting his rocks off by tormenting him rather than killing him outright.

He gripped his grandfather's medallion through his shirt and rubbed it for a little extra luck. Going after Likho alone and winging it was not how he'd wanted this to go down, not when there were two gods around somewhere who owed him big time.

Headed for the north end of town, a flatbed construction truck loaded with tar paper, roofing shingles, and other supplies changed lanes in front of him, making it hard to see ahead. He signaled a move to the opposite lane but changed back immediately to avoid a large pothole. In front of him the truck took a dip in the road too fast, bounced as the back tires hit bottom, and spat a small, unsecured box off the tailgate. Roofing tacks detonated in every direction. Alex swerved instinctively, nearly sideswiping a car, and threading the needle between the cluster of tacks and the lane line. It made him wonder whether his good luck charms were already at work. Or the broken mirror. Maybe both.

With adrenaline still burning his fingers from his near misses, he passed the Four Winds and turned suddenly into the driveway when he saw a gray four-door parked in the corner of the lot. The car was parked a good distance from their old rooms, but he knocked on both doors anyway, then checked with the clerk again even though the car wasn't the right make and bore no license plate cover with Stribog's rental agency logo.

Confirming that Stribog and Morana hadn't returned, he started his bike with a hollow hopelessness settling in the pit of his stomach, ready to head for the trail he had in mind off Highway 199. He walked the motorcycle back far enough to make a U-turn but it felt unusually heavy and sluggish and he knew before he looked down what he'd see. The back tire was nearly completely flat. Apparently, he hadn't missed all the tacks in the road.

"God damn it." He took his helmet off, walked past the U-shaped motel, and looked up and down the street. In a rare stroke of good fortune, there was an old-fashioned gas station on the same side of the street at the end of the next block. The sandwich board out front said Ted's.

It was perfect. Two old gas pumps and a rundown-looking service garage attached to the customer service side; no big chain business, no minimart. A tow truck sat parked in front of the garage door with "Ted's Tow" in black lettering against gold paint.

The businesses between the motel and the station had a series of unconnected driveways with no sidewalk and cars parked here and there along the curb. He ended up pushing the heavy bike on its flat tire across the street, down the open parking spots, then back across the crosswalk to the gas station. He was sweating buckets by the time he booted the kickstand down.

There was no one behind the front desk and no bell. The paint on the thin wooden counter was so smeared with dirt and grease it was hard to tell if the original color had been white, cream, or light yellow. Dirt and mud spattered the linoleum floor and congregated thickly at the edges and corners. An odor of motor oil wafted in the air from the spotted concrete in the bay, plus the years of it tracked into the front office and oily hands coating it on every surface. A heavy black phone with a circular dial sat on the desk, and a swinging, full-length vinyl door separated the tiny front office from the garage beyond.

The phone began to ring with a jarringly loud peal. With no answering machine connected to it, the phone shrilled for long enough that Alex was tempted to answer it just to make it stop. A toilet flushed somewhere in the garage and a heavyset man emerged. Without so much as a flick of his eyes toward Alex, he picked up the phone.

"Ted's," he answered gruffly. "This is Ted." He paused. "Do you have the mile marker?" A pad of paper lay near the phone with a pencil resting atop it. He pulled it to him with one thick finger and scribbled notes. He listened for another minute without speaking. "You've got to be shitting me." Pause. "Yeah, well, life's stranger than fiction, right? Okay, I'll get Bill on the way."

He pushed the swinging door open to the back and yelled into the service shop over the sound of an air compressor. "Billy-boy. You got a call." The compressor stopped and a man of similar age came to the counter and took the slip of paper he was handed. He wore a work shirt with an embroidered patch over the left breast stating he was not Billy-boy, but Bill.

"You aren't going to believe this," the man said to not-Billy-boy.

"What's that?"

"Some guy had a driver's-side blowout on northbound 101, just this side of Smith River. He steered to the shoulder, got stopped okay, set up hazard triangles, and was changing his tire when a semi loaded with—get this, car tires—passed him just as a tiedown on the truck came loose. A tire came flying off and hit the poor sap in the back of the head, killing him dead."

Bill scoffed. "Bullshit."

"Swear on my granny's grave." He held his hand up, palm out.

"Damn."

"CHP wants you to tow the car to the holding yard."

"Got it."

Bill folded the paper and stuck it in his shirt pocket. He pushed through the short wooden barrier next to the counter and out the front door to his truck.

Ted turned, at last, to look at Alex. He wore baggy jeans belted below his belly and a plain navy T-shirt despite the drafty building. No name stitched over his breast. "What can I do for you?"

"Got a flat tire I need patched."

Ted looked wistfully out the large front window to the tow truck just pulling out. He chewed the scruffy gray hairs of his beard just below his lip. "What kind of car?"

"Motorcycle."

"Oh. Hell, I guess I can do that. I'll open the bay door. Push it in for me, will you?"

"Sure thing."

Ted lifted the bay door by hand, giving it a shove to roll it up the last few feet. Alex maneuvered his bike inside and offered to help, but Ted waved him off. With no waiting room or chairs, Alex went back out front and sat on the curb stop in front of the tow truck's parking space.

Watching the flow of traffic, he wondered again about the coincidence of swerving around the pothole just as the construction truck hit that dip and dropped tacks into the road. He'd thought himself unlucky to be behind the truck, then lucky not to wreck, then unlucky to have a flat, then lucky to find a service station so close.

He didn't know if the talismans he'd collected had anything to do with it, but the last few days had left him open to believing just about anything by now. The overheard story beat all, though. The guy with a flat tire getting hit in the head with a tire from the semitruck carrying tires that came loose just as it passed him? If that wasn't Misfortune at work, he didn't know what was. And there he'd been, in the gas station with a flat tire, at just the right time to hear the call and the address. Maybe instead of drawing Likho to himself, he'd instead had the luck to stumble into a way to track the creature.

By the time Ted had the tire fixed, Alex's mind was made up. He'd head up to Smith River. He paid the man, drove out to the main road, turned right on Third then left on M, and followed the business stretch of 101 out of town.

Chapter Fourteen

THE ACCIDENT HAD caused traffic to back up on the two-lane highway starting a couple of miles south of the little town. Alex made faster progress than most, able to weave between cars and along the shoulder. When he got close enough to the scene, it looked like the ambulance or coroner must have already left with the body, but highway patrol officers and Bill, the tow truck driver, were still on site. He eased back into the traffic and crawled forward with the cars.

There were three officers on scene—one slowing the approaching traffic, one pushing a measuring wheel to record data for the report, and one talking to Bill as he set up to load the car on his truck. A tire iron was still plugged into one of the car's lugs. A spare tire lay to the side, and another larger tire lay halfway across the white line of the shoulder. He was pretty sure he saw blood on the fender over the flat tire. Alex studied the woods surrounding the area, looking for any sign that Likho had hung around to enjoy his handiwork.

In a few minutes he'd be past the wreck and Alex wondered if he should write the whole thing off as coincidence until a CHP radio squawked to life through a partially rolled-down car window on one of the patrol vehicles. A dispatcher's static-filled voice echoed in all three officers' portable radios.

"759, are you available to respond to an 1181?"

The female officer talking to Bill answered on the mic clipped at her shoulder. "759, available." She nodded to Bill and headed for her car at about the same pace Alex progressed past the accident.

"759, respond to an 1181, Highway 101, mile post 808. Be advised, sheriff's department is on scene with a homeowner involved in an accidental weapons discharge that caused the traffic accident. Allegedly cleaning a gun on the porch. Homeowner is in custody. Scene is secure. Ambulance is en route."

A bizarre shooting accident causing a wreck that close in time and location to the bizarre tire fatality; it certainly sounded like Misfortune still at work. Either that or Alex was fabricating a wild goose chase for himself.

The officer confirmed the information and got in her car. She left her emergency lights on and pulled into the snarl of traffic, Alex only three spots behind her. Everything about this felt like a genuine lead and had him wound tight as a watch spring. Just ahead, traffic broke free and returned to normal speed. The officer tapped her siren and pulled away from him.

Keeping the officer in sight wasn't essential, but timing this to catch Likho was—if he was even there at all. Mile marker 808 had to be fairly close; Crescent City was in the 790s, and Alex was already a few miles north of town. He weighed the advantages of keeping the officer in sight against a parolee getting pulled over for speeding. His hands clenched the handlebars with a grip he wished could be around Likho's throat, but he backed off the accelerator.

Seven miles later, he saw the highway patrol car and a sheriff's vehicle parked on the shoulder behind what looked to be a fender bender accident. Two people were talking animatedly to the highway patrol officer, one of them pointing to a third person in custody in the back of the sheriff's vehicle. Another person was stretched out at the side of the road and the sheriff's officer held a wad of something to their arm. The best he could piece things together from what he'd heard and what he saw was that someone from the trailer home set back off the road must have accidentally fired a gun and the bullet had gone through a car window, hitting a person in the first car. First car hit the brakes, and the car behind rear-ended them.

Alex passed the wreck and searched along the heavily tree-lined road and thick undergrowth for any sign of Likho, as well as for a pullout or side road where he could park and be less obvious. A green and white Welcome to Oregon sign, half blending into the roadside trees and shrubs, registered in his brain at the last minute.

He jammed on his brakes and jerked the bike to the shoulder, still in full sight of the officers. When the police had first put his ankle monitor on, he'd been instructed that he was free to travel within Del Norte County but could only leave the county for up to two days with permission and a travel pass. Crossing a state line was forbidden except in case of emergency, and only then with a written exemption.

If he'd crossed into Oregon just now, his ankle monitor would have sent an alert to the Crescent City police station. He knew from his ranger days that GPS could track within three feet or so, but he had no way to know if the welcome sign had been erected on the geographical state line. It might be off by a hundred feet or more. Across the street and twenty feet south sat the blank, gray backside of another sign, probably the California marker.

"Fuck!"

He turned and rode back far enough to feel safe, then U-turned and parked again on the northbound shoulder— about equidistant between the officers and the sign— risking attracting their attention with his odd behavior. Removing his helmet, he scanned his surroundings: a few scattered buildings set back along the road, the thick brush and trees, and the border. Looking back the way he'd come, only now did he realize he'd passed the state border agriculture inspection station on the west side of the road without even noticing it, focused as he'd been on the accident. He seriously needed to get his head in the game if he was going to attempt taking on a malevolent supernatural entity.

Scanning again to the Oregon border sign, probably less than a hundred feet ahead, something between the bottom of the sign and the ground caught his attention. He stared, trying to make out if he saw a pair of thin legs. Yes, definitely legs. They walked to the side nearest the road and Likho's grinning, boyish, one-eyed face appeared around the edge of the sign on the Oregon side.

Holy shit. Alex sat in numb astonishment. It had worked; he'd actually managed to track Likho down. The boy was too far away for Alex to see his expression clearly, but his posture looked hunched and contrite, like a child caught in the act of finger painting on the kitchen walls.

Alex's astonishment lasted only a moment before anger replaced it, then rage. He'd been a peaceful person before prison and a cautious one after. To hunt someone down to harm them was anathema to everything that defined him, but he'd run out of options. With the frustrations and terrors of the last few days swelling in him, he felt a sudden certainty that if he could lay hands on the creature, he could do to Likho what someone had done to Fabick three years ago. A thing so far from his normal nature that he hadn't understood how people had believed it of him back then.

Springing into motion, Alex swung off his bike. He glanced back, but the officers were still busy. The side of the road was unfenced, and the tall trees and thick foliage would provide cover if he could entice Likho in there. He stepped off the shoulder, hoping Likho might shift them both into the woods somewhere, maybe all the way back to Boy Scout Grove. Nothing happened.

"Stribog found the horn this morning," he lied, speaking in Russian in a voice just loud enough to be heard during a lull in the traffic.

As hoped, the creature straightened in surprise.

"That's right," Alex continued. "They found it a few hours ago. You'll all be going home soon. You want a bite out of me before you go? This is your chance. Come and get me."

Likho glanced around and licked his lips. He emerged from behind the sign.

"Or maybe you're just hot air? A pawn for the gods? I think Perun woke up on his own and you can't do anything worse than getting me turned around in the woods. If that's all you've got, you're wasting my time."

He turned his back on Likho and started walking. A moment later, the hairs on his neck prickled and he glanced back. The one-eyed boy had closed half the distance in an instant. His face held a sinister smirk.

The distant wail of a new siren grew in the north, no doubt an ambulance from Brookings headed for the gunshot victim as the Oregon town was closer to them than Crescent City.

"Better hurry," he said, knowing it was actually him that needed to hurry. Once the ambulance arrived, the paramedics would take over medical care and the CHP officer might decide to come check out why Alex was parked on the side of the road. His chance at Likho would be gone. He needed the thing to come just a little closer, so he didn't risk crossing that state line. How he'd handle the rest, he still wasn't sure.

Likho had closed to twenty feet and Alex eased farther off the shoulder, half behind a tree. The ploy to get him to follow was far from subtle, but Likho couldn't know what else he had in mind. The taunts seemed to be working, bringing Likho to him. The boy-goblin closed to ten feet, but remained stubbornly at the side of the road, in sight of the officers.

"Forested land," Alex said, desperation making him more blatant. "Step in here and you could probably get me lost again."

Likho looked intrigued but wary. Alex was going to have to make his move in the open. He glanced back. Both officers still had their backs to him, busy with the victim and the traffic. The siren had grown louder, but there were no cars near them in either direction. Whatever he was going to do, he needed to do it now.

Gripping fistfuls of the items that he'd gathered this morning, he pulled both hands from his pockets. He channeled every ounce of skill he'd possessed as a pitcher in junior high into his aim, sliding the double handful at Likho: the rabbit's foot and four-leaf clover in acrylic, the jade, the bag of herbs, all the good luck charms and counters to misfortune he'd found. They skittered along the pavement to Likho's feet. The throw couldn't have been more perfect. Some items bumped the boy's feet or wrapped around an ankle; some slid to either side, nearly encircling him.

Likho bent his knees to launch backward, then gave a small shriek of fear, seemingly unable to move. Alex hit him like a freight train. He pulled the medallion from his neck and wrapped the sturdy chain around the boy's throat. With one hard jerk, he pulled Likho from his feet, both of them falling off the road and into the trees and brush.

They were hidden from the officers now, but still visible from the road. If someone looked to the side as they passed, they'd see him choking the life out of a young boy. Pulling the chain like a garrote and praying it didn't break, Alex dragged Likho another few feet into the thick cover. The boy's legs thrashed and his breath came in strangled gasps. Alex pulled the final item from the back pocket of his jeans, the thick railroad spike. He might not be able to kill an immortal, but blinding Misfortune should be almost as effective. Even if the eye regenerated, it would probably take long enough that Likho would be back in Russia or wherever, and Alex's family would be safe.

He pinned the boy to the ground by the throat with his left hand and raised the spike in his right. Alex forced down thoughts of wrestling with his nephew David, the same size as Likho now, the same slender limbs under his hands. This was no boy and he knew it, no matter what his brain told him.

Alex slammed the spike down, but Likho wriggled with unexpected strength and twisted his upper body free. From his knees, Alex launched himself again, elbowing the boy across the face. Tree limbs and azalea branches scratched at his arms. Small stones dug into his shins and knees as he levered onto the boy's chest. He raised the spike again, stabbing down toward Likho's good eye with all his strength.

Likho shifted into his goblin form at the last second. The neck grew thick under Alex's grip and sparse, coarse hairs rubbed against his palm. The body expanded to nearly Alex's height but heavy with ropey, lean muscles. The teeth grew long, as yellowed as the rough skin. Likho jerked his head with startling force and the spike grazed his cheek. The chain tore through Alex's hands. The body twisted beneath him, but Alex hung on. The ambulance passed them on the other side of the brush, the siren deafening. He yanked the chain tighter and raised the spike a third time.

The goblin kicked out, catching Alex in the hip. He fell back, his grip on the chain lost. Likho turned, gasping with a throaty gurgle, and crawled down the embankment and through the trees toward the road. Alex lunged after him, also on all fours, grabbing for the thing's ankle. He missed and the goblin tumbled free of him, down to the road, shifting back to a boy as he cleared the foliage. The boy-Likho pushed to his feet and ran up the unpaved shoulder.

Alex, manic with his near success, raced behind. He reached for the collar on the boy's windbreaker and brushed the nylon with his fingertips. One grab, one hard lunge to the right, and he could finish this. He'd been so close, had felt so certain he could win.

A car passed within feet of Alex. The close rush of air, the weight of the metal chassis rumbling by. The passenger turned to stare at him. Alex came back to himself with the sudden alertness of waking from a nightmare. Another car passed in the other direction. He stopped and took his bearings, the spike still gripped in his fist. He stood exactly opposite the California marker. Alex glanced back. The paramedics were attending to the gunshot victim. The sheriff's officer was getting into his car. The CHP officer was staring up the road. At him. He wondered how much she'd seen.

Likho stood no more than five feet ahead of him, eyes wide. The boy took one step back, then another.

But if Likho were truly frightened, why was he standing there? Why hadn't he kept running?

In a moment of stunning clarity, Alex's perspective spun as he realized which of them had been the hunter all along and which the prey. He felt sick. It had all been an act. Hiding behind the sign. The fight Alex shouldn't have been able to come so close to winning. The fear in Likho's gaze.

No, more than that. The overheard police calls. Probably all the way back to the tacks in the road and his flat tire and having to push his bike a block and a half. Likho had been toying with him the whole time. Hearing the call at the gas station hadn't been a lucky coincidence. Just like the gathering of law enforcement here and the border being so close hadn't been unlucky coincidences.

Everything, every bit of this farce of a day, had been part of Likho's game to see if he could bait him across state lines or have him attack a young boy in sight of the officers. Better still, both. Likho had played him like an instrument.

Alex wanted to say to hell with the state border and to hell with the officers behind him. He ached to finish this, but his feet wouldn't move. He hesitated, tallying the consequences: The remainder of his sentence hung over him still, along with the certainty of additional time for breaking parole. On top of that, a new sentence for assault. Five years? Eight? Ten? The sounds of metal bars clanging shut haunted his dreams. Concrete rooms. Guards. The constant vigilance to stay safe. He clenched his jaws. Tears of frustration burned his eyes. Inertia gripped him like a fist.

The boy's expression shifted from alarm to a sneer to a smile. He began to laugh.

With sudden cold certainty, Alex guessed the creature's next move. His hesitation evaporated. Electrified into action, he sprinted for the border shouting, "No!"

Likho vanished.

Chapter Fifteen

DAVID TRIED TO shove the sparkly purple hat that his mom had worn last Halloween back between the dog's ears but Bonkers turned his head again.

"Mom," he said, frustrated, "the hat keeps falling down."

"The elastic strap's too thin," she said from where she sat on the porch steps while he and Jake played in the yard. "Just push it back up."

The pointy princess hat with its flowing veil hung nearly upside down under Bonkers' chin. David tried to hold him by the collar and shove it back in place while Jake pulled the veil over their dog's shoulders for the third time.

"I want to be the prince now," his little brother said.

"Let Jake have a turn," his mom said.

Jake always got his way. It wasn't fair. David hadn't even had a chance to fight the evil queen with the princess yet because Bonkers' stupid costume kept falling off.

"We have to get out of the castle first and then you can be the prince," he said, adamant to finish his turn. The game had been his idea, anyway.

The phone rang inside the house. His mom stared at the back door but didn't get up. On the third ring she said, "I have to get that. It might be your Uncle Alex. You two stay *right* there."

She was barely inside the door when Bonkers shook his head, slinging the hat back under his jaw. He pulled from David's grip and ran toward the steps to follow her inside. David grabbed him around the hips and they both fell onto the stairs. A rabbit suddenly dashed out from its hiding place in the shrubs next to the steps and sprinted across the lawn. Bonkers turned so quickly that he jumped on David's arm then lit out after the rabbit.

David yelled for him to come back, but Bonkers didn't stop. The rabbit raced up the yard and darted through a small hole in the blackberry bushes. Bonkers tried to follow but the hole was too small. He backed out and ran to the end of the hedge next to the road. David ran after Bonkers and Jake ran after him. "Go home," David yelled to Jake.

Reaching the end of the yard, neither the rabbit nor his dog were anywhere to be seen. Something bumped his right arm. He looked down to see his brother.

"Go home," he said again. "Mom told us not to leave."

"You did."

"Hey, are you looking for your dog?" a new voice said. Standing on the road in front of the next-door neighbor's house was the boy with one eye. "He went this way. Follow me. I'll show you." The boy ran, angling across the neighbor's lawn and into the side yard, then stopped and looked back. "You better hurry. If he goes into the woods, he could get lost."

David knew his mom had been upset the last time they played with the boy, but this was different. He wasn't playing, he was catching Bonkers.

David ran after him. Jake ran too. "Go home!" he yelled. He heard his mom call his name.

"I'll be right back," he hollered as the boy vanished between two apple trees. David grabbed Jake's hand to make him run faster since he wouldn't go home. Together, they ran into the shade between the trees but instead of coming out at the next house over, tall redwoods suddenly surrounded David on all sides. He stopped, still holding Jake's hand. The neighbor's yard must have a shortcut to the woods at the end of the road. Ahead, in the half-light, he spotted the boy running between the trunks.

"I'm not supposed to be here alone," he shouted.

"You're not alone," the boy called back, also stopping. "I'm here too. Besides, I know my way around in here really, really well. Hey, look. There's your dog." He turned and pointed.

David didn't see anything, but he called Bonkers' name and ran again to catch up, still dragging his little brother behind him. The one-eyed boy sprinted to the left, flashing in and out between the trees. David was afraid to lose sight of him, especially as he'd never been off the path before. He dragged his brother into a run again.

"Hey! Where'd you go?" He shouted Bonkers' name as well, but there was no response to that either. Jake parroted his call for Bonkers to come.

Not seeing his dog or the boy now, he stopped once more.

"We better go back," he told his little brother.

He'd thought they'd only be gone a minute. They were going to be in big trouble for going into the woods. He turned and walked the way he thought they'd come but saw only ferns and wide-spaced trees in all directions.

"Where's Bonkers?" Jake whined.

"I don't know. Maybe he already went home."

David's mom and dad and uncle had taken him for walks in these woods since he was a little boy, smaller than Jake. He was so close to home he was sure he couldn't get lost, but his mom had told him lots of times there was a nasty lake up north and he should never go that way.

He turned in a circle, unsure which direction was north, or which would lead him back home.

"Mom," he yelled, but there was no answer. His mom would be looking for them. He hoped she'd find them soon; he didn't care anymore about getting in trouble.

A rustling came from behind him and he spun toward it. "Mom?" The rustling grew louder. "Mom!" he yelled.

A woman emerged through the trees. For a moment he

wondered why his mom was wearing a funny old, patched dress, and then he saw her clearly. She was blonde like his mom but shorter. Her shoes were funny, like the clogs a lady wore once at a dance she did for a school assembly. She wore a scarf over her head like the girls in his class had worn during their Trapper's Days play. He was used to seeing other people walking here and hoped maybe she could help.

"Have you seen my dog, Bonkers?"

He didn't know what she said but he was pretty sure it was in Russian. His mom and his uncle talked Russian sometimes and his great-grandfather Oleg had talked Russian all the time before he died. David could say mom and dad and brother and dog and car and a few more words—more than Jake knew—'cause his mom had taught him, just like his dad had taught him some Japanese words. He didn't know how to say what he wanted, though, so he asked in English.

"Do you know the way to Jackson Street? I followed my dog, and I don't know where home is."

The woman put her hands on her hips and replied in Russian again.

"What'd she say?" Jake asked him.

"I don't know."

"I think home is that way." Jake pointed straight ahead.

"I have to find Jackson Street and my dog," he told the woman. She narrowed her eyes and a sudden mistrust flared in him. He gripped Jake's hand tighter, ready to run from the woman.

A heavy stomping noise came through the trees and a little house, smaller than his uncle's cottage, appeared behind her. It was made from sticks and branches stuck in all directions and it walked on little skinny brown legs ending in big bird feet. A house-shaped shadow spread across the ground in front of it, the dark point of it nearly touching David's shoes when it stopped. The tree branches overhead let only little bits of sunlight reach the ground here and there. Nothing else in here cast a shadow, not him or Jake or the lady.

It was the hut with the grass roof he and his friends had seen that day from the schoolyard. That day they'd been half playing when they told each other it was a house walking on legs. But now he was close to it, and it was real, and it was weird, and the lady wasn't acting like his teachers and the other people who walked on the trail acted.

He wanted more than anything to run home with Jake, away from the lady and her creepy house on its creepy legs, but he didn't see the path anywhere and the house might run after him and stomp him dead.

"It's like Mr MacKenzie's rooster," Jake said, pointing to the knobby, scaly legs that were nearly as tall as the lady.

David shushed him. Jake was only little and didn't know to be scared. Like the time they took an airplane to Montana to get Uncle Alex's belongings out of storage and Jake didn't know what a plane was and how high up in the sky they were.

The lady stepped closer. She smelled like the redwood trees and campfire smoke and the salty grease in the pan after his mom made pot roast. She took his chin in her hand, turning his head to one side and then the other. Her skin scratched his face and her grip hurt. He tried to pull away but couldn't. Then she reached down and grabbed him hard by his free hand. She pulled him in the opposite direction he'd been turning and strode off, talking to him again.

He knew he and Jake shouldn't go anywhere with a stranger, especially one with a creepy walking house. But he was lost and unsure of everything now and he couldn't get loose anyway. Maybe she'd understood him after all and was taking them to his dog or his mom or his home.

She gripped his hand and he gripped Jake's, and together the three of them threaded through the seemingly endless trees with the little hut following.

Chapter Sixteen

ALEX DIDN'T CARE if he wrecked his bike riding hell-bent, twenty miles an hour over the speed limit between Smith River and Crescent City. He didn't care if he got arrested. If he'd cared less about himself when Likho had been in arm's reach, he wouldn't be worried about his family now.

His heart tore at his chest and pounded painfully in the arteries at his neck, like too much blood forced through with each beat. He'd hated himself three years ago for being too insipid to fire his lawyers before his case went to court, and for not calling out his girlfriend Anjali when she didn't support him during his trial, but his self-loathing then didn't hold a candle to what he felt now. What the fuck did it matter if he'd stepped across the border to catch Likho? What would it have mattered if he'd throttled the boy in full sight of the officers? Nothing should have been more important than keeping his sister and her children safe. But he'd hesitated, and now there was no telling what Likho might be doing this very minute.

Traffic forced him to slow when he reached the city limits, but he weaved through the cars stopped at red lights and accelerated to the front the second they turned green. His vision tunneled with stress when he finally turned onto Jackson and saw the house on the next block. Dan would be at work, but Alina's car was there, parked by the kitchen door.

Roaring up to the farmhouse, he skidded into the gravel driveway, scanning for signs of anything amiss. He yanked off his helmet with its sweat-soaked forehead pad and ran for the kitchen door. Tuned in to the sounds around him, he made out the rumble of a small plane taxiing at the airport just out of sight, a neighbor trying to pull start a lawnmower, seagulls crying out to each other.

He saw before reaching it that the door was standing open. Trying to watch in all directions at once, he leaped up the steps and called out for Alina. From inside, he heard the shrill, rapid beeping of a phone off the hook. Goosebumps rose on his forearms. His pulse accelerated again to its former burning, staccato beat. He followed the sound to the living room and lifted the phone from the floor. Pressing the caller ID for recent calls he saw the toll-free number of a marketing group and replaced the phone in its cradle.

A fast-moving something caught his eye out the window and he flinched before realizing it was Alina, running toward his cottage. He dashed out the back door, calling to her.

She spun toward him. "Do you have the boys?"

The shock of her words confirmed his worst fears. His breath caught in his chest, as if he'd fallen through ice into a freezing pond.

"The boys," she repeated, "do you have them?" She was in front of him now, shouting the question.

"No," he said, finding his voice. "I just got here."

"They were playing with Bonkers in the yard. The phone rang. I thought it might be you. They were only out of my sight for seconds."

She was talking in short beats, as if her brain couldn't feed more than snippets of information to her speech center at a time. Her eyes were distant. She wasn't moving. She wasn't forming theories or taking action or doing any of the decisive things Alina would normally do.

Alex grabbed her by the shoulders.

"Alina. What was the last thing you saw?"

"I thought I saw Jake running toward the road. But I couldn't see them once I left the window. And when I got outside, they were just... gone. They would have heard me if they were near and the woods are more than a block away. I don't know how they could've been out of sight so fast."

Alex knew.

She looked into his eyes but still seemed only fifty percent with him. He remembered from his early prison days what dissociation felt like. Before he'd been moved to minimum security, he'd been cornered once by two inmates at the back of the laundry room. His mind had gone blank. He didn't keep his cool and talk to them. He didn't look for a guard or a way out. He didn't brace himself to fight. He just froze and everything around him seemed unreal. It's how his sister looked now.

"Do you think they're in the woods?"

Tears formed and spilled down her cheeks.

"I don't know. David should have answered me when I called for them. They'd been gone less than a minute. And then I heard your motorcycle and I thought... I don't know... I guess that you had found them, but you didn't even know they were gone."

"Did you see Likho?"

A trace of alertness returned to her eyes. "The boy? No. But he could have shown up when I took the phone call." His hands were still on her shoulders. She gripped his forearms now with vice-like strength as her thoughts visibly kicked into gear. "We need people to help us search the woods. You go to the neighbors." She let go of him to pat her pockets and pulled her phone from one. "I'll call Dan." Her voice grew more certain, her concentration sharper. "I'll go back and search the trail that goes straight from this side to the school side, and you come as

179

soon as you can. And look for signs of Bonkers too." Her eyes widened. "Or the princess hat. That purple princess hat. The boys had it on Bonkers. It kept falling off."

He wanted to slow her down and let him explain how they should run the search, but he knew he wouldn't be able to stop her now her momentum had returned. Better all round if she kept looking and left him to direct any search volunteers they got.

"Okay, you call Dan and I'll get what neighbors I can. Stay on the path. Try not to step on any footprints that might be theirs. Are the boys wearing their sneakers or boots?"

"Sneakers."

"I'll meet you along the trail."

She pulled away from him and ran.

ALEX HAD BRIEFLY met the couples to either side, but only knew the rest by sight. There was no answer at the nearest house, but at the house west of Alina's he found Jack Anderson in the backyard, crouched over the open casing of his lawnmower, tinkering with the motor. Filling him in as briefly as possible he learned that the man's wife, Sarah, ran the neighborhood watch and had phone numbers to at least a dozen homes in the area.

Alex let him know about the dog and the princess hat as well. He wondered if he should warn the man about Likho but had no idea how he'd convince an adult that a one-eyed seven-year-old might be dangerous. Instead, Alex asked him to tell everyone to meet at the trailhead at the end of the road and to wait for him and his sister there. He didn't need a bunch of inexperienced people wandering around haphazardly destroying evidence—if any evidence existed.

That done, he ran to meet up with Alina. In a normal situation, it would make more sense for him to start at the house and try to track the dog and the boys. But if Likho was behind this—and the way he'd baited Alex this morning, it was hard to believe anything else—then this was no normal disappearance. Likho was a forest spirit, and one who could get people lost in the woods, so the trees at the end of the road seemed the reasonable place to start. It was hard to hold despair at bay, though, remembering how effortlessly Likho had cast him around different parts of Jedediah Smith State Park with every step. He tried not to think how far Likho might be able to transport David and Jake. To the farthest end of the woods? To another grove altogether? To another state or all the way to Russia?

He scanned the road as he ran toward the woods but saw no obvious tracks from the children. Once on the trail, he took no branches. If he met Alina coming back toward him then they'd know they were in for a longer, more involved search. At that point, it would be worth stopping, regrouping, and calling the authorities. He wished with every fiber of his being that it wouldn't be necessary; that at the next bend or rise in the trail, he'd see her with the boys. That this would turn out to be a normal, non-supernatural, kid thing. Boys being boys.

He hadn't jogged this far in months. Not since running the track at the prison. His breath wheezed and his thighs burned. His fears were realized a few minutes later when he encountered Alina, wild-eyed, running toward him.

"Did you find them?" she asked, her voice loud, her words quick.

He shook his head no, and tears welled in her eyes. She brushed at them angrily. "You should be... we're covering the same ground."

He gripped his sister by the shoulders again to keep her from running off. "Alina, let me help you with this," he said, still trying to catch his breath. "I've done this, remember? Looking for people lost in the woods was part of my job. A hasty search like this is good. We needed to know if they were on the main trail, but they weren't. Now we need to be organized and thorough. Jack and Sarah are on their way. Sarah is calling the other neighbors. We need the police involved. They wouldn't come out this quick for an adult, but they might for children."

She nodded. A fresh tear rolled off her chin and fell to the trail, taking his heart with it down into the dust.

"Did you reach Dan?"

"I had to leave a voicemail. He called back a couple of minutes ago. He's on his way now."

"Good. Do you have any phone numbers for teachers or parents from the school?"

She nodded again.

"Call the police first, then start calling them. The school and the police are probably your best bet for getting enough people here for a proper search. First, I need you to head back to the house and double-check that they haven't shown up. If not, connect with Jack and Sarah and tell everyone to gather on the road at the trailhead. Besides," he said, addressing the panic growing in her eyes, "if you're on the road, you'll be able to see the boys or Bonkers if they head home from any other direction."

Her gaze moved restlessly over him and their surroundings as her anxiety ratcheted up at his suggestion she stay in one place rather than search. Seeing her like this sent a new spear of regret lancing into his chest. His fault. All of this. He was the one who'd stayed involved with Stribog and Morana. Who'd first caught the attention of Likho. And who'd been too spineless to attack Likho in front of the highway patrol officer. Maybe Likho's big end game had been Alex getting arrested again. And if he had been, maybe his nephews would be safe at home with their mom right now.

"I'll have a quick look down the side trail just up ahead while I call friends from work to see if they can help. You need to get going to meet up with Dan and catch the neighbors showing up. And don't let anyone start searching until I get back to the trailhead." She nodded once more and left without objection.

A hundred feet down the path he took a small branching trail to the north, pulling up his contact list as he went, and noting that it was nearly two in the afternoon. A couple of hours of decent light in the woods and three until full dusk. Ida answered his call and said she and Jim had gone out of town for the holiday weekend. She asked if they should head back up from the Bay Area, for which he felt an immense gratitude, though he told her no. Stan didn't answer and was probably in his cups anyway. Mike Murphy picked up on the first ring.

"Hey, Mike. Alex. Am I catching you at a bad time?"

There was an unexpected pause at the other end before Mike said no.

"My nephews have gone missing. We're afraid they might be lost. We're looking for people to come help with a grid search."

"They're little, aren't they?"

"Five and seven."

"Where do I meet you?"

"Come to my house."

"I'll be there in ten minutes." Mike hung up without signing off.

The neighbor, Sarah, must've reached people too, because he could hear car doors and voices in the distance. Keeping his own counsel, he returned to the road when he saw no footprints or paw prints going up the side trail. By the time he got there, a handful of people had gathered around Alina.

He asked her to pull up a satellite view of the woods on her phone and helped her divide it roughly into sections, then instructed the group on search techniques in case the police were slow to show up. He covered how close to stay together and details to look for that people might not think of. Also, what to do if they found anything, how far to go, and when to come back and start a new grid.

A proper grid search required a huge number of people—maybe a hundred individuals. Twenty highly trained searchers could cover the same ground in a fraction of the time. Hopefully, when the police arrived, a more professional effort could be coordinated, but even that might be futile. Everyone would assume the boys to be in easy walking distance. But they had to do what they could and hope that maybe the boys really were nearby. At least this volunteer effort would be likely to turn up any signs they'd left in this area.

Alex heard the rumble of Mike's Trans Am pulling onto the shoulder of the road. The big man got out and headed for them. Mike's face appeared haggard, like he hadn't slept. His eyes were sunken, and white gauze wrapped one of his forearms. It looked like Mike's Thanksgiving had been nearly as rough on him as Alex's own. He shook Mike's hand and thanked him for coming, then introduced him to his sister. Mike sounded every bit the naval officer he'd once been.

"I'm sorry about your kids, ma'am. I'm sure they'll be fine."

She swallowed hard and nodded her thanks.

"Alina," Alex said, "I should start back at the house and do a more thorough look before too many people get here. See if I can find a solid starting point."

"I can come with you," Mike said. "I did combat search and rescue training in the Navy."

Alex, once again, realized how little he knew about the man he'd worked alongside these past months.

"I'd appreciate that," he said. Alex squeezed Alina's hand. "Wait for just a few more people before you get them started on the first grid, okay?"

"I will," she said.

He and Mike took off.

Glad for the extra set of eyes, Alex moved quickly but carefully as they each scanned one half of the road. Two cars passed, volunteers answering the call for help, and he grimaced at the tire tracks and dust accumulating. A few minutes later, level with the next-door neighbor's house to the east, Mike yelled, "Here."

Alex jogged over and Mike pointed. It was little more than a heel print, but the right size for a child. He and Mike scanned the area closely and soon found dog tracks and David and Jake's prints. Searching back toward the woods, the tracks vanished. They combed the area where they disappeared and determined the boys had cut through the neighbor's yard.

"They may not even be in the woods," Mike said.

"I have reasons for believing they are." Mike waited for more, but Alex left the statement hanging.

Between the thick lawn and lack of rain the past day or so, the tracks were difficult to follow. A flash of purple caught Alex's eye. He turned back. The purple fairy princess hat and veil hung from a low branch on a spreading azalea bush, a few dead leaves caught in the net of the veil. Following the sparse signs, they tracked a weaving pattern diagonally across the yard.

"Here," Alex said, when he saw prints from both boys in a patch of loamy soil. They led between two apple trees. On the other side of the trees, all traces vanished. He and Mike spent precious time scanning and rescanning the area.

"Find anything?"

Mike shook his head. "There's enough dirt between the undergrowth here we ought to be seeing something."

"Agreed." Under normal circumstances, anyway. But Alex felt certain his own prints had ended just as abruptly near Boy Scout Tree Trail when Likho spirited him off. "We should go back and check in with my sister."

Mike's brow furrowed. "Sure you don't want to keep trying to pick up their trail here?"

"I'm sure." Alex turned to jog back to Alina.

"Alex." The tone of Mike's voice stopped him. "Have you seen anything unusual lately?"

Alex tried to keep his voice casual as he asked, "What do you mean by 'unusual'?"

"Standard definition. Out of the ordinary. Strange."

"Yeah. A little bit," he said.

"Like that night at the diner?"

"Like that. Yeah. Why? Have *you* seen anything unusual?"

"A little bit."

"Anything to do with that?" Alex gestured to the gauze wrapping Mike's arm. Mike looked down.

"Yeah."

They were dancing, neither one wanting to lead.

"Feel like telling me about it?" Mike remained silent, so Alex continued. "Do you remember the people you met at the motel that night you took me to the diner?"

Mike nodded.

"They brought some… friends here with them. One of them has been hanging around the boys. He doesn't have good intentions. It wasn't him that made me ill that night, but it *was* someone else they knew. I've seen one or two more folks since then who… well, who fit the definition of unusual. How about you?"

Mike nodded slowly. "I think so. A dog. Last night."

Alex's face and shoulders relaxed in surprise. "A dog?"

He couldn't think of any evil dogs in Russian mythology and wasn't sure why Mike would be alarmed by something so mundane.

"A dog first. Then it was an owl. Or maybe it was an owl first and then a dog and then an owl." Mike eyed him warily, waiting for his reaction.

"Shit."

The standoff eased. "What do you know about it?" Mike asked.

"It's going to sound unbelievable."

"Seeing a dog turn into an owl two feet from my face is pretty fucking unbelievable. Try me." Alex hesitated and Mike pressed him. "Look, something tried to kill me last night. If you know anything about it, I need you to tell me."

"You're right. I do." Dan's Camry barreled down the road and past the neighbor's lawn where they stood. "That's Alina's husband. I need to be there to help fill him in. Walk up there with me and I'll tell you what I know."

He shared his heritage and explained that he'd grown up on Russian fairy tales but that most of the things he'd encountered this past week, he'd never heard of before.

"I have no idea what might be after you, Mike." They reached the road and turned toward the woods. Ahead, Dan parked the car haphazardly and sprinted toward Alina and the growing number of volunteers. "I've never heard of anything like your owl-dog. All I can tell you is that a creature named Likho is most likely what took the boys or led them away. And that Stribog and Morana are more than they seem. They're the ones at the root of all this."

"What does being Russian have to do with anything?"

In for a penny... He told Mike who Stribog and Morana really were. Into the silence that followed, he said, "You can believe me or not, but I've seen the proof."

"Why are you involved? Are you some kind of Russian god too?"

"What? No."

He gave him the short version of the celestial battle between Stribog and Morana against Perun and how it had attracted the other creatures here. Alex wondered if he'd ever had a weirder conversation, and that was saying a lot lately. But Mike was still listening.

"So this happened to me because I took you to the motel?"

"Maybe. Or maybe just knowing me was enough, like what happened to my nephews. Likho never met either of them. Neither did Stribog or Morana." He stopped walking, shoved his hands in his jacket pockets, and eyed Mike incredulously. "So, you believe me?"

"Hell yes, I believe you. A mangy dog tried to kill me then turned into a scruffy owl with a beak full of teeth. I'd rather believe you than think I'd lost my fucking mind."

Alex could relate.

They were still only halfway to Alina and the volunteers clustered around her when Dan led a group of searchers into the woods to the right of the trail. The others broke into teams and spread out to search other sections. He'd told Alina to keep everyone there till he got back, but this was probably for the best. He was likely to be the last person Dan wanted to see right now. And having seen the boys' footprints vanish so abruptly only confirmed his earlier fear that they were unlikely to be anywhere nearby where his search and rescue skills might help.

"So, how do you find your nephews and how do I fight a dog-owl out of fairy tale?" Mike asked.

"I don't know." They walked a few beats in silence. "I have one idea, though." It had been brewing for a while. Mike gave him a questioning look.

"I think Stribog and Morana can help, but they've

checked out of the motel and I don't know where they are anymore. But the same day I first met Likho, I met another folklore character. Koschei." He looked at Mike expectantly, but Mike returned a blank stare. "He's some kind of sorcerer, but he's been working with Stribog. I'm thinking that maybe if I can go back and find Koschei, I could ask him to get a message to Stribog for me."

"Okay. Do we look for the boys first or this sorcerer?"

Alex shook his head "Not 'we,' buddy. Me. I've been reading up on him lately. If the fairy tales are at all accurate, Koschei's a nasty piece of work."

Russian tales were full of characters that would drown, torment, or harm people. Koschei was one of the worst, consistently depicted as a personification of both greed and a fear of death, and someone immensely powerful and thoroughly evil.

"I can either come with you or I can follow you," Mike said, leaving no room for argument. "This Koschei thing hasn't tried to kill me yet. The other one has. If Stribog can help you, maybe he can help me."

He had a point.

They were approaching Alina, who stood alone at the trailhead now. Another car was coming up the road behind them but there was no sign of the police yet. He wasn't all that surprised. Even though children were involved, they were near home and had been missing probably no more than an hour. They wouldn't rush out just to find that the kids were off playing somewhere.

Alina's eyes tightened. "Did you find anything?"

"I saw the hat in the next-door neighbor's yard. The one on this side of your house. I left it there for the police. We found some tracks near it, but only a few." He hurried on before her hopes rose again. "They didn't lead anywhere. I don't mean we lost the trail. I mean they just stopped."

Mike glanced at him, probably surprised he didn't lie or couch the information in more comforting terms, but Mike didn't understand their relationship. Withholding information from his sister this past week had only created more anguish; he wouldn't do it again.

"How many searchers so far?" he asked her.

"It wasn't as many as you suggested, but when Dan got here, I couldn't stop him. I told the volunteers everything you told me about how to conduct the search."

"That's fine. You did well. The best thing you can do is what you're already doing, and I'm sure more people will show up, as well as the police. I've been thinking about something. I still think Likho, that boy, is behind this. If so, I think Stribog might be able to help. Mike and I are going back to the area where Likho was jacking with me the last couple of days."

"You're not going to search here first?" Her voice rose. "The two of you have the most experience."

"Believe me, Alina, I would if I thought I'd make any real difference, but there's a lot of ground to cover, and with the tracks disappearing, we don't have any starting point. If the boys are anywhere near here, they'll hear the searchers. If they're not nearby..." He trailed off, reminding her what they were most likely up against. "If they're not, then I think we're going to need Stribog and Morana's help."

The car behind them had parked and a young couple hurried toward Alina. He heard gravel crunch under tires down the road and turned to see a police cruiser approaching.

"We should get going," he said. "I've got my phone on me. I want you to call me if you see or hear or find anything. Anything at all. And I'll do the same, okay?"

"All right." The words came out mumbled, weighed down with her stress and anxiety.

He hated leaving her like this, but he had to do whatever was most likely to help David and Jake.

"Ready to hunt down a couple of gods?" he said to Mike.

Chapter Seventeen

THE IMMENSE OLD-GROWTH trees on either side of the narrow dirt road shadowed thick brush and vegetation that all seemed the same, but Alex had developed a strong memory for natural landmarks during his years with the Forest Service. He pointed for Mike to pull over at a spot on Howland Hill Road where the curve of the road and drop-off beyond the right shoulder looked familiar. A sign a short way back had indicated Boy Scout Tree Trail lay not far ahead, and he felt certain this was where Stribog had suddenly sensed Koschei the other day. Getting out to check, he found the dried mud ridges behind the Trans Am from old tire marks where he'd parked Stribog's rental two days ago. He motioned for Mike to cut the engine and join him.

"The things we're looking for may not leave tracks. Watch for my footprints and keep an eye out for small creatures. Koschei's attendants. Minions… whatever." He gestured about knee high. "I think they were dressed in brown and green last time. Brace yourself. They have human features and are creepy as hell."

He didn't glance back as he described them, and Mike made no reply.

Alex called out once but felt so absurd yelling into the forest for Koschei the Deathless that he didn't do it again. Moments later, though, one of the small creatures appeared from between the thick ferns a few yards ahead. It peered up at him with its wizened face and rheumy eyes. Mike froze at his shoulder. Alex could feel the man's tension in every line, but impressively, Mike said nothing.

"I need to speak to Koschei," Alex said.

The thing stared defiantly at him without replying. Age spots and moles stood out brown on its pale skin. Darker, purplish marks at one temple and cheek made Alex think Koschei might not be the most benevolent of masters.

He repeated himself in Russian.

The thing considered for a moment, then turned and ran. Alex jogged after it at first, then ran, Mike right behind him. Inexplicably, on legs less than a foot long, it outpaced them and vanished into the underbrush.

"Damn, that thing was fast," Mike panted when they both stopped, unsure which way it had gone.

Alex lowered his voice. "I'm guessing it doesn't want us to follow. I say we try anyway."

He searched the ground. As he'd expected, the creature had left no footprints. Squatting down where it had dashed beneath the undergrowth, he saw a freshly broken fern leaf. He pointed to it and began moving forward. He lost the trail again quickly, but Mike spotted the minute clue of a leaf pushed back out of place and hooked on another to their right. They moved forward slowly but surely; a hundred feet, two hundred.

A blaze of heat hit Alex in the chest and face.

"Do you feel that?" he whispered.

"Feel what?" Mike said just as softly.

It ended as quickly as it had started, but for a moment it had felt as though the damp, coastal November chill had fallen away and the warmth of an inland summer sun had broken through the clouds. He searched his surroundings for any clues as to what had just happened, but the sky remained as cool and overcast as usual.

Still scanning, Alex caught a flash of movement in the corner of his eye. Following it, he spotted a shadow about a hundred yards ahead, high up in a tree. Something big scuttled down the trunk like a giant squirrel. It was difficult to make out the details among the branches of a tree as tall as a thirty-story building, but Alex would have sworn the figure was human and clothed in midnight blue, descending rapidly... headfirst. A second later it had scampered around the far side of the tree and out of sight.

A heavy hand slapped his shoulder. Alex startled, snapping out of his reflections, and heard the light footsteps that Mike had alerted him to. Standing from his half-crouch, he tried to appear as if he hadn't been sneaking after the little creature or seen something he perhaps shouldn't have. He strode forward noisily, hoping Mike would pick up on the body language, and feigned surprise when the troop of six little creatures appeared leading Koschei toward them.

The emaciated sorcerer wore the deep blue robe trimmed in gold he'd worn before—the same hue Alex had seen against the treetop moments ago. His beard of bright copper strands against the dark-blue garment made the robe seem old and faded. His upper eyelids rippled in folds flowing down over his eyes.

Alex's heart beat faster and his fists clenched and unclenched as Koschei drew close. He felt the absence of the two gods at his side suddenly and acutely, and the full impact of just how foolish it had been to come here without them. Too late now.

He spared a quick glance at Mike. "You okay?" he mouthed, but Mike's gaze was fixed on the approaching procession. An expression between wonder and horror painted his features.

Finding his intruders closer than he must have expected, Koschei scowled. Not good. Some of the reading Alex had done last night in his cottage, while the domovoi snored under his desk, included what little he could dig up on Koschei and the other folklore creatures. He almost wished he hadn't chased down old stories in their original

Russian. The ones that explained that Koschei was no mere sorcerer, but one who ruled his own realm of unholy creatures. This was not someone he wanted to piss off.

Putting on the exaggerated airs of a petitioner, Alex bowed, in case the Deathless One could sense or somehow see the gesture.

"Thank you for meeting with us," Alex said in English for Mike's benefit, remembering Koschei had spoken it fluently. "Likho attacked my family today. I think he's abducted my nephews. I've come to ask your help to find Stribog and Morana."

Koschei took so long to respond that Alex struggled for what more he could say when the sorcerer at last answered in his slow, indifferent fashion. "I have not seen Stribog since he was here at dawn."

Alex waited, but Koschei said no more.

"Do you know where either of them are now? Or where my nephews might be?"

"No."

Crazed with fear for David and Jake, Alex hadn't thought things through beyond this point. Belatedly, he racked his brain for anything he might be able to offer someone of this power. Koschei had a fondness for abducting young brides. Alex had none to barter, not that he would, but Koschei was also said to hoard treasure. Alex dug in his jeans pockets. He opened his wallet and took out the twelve dollars in cash. Koschei made no move to take it. Putting his wallet back and trying his jacket, he felt something still lodged deep in one corner. One of the trinkets he'd bought this morning to throw at Likho. Wrapping his fingers around the cord, he pulled the Turkish nazar boncuğu free; a cheap, blue bead painted like an eye and strung on a black cord. The gift shop sales lady said it protected against the evil eye.

Two of the little creatures quickly scaled Koschei's heavy robes and perched on his shoulders. Each hauled open one heavy eyelid until their small arms were filled with the wrinkled skin. Koschei's bright blue eyes examined the offering Alex held out.

He lifted it by the cord and studied the bead closely. "I possess few charms from foreign lands." Alex suspected it had more likely come from China than Turkey, but whatever, as long as it pleased Koschei. "You may soon wish you had kept some of your protections." The cryptic statement hung in the air as the charm vanished into a pocket of his robes. "What else?"

What else? Alex patted his empty pockets.

"I will accept this and gold for your information."

His grandfather's amulet had been lost in the bushes up by the state border, but it was unlikely the gold on it had been anything more than paint anyway.

"As soon as I've taken care of Likho, I can bring you gold." He'd find something. A pawn shop engagement ring or brooch, maybe.

"You will owe me, then?" The word "owe" carried a weight that sent a chill through Alex.

"Yes," he said, with a hard knot in his throat making the word catch. The spirits Koschei was said to rule included humans turned into creatures after they died, and he could guess at least some had reneged on bargains with Koschei.

"Stribog searches for the horn. Morana distracts Perun for him. Stribog plans to return here at dusk. I cannot say if he will."

"Thank you, Tsar Koschei," he said, hoping the honorific for a ruler was the appropriate one. He started to add, "I'm in your debt," but choked the words off, reminded of the literal contract he'd made. Instead, he gave another small bow and turned to leave, anxious to be gone from here and away from the sorcerer. Mike was in his way and Alex pushed lightly at his arm. He might as well have pushed at a boulder.

"Do you know what's been after me?" Mike asked Koschei.

The little creatures continued to hold the sorcerer's eyelids open, and the piercing eyes shifted to him. Mike unclipped his dive watch—the one he'd told Alex he bought with the first and only pension check he spent on himself—slipped it off and held it out. Koschei took it without so much as glancing at it. Instead, he leaned forward and stared at Mike's now-closed mouth more obviously and rudely than Stribog had.

"There a problem?" Mike said, in a decidedly undeferential tone.

Alex chewed at his upper lip, wishing he could warn Mike to be cautious.

Koschei nodded, making the little creatures on his shoulders struggle for balance. The nod seemed less affirmation than having verified something to himself. "This explains the stryga," he said, pronouncing it as sTREEga.

"What's that?" Mike asked.

Alex didn't know either, familiar with only the most basic Russian folktales. The old stories, the ones long ago lost to Christianity and the march of time, must've been rich with characters, probably many that modern scholars would never know.

"Ask your friend," Koschei said, "unless you also wish to strike a bargain with me for more information."

Alex thought Koschei meant for Mike to ask him, then realized he referred to Stribog.

"We will," Alex answered for Mike, eager to be gone. "If you see Stribog or Morana before we find them, please tell them we're looking for them. Tell them I need their help."

The little creatures dropped Koschei's eyelids, and they fell in a small avalanche of loose skin. With two still perched on his shoulders and four leading him, Koschei turned and strode away.

Chapter Eighteen

"SUNSET'S ABOUT HALF past four, isn't it?" Alex asked when they reached the relative safety of the car. He pulled out his phone and checked the time.

"Closer to five," Mike said.

"Fifteen minutes to go."

"Till sunset. Dusk could mean anything from sunset to near dark. If he shows." He leaned against the hood and Alex did the same.

"I better check on Alina." He tapped her speed dial, and she answered on the second ring. "What's happening there?"

"The police found the tracks and the hat that you saw at Phil and Dianne's, but they haven't found anything in the woods. Nothing at all."

Mike probably inferred from his expression that the news wasn't good, but Alex shook his head to confirm.

"They're going to stop searching at dark, Alex." Her voice vibrated with tension. "They're going to leave my babies out here alone all night." She sounded closer to breaking now than she had the final night they'd spent at the hospital with their mother years ago.

"We'll find them, Alina. I promise you. Mike and I have a lead on Stribog. And don't forget, Likho fucked with me, but he never actually hurt me. I'm not sure he's able to—not directly, anyway. This is more likely to be some new way for Likho to screw with me rather than him out to hurt the boys."

"And what if Likho didn't take them? What if it's the other kind of monster?"

"I don't think it is, Alina. Everything points to Likho having Pied Pipered them off somewhere. Him leading me on that chase this morning. How fast the boys got out of your sight today. The tracks vanishing in the neighbor's yard. The important thing is that you and Dan stay safe and keep it together while I track Likho down and find out where the boys are. How's Dan doing?"

"Not good." She didn't elaborate.

Alex wanted nothing more than to divide himself in two—to stay and meet with Stribog here and to be there with his sister.

"I understand. I'm working on it, Alina. I'm really hopeful I'll know something more soon."

Despite his reassurances, he felt nauseous with stress when he hung up. Having missed lunch wasn't helping, either. Alex said nothing to Mike about Alina, and his friend didn't ask.

"So you've never heard of this thing either, this stryga?" Mike said after a minute.

"No, sorry. My grandfather knew so many stories. I wish I'd listened better." He crossed his arms against the evening chill. "I feel like all of this is my fault. If I hadn't laid my motorcycle down that morning or stayed and talked to Stribog…"

"You stepped into a fairy tale like someone stepping in a pile of dog shit. If you'd known it was there, you would have avoided it."

"I knew what I was dealing with this morning, though. Maybe I could've prevented my nephews from being abducted if I hadn't been such a coward."

Mike said nothing. Not a judging and weighing silence, just a quiet into which Alex continued to talk while he stared off into the deepening shadows in the forest.

"I tracked Likho today. I planned to blind his other eye." He pulled the heavy railroad spike from his back pocket.

The flattened head and thick metal shaft had seen use and bore light orange rust stains and small pockmarks. He turned it over in his hands. "I got iron, in case that hurt him, like fairies or something. But when it came down to it, I couldn't move. I was too scared of breaking my parole and going back to prison. A few hours ago, I thought prison was the worst thing that could possibly happen." The spike blurred in his vision. He turned his head so Mike wouldn't see the hot tears brimming in his eyes.

"This rodeo ain't over yet. Not by a long shot. You're going to keep searching for those boys, and so am I."

The chill in the air deepened. Alex paced the road, battling a rising panic that Stribog wouldn't show. When twilight edged to dark under the trees, he finally heard the rumble of a car on the gravel road and his heart leapt with anticipation. Mike stood from where he'd been sitting against his front bumper. A gray Dodge Avenger came into view, careening down the road, headlights off. Alex and Mike both stepped well off the road, but the car fishtailed to a stop behind Mike's Trans Am.

Stribog emerged from the car, his gray suit and black ushanka hat blending into the shadows, leaving only his face and hands pale in the faint light. He leaned on the open door, one elbow resting on the top, apparently unsurprised to see Alex and Mike there.

"Good. You came to help?"

Alex shook his head. "I have troubles of my own. Likho has my nephews. I need your help getting them back."

Stribog made a dismissive grunt. "Likho has no interest in children. They have natural misfortunes, but he never targets them. Baba Yaga, though. She's here, and children are her interest. I suspect he's led Yaga to them, or them to her."

"Even I've heard of her," Mike said. "An old witch or something, right?"

"Yaga is only old in the sense that all of us are old. She can be any age. She's neither hag nor witch, as your Christianity painted her. She is teacher. Teaches children to be strong. To fight, to survive."

"Where is she?" Alex asked, excited at the possibility of a real lead.

"Somewhere near." He raised his hands and spread them to indicate perhaps the entire county.

"So the children aren't in danger if she has them?" Alex asked, grasping for any hope now.

Stribog pursed his lips then shrugged. "Depends on children. She's a stern tutor, not one forgiving of fools or failure."

Alex's forearms pebbled with gooseflesh. "Stribog, I need your help finding her. Finding them."

"There is more at stake than your nephews. Once I have my horn, if I can help you, I will." He stepped out from behind the door and closed it, ending the conversation with a final bang. "Have you seen Morana?"

"Koschei said you were out searching for the horn and Morana was distracting Perun. I saw Likho this morning and Koschei a little while ago, but that's all."

That's all? What even was his life now?

"She has been gone longer than I expected." Stribog stared at Alex's midsection as if he could see inside him. "How do you feel?"

Shredded, emotionally and physically. Foolish. Devastated. Ashamed.

"Okay."

Lost in thought, Stribog didn't seem one bit the comical old man he pretended to be. He looked dangerous, gazing at Alex like a predator with sharp eyes and coiled strength that belied his size. He looked like a god.

Stribog met Alex's gaze. "Do you know where Perun is?"

"No. I haven't seen him since that morning he tore out of me." Alex waved a hand vaguely in the direction of Boy Scout Tree Trail.

"And the horn? Do you know where it is?"

"No," he said, unnerved by what had started to feel like an interrogation. "I have no idea where it is." He backed up a step without meaning to, before summoning his resolve. "Look, I'm just trying to find out where my nephews are. If you can't help me, can you at least tell me where Likho is? I tried to trap him this morning, but he got away." It sounded better than the truth. "I have no idea where to find Baba Yaga, if she even has the boys, but if I can find Likho again, I can try to make him tell me what he did with David and Jake, or take his other eye, so maybe he can't hurt us anymore."

Stribog crossed his arms over his stout chest and leveled his stare at Alex. "You found Likho how." His tone didn't rise at the end, making it more a statement than a question.

He hadn't "found" him at all. Likho had baited him, playing cat to his mouse from the start. His silence answered for him.

"I will tell you some things about Likho," Stribog said, his voice strong, his diction clear. "If you found him, he wanted to be found. I suspect you will encounter him again soon enough whether you seek him out or not. But know that what he's done so far is nothing to what he can do. I blinded one eye to punish him, but even I can't kill him. He's part of the pattern of life and can never be unwoven from it." He took a step closer. "*I* blinded his eye. You can't. A mortal with a piece of simple iron." He gestured toward Alex's back pocket. "Help me find my horn instead, then it's over. We'll all go home."

"If I had even the faintest idea how to find your horn, I'd have done it already. Perun and the horn are your problem. My priority is getting Likho away from my family and finding my nephews. After that, I'll help any way I can if you give me something I can actually do. Once you find Perun, you can put him back inside me. I won't fight it."

Stribog waved the idea off like waving off a fly. "Morana was right. He wouldn't succumb to the same trick twice." He stepped so close that even in the pale light Alex could have counted the mottling of light and dark hairs in the man's gray beard and eyebrows. "I will make you this promise, though. You find my horn, and I will take care of all your problems."

"How am I supposed to find your horn if you and Morana can't? You're *gods*. I can't even hold my own with your "lesser beings" like Koschei and Likho."

"Pffft. You're stronger than you think. You held a god inside you for eight days. How do you think you did that, eh?"

"Yeah, I'm an eagle. Whatever." Anger and helplessness welled up inside Alex stronger than anything he'd known since the day he'd first been arrested. "My nephews are innocent in all this."

Stribog shoved his hands in his suit pockets and shrugged. "All of Likho's victims are innocent. It wouldn't be misfortune if they weren't. It would be justice." Ending the discussion abruptly, he turned to Mike. "Okay, now you, before you burst with your questions."

"Koschei told me some stryga was after me," Mike said. "Is that another name for Likho?"

"No. But I suspected the stryga would find you."

Mike narrowed his eyes and waited for more.

Stribog sighed. "Stryga are born with two hearts, two souls, and two sets of teeth, but are not yet monsters. When they die, one soul goes to the afterlife, but the other brings the body back to life again. Now it's a creature that hunts by night and eats its victims for blood to sustain it. You have come to its attention through your friend, but perhaps it hasn't killed and eaten you because it's curious about you. Or perhaps it plans to steal one of your souls, so it will again have two and be complete."

"I don't have two souls."

"No, but you have many teeth, and dead things are not very bright."

"What do I do? How do I fight it?"

Stribog shrugged. "Kill it," he said matter-of-factly. Removing his hands from his pockets, he waved off more questions. "And now, I must go. I have my horn to find and my brother to kill." He headed for the embankment.

"They're your grandchildren, aren't they—the eight winds the horn summons?" Alex shot at his back. "They're your family?"

Stribog turned. "They are."

"So if Perun gets the horn, he captures your grandchildren."

Stribog waited.

"My nephews are just as important to me. And Likho's already abducted them. They're just little boys. My sister is nearly crazy with worry. You're the one who dragged me into this war with your brother and got my family involved. You're a god and you're really telling me there's nothing you can do to help?"

Stribog stood half turned so long that adrenaline surged in Alex's hands and thighs when the old man suddenly strode back to him. This time Alex didn't back up. Stribog held out one hand. "Give me the weapon."

Alex pulled the railroad spike from his pocket and placed it in Stribog's palm.

Stribog examined it. "This will do no more than poking his eye with a stick." He closed his fist around the spike, squeezing it until his fingers blanched and his brow furrowed. The night seemed to grow darker around them and Stribog grew somehow larger while staying the same, like a person casting a giant, late afternoon shadow. An invisible aura of warmth and energy spread around them all. The breeze picked up. In the murky light, Alex saw a faint glow lighting Stribog's gray eyes. The ends of the spike turned flame gold, then forge red. Alex could feel the heat from where he stood, and still Stribog squeezed the metal shaft.

The god eased his grip; his shoulders relaxed and his brow smoothed. He opened his fist and handed the dull brown spike back. Alex took it carefully, but the metal was cool to the touch. The shaft was slightly irregular now, as if it had molded to the grooves and curves of Stribog's hand.

"There. I have siphoned what strength I can into your weapon. That is all I can do. It is more than I should have done. An act that will alert Perun and every other thing to my location. A drain of strength that I should have retained. Strength I need and cannot renew in this foreign land."

Alex stood speechless as Stribog left the road and clambered down into the trees, moving like a man of the years he appeared to be.

"I didn't think it would cost him anything to help me," Alex said, staring at the spot where Stribog had vanished into the gloom.

"If it helps your nephews, do you care?" Mike asked.

Alex didn't answer.

"So now you have that, what's next?" Mike said.

The question shook him free of the encounter and he turned his thoughts to the present. "Figure out how to make myself bait for Likho, I guess. How about you?"

"At least I know what's after me and what it wants. No point sitting around and waiting for it to find me again, though. Give me your sister's number and I'll see how I can help her until you get back."

"I appreciate that, Mike," he said. The words felt entirely inadequate to his gratitude. "Do me a favor," he added. "Tell her we found Stribog and I'm still working on things, okay? It'll save my phone battery."

One call would do nothing to his battery and they both knew it, but he didn't think his heart could take hearing his sister's desperation again.

"All right," Mike said. Alex pulled up Alina's contact screen and held out his phone while Mike tapped the number into his own contact list. Typing slowly, he asked, "So how are you planning to make yourself bait?"

"We're near to the place I first saw Likho. He's a forest goblin as well as Misfortune, and Stribog said these ancient trees have strong magic." Alex shoved the spike deep in his back pocket and placed his phone back in its case, making sure the magnetic clasp caught. The last thing he needed tonight was "misfortune" causing him to lose either one. "There are a lot of old-growth forests around here, but Koschei and another creature that Stribog talked to seem to be hanging out in this area. I'm hoping maybe Likho will have come back here too. Stribog's probably right, that he'll find me anyway sooner or later. But maybe I can tempt him somehow and bring him to me faster."

His original plan this morning had been to drive out to an area of narrow trails and cliffs. It turned out he hadn't needed to put it into action, but he was confident he could find something appropriately hazardous nearby and test the theory now.

"Do you want to go back and get any supplies?"

Alex shook his head. "The less prepared I am, the more likely I am to lure him."

"You should at least have a flashlight."

Mike opened the car door, the brightness of the interior light demonstrating just how dark it had gotten in the last few minutes. He sat sideways on the seat, rummaged in the glove box, and handed a small but powerful tac light to Alex.

"The batteries are fresh." He reached back into the glove box. "You should have this too." He pulled out a holstered gun and held it out, grip first. "I have a concealed carry permit."

Alex chewed his lip then shook his head. "You heard what Stribog said about him. I don't think a gun can kill him. Besides, convicted felons aren't allowed to carry. I don't need any more trouble than I've already got."

Mike returned it to the glove box and stood.

"All right. Call me when you need me to pick you up, then. Good luck to you."

They shook, Alex's hand vanishing into Mike's grip.

"You too, Mike."

Chapter Nineteen

ALEX STOOD BACK while Mike started the Trans Am. The motor rumbled loudly in the still forest. Mike pulled a U-turn and the yellow light of the headlights retreated, then disappeared around a curve. As the shadows and turns in the road swallowed the last of the light, Alex realized full dark had fallen while they'd talked. Thankful for the loan of the powerful flashlight, he started down the road toward Boy Scout Tree Trail, the path that led to the forest spirit—the leshy—and hopefully to Likho's home base.

It was barely suppertime, but the thin sliver of moon rode high already as it scudded in and out of the clouds above breaks in the canopy. With no distractions now, Alex could clearly hear the nocturnal sounds of the forest around him. A light breeze swished through the branches high overhead. A faint scent like warm Fritos drifted to him; the salty, earthy odor of a large animal nearby. Twigs crunched underfoot no more than a hundred yards away, fell silent, then crunched again; likely a big mule deer browsing. Something small skittered through the dead leaves, hiding from his approach. Camping in Montana, he would've found the noises soothing. Here, they set him on edge.

He considered his options for the kinds of risks that might summon Likho. His immediate surroundings held none of the dangers of extreme outdoor pursuits: no ice crevasses to fall into, no rock walls to scale, no whitewater rapids to navigate. There were bears, but only black bears—not usually confrontational with humans.

Mountain lions were exceedingly rare in this area, and probably even less common in a state park. Even the trees here were unscalable, with branches starting a couple hundred feet up. Still, he was walking through the woods alone at night; how hard could it be to tempt Misfortune to visit him? Hell, even turning off the flashlight and leaving the road to run through the trees pretty much guaranteed at least a sprained ankle. And the assortment of fairy tale characters milling around in these groves definitely upped the ante.

Magical creatures out of Slavic mythology sharing these woods with him made him uneasy, but it also gave him a thought. Aggravating the leshy, if it was still nearby, might put him in enough danger that Likho would take an interest. He could try setting a fire at the base of a tree, sure that it wouldn't catch enough to do real damage. The tricky part was that Alex wanted to take a risk, not end up dead. Perhaps better to see if he could speak with it rather than aggravate it. If Likho didn't show up, maybe the leshy would know where to find him—or, better still, find Baba Yaga. It might even know the location of his nephews. Having decided on at least a first course of action, he stayed on the road and picked up his pace. If he remembered correctly, he should only be a half mile or less from the trail. Even traveling in the dark, he could be there in ten or fifteen minutes.

A few minutes into his walk down the road, the moon sailed behind clouds or branches, deepening the surrounding shadows. A northern spotted owl hooted its four staged hoots somewhere ahead and to his right, high up. The pleasure he'd normally take in hearing one of his favorite birds withered under the concern that it might be Mike's owl, the stryga. Dry twigs crackled again somewhere under the trees and the hairs raised on the back of his neck. He'd never in his life been nervous in the woods. Until now.

Walking the half mile felt more like five miles, but eventually the wide beam of the flashlight caught the bare gravel of the parking pullout on his left and the gleam of white lettering on the dark signboard at the trailhead.

"*Dobriy vecher.*" A young voice greeted him with a good evening.

Alex jerked to a stop and swung the flashlight quickly side to side. Likho stepped into the beam of light. He still wore little boys' pull-up jeans, sneakers, a striped cotton shirt, and his windbreaker. The unbroken skin from forehead to right cheek shone pale, like the white skin of a newly healed injury.

"You seek me?" he said, continuing to speak in Russian. "Here I am."

When Alex made no move, Likho sauntered closer, nearly coming within arm's reach. So, he hadn't needed to summon Misfortune after all. He'd been waiting here for him. Alex remained still, his mind whirling as he tried to figure out what game the thing played this time.

He wasn't left wondering for long. In the next instant, a blue light flashed across the trailhead sign and the giant bole of the tree next to it. A red light followed, painting the shadowy undergrowth in hues of blood.

Alex risked a quick glance down the road at two approaching vehicles as understanding dawned on him. Mike and Stribog had both driven in and out past the "road closed" sign this evening, and Likho had made sure someone would report seeing them.

And here they all were again, him and Likho and the law enforcement officers, just like this morning at the Oregon border. Likho resuming his game, testing which tribulation Alex would choose: his nephews' abduction or prison. Except Likho didn't know that the game had changed. He couldn't know that the threat from the spike was greater than it had been this morning. And Alex had changed as well. He would risk anything now. Anything.

"Yes. I seek you," Alex said. The words came out in the rough, gravelly tone he'd picked up in prison. His don't-fuck-with-me voice he'd learned to use whether he felt equal to his aggressor or not. "Where are my nephews?"

Likho gave him a sly smile and stepped onto the road and into the flashing lights and headlights.

Alex pulled the spike from his back pocket and followed Likho onto the road.

"This again?" Likho said, circling him lazily.

When Likho drifted almost close enough to brush his chest, Alex dropped the flashlight and his arm shot out. He saw a flicker of surprise and excitement when he grabbed the boy-Likho by a fistful of hair and jerked him down onto the road. It didn't matter that he knew the creature had allowed it. He set the spike in the hollow of the boy's throat to keep him down and pushed slowly, sliding one knee onto his chest. Likho smiled.

Despite his conviction to see this through, a small hope tickled the back of Alex's thoughts. Maybe he could win the location of the boys and then flee into the forest. He imagined himself evading the officers, avoiding getting either shot or captured. Avoiding jail.

He spared another quick glance down the road and estimated he had less than a minute before the officers were close enough that there'd be no chance of escape. Alex held Likho firmly and moved the spike from his throat to his good eye. Likho squirmed in his grip. Alex clenched his fist into the handful of hair, leaned more weight onto his knee, and held him still. In the glaring headlights of the oncoming cars, he pressed the spike firmly against the boy's eye. The sound of tires on gravel grew louder than his panting breath.

Likho at last felt the magic that permeated the spike. The act of pretending to wriggle free dropped from him like a discarded cloak and his strength tripled. Recentering the spike, Alex pushed hard enough that he yelled out and stilled.

"Yaga has them at…" Alex interpreted the rest as "the lake of dead things." He maintained the pressure. "I'll take you there now," Likho said. "I'll tell her you must take them home. She will allow it. I promise." He ceased his struggling then and gave a smile, as if to say, "There. You've won the game." *This time.*

Against the odds, Alex had achieved his goal; he felt certain "the lake of dead things" could only mean one place. It was everything he could have hoped for. Likho could transport them away from the approaching officers in a single step. There'd be no reason for anyone to suspect him or search his ankle-monitor history. He could be hugging his nephews in the next few moments.

He didn't move, realizing that it changed nothing in the long run. Alina and the boys would never truly be safe with this creature on the loose and now that Likho knew he possessed a weapon that could hurt him, he might never get this chance again. He glanced once again into the woods, wishing he could have it all and knowing he couldn't.

The enforcement vehicles skidded to a stop, gravel crunching: a county sheriff's car followed by a Redwoods State Park ranger. Headlights framed him. A loudspeaker clicked. Car doors opened. Guns cocked. An officer shouted at him to drop the weapon.

Alex rammed the spike home.

Chapter Twenty

"DAVID! JAKE!"

Alina swung her flashlight in a nonstop, one-hundred-and-eighty-degree arc and called out again for the boys. After hours of shouting, the names rasped from her throat in a croak, like a heavy smoker with laryngitis. Mike, at her shoulder, repeated her in a voice that carried so far it echoed faintly off the tree trunks.

She'd been relieved when Mike phoned to say he was on the way to his house to pick up extra supplies and would join her again soon. They'd met up at the trailhead nearly two hours ago, and she'd at last gotten an update on their meeting with Stribog and learned that Alex had set off to try and find Likho in Jedediah Smith State Park.

Her hope that her brother would find the creature and force information out of him on the boys' whereabouts had progressively faded with the twilight. For the past hour of stumbling through the woods in the dark, Mike had been the life ring she'd clung to. He'd taken charge of the few volunteers they'd encountered and then had led her off the trails and deep into the trees, past where the police had ended their search at nightfall. A gun was tucked into the large front pocket of his jacket, and a hunting knife hung from his belt. His confidence, skill, and calm reassurance had been a granite cliff for her terror to break against, giving her the will to keep going.

She swung her flashlight side to side and called out again.

At the far left of the arc, the beam fell across a pale lump under the ferns. A noise squeezed from her mouth like no sound she'd ever made: a choked and gasping grunt in place of the words that stuck painfully in her chest. She ran toward the still form with a heart clenched so hard it burned like it might burst. Her arms pumped, sending the light swirling wildly over trees and the night sky. She tripped over a downed branch and landed heavily.

"It's okay," Mike said, jogging to her and taking her arm to help her up. "It's okay."

She twisted in his grasp to reach the small, naked body curled in the undergrowth.

"It's a rock," he said, gripping her arm more firmly. "Look at it." He pointed his headlamp at it. "It's a rock, see?"

She inhaled deeply and a sob rose from her solar plexus into the hand she held to her mouth. It seemed obvious now. A pale, rounded rock, half the size of Jake, partially covered by ferns.

Her right knee throbbed, and a tickle of blood dripped down her shin beneath her jeans. Her voice choked on fresh tears. "What if they went past the school and into town? What if they made it to the highway?"

She didn't care that she'd asked this before, along with all her other "what-ifs." This stretch of woods wasn't endless—like some places in the county where, if you headed in the wrong direction, you could travel for miles without emerging from the forest or hitting a road—but still, the boys could be going in circles. They could have run into strangers. And worst of all, her brother's fear could be right that Likho might have spirited them far, far from here.

"If they come to the highway or to town it increases the chances someone will see two young boys on their own after dark and report it to the police," he answered patiently, though he'd said the same before. "And you know the police are on the lookout for them on the roads."

She walked to the rock and touched its cool, gritty surface, reassuring herself there was no mistake, that she wasn't leaving her child half buried in the forest loam. Convinced beyond doubt, she straightened her shoulders and lifted her head.

"I'm okay. I'll be okay."

She wasn't, though. Desperation and panic had turned her stomach to a small ball of lead and reduced her thoughts to cycles of near catatonia followed by adrenaline-fueled energy with no outlet. She couldn't afford to keep falling apart. She had to do better, be stronger.

Dan had fared even worse. His stress had transformed to mania hours ago and he'd run the trails so many times she'd lost count. After that, he'd begun canvassing the woods bordering their school to the north and south, still certain the boys would stay near the places they recognized. He hadn't registered her inability to keep up with him or the fact that he was obsessively covering the same ground. She didn't even know where he was at this moment, but she heard him sometimes in the distance, calling out into the oppressive silence of the woods.

Worry for her husband occupied the only corner in her brain not filled with fear for her children, but at least the last of the neighbors and volunteers still searching were near him. She and Dan needed each other tonight, but even more compellingly, they needed to follow the separate paths their worst fears led them down.

Her phone rang and she pulled it from her pocket. She wished again that she'd gotten a phone for David when she and Dan had discussed what age he might be responsible enough to carry one. The screen said the call was from the Del Norte Sheriff's Office. Hope and fear for her children squeezed like a tight band around her chest as she answered.

"Dead Lake." It was Alex's voice, filled with urgency. "You need to go to Dead Lake."

She took a second to register the words and make sense of them.

"Are you there? Are you with them?" she said just as insistently.

"I'm in the county jail. I'll fill you in later. I only have a few minutes to talk. That *boy* who's been hanging around with them said they're at the lake of dead things, with *Aunt Babs*." He stressed the name, to make sure she put the pieces together. "I'd bet my life he was telling the truth. It all fits. The lake being just north of those woods. The boys seeing her and her house across from the school. I'm certain it's the place he meant. I tried telling the officers who arrested me to search there, but they wouldn't listen. Maybe they'll listen to you if you call. I don't know. Don't go up there alone, though. Did Mike show up?"

"Yes. He's here with me."

"Let me talk to him for a sec."

"Put it on speaker," Mike said. She did and then held the phone out in front of them.

"I heard most of that," Mike said to Alex. "I think we're near the north end of the woods, straight up from the finger that runs east of your house." While he talked, he shone his headlamp on the compass he'd brought along as a backup to his phone GPS, checked the time, and briefly studied the map. "I'd say we're about due east of the bottom edge of the lake, probably less than half a mile from it."

"Have you been there before?"

"No."

"Alina has. The road and boat launch are on the west side and the north end is pretty open. I don't think they'd be there. The southeast is swampy and the lower half of the eastern shore is wooded. That east shore would be my guess."

"Got it." Mike took a bearing on his compass and started walking. Alina stayed at his side, still holding the phone out in front of them.

"Be careful, both of you," Alex continued. "More than just Auntie could be out there."

"We will," Alina said. "How about you, Alex? Are you alright? Why are you in jail?" Her overstressed brain fired a few neurons of memory from the days of worry and strain they'd both endured the last time he'd been arrested: the trial, the lawyers, the money, the anxiety. So much anxiety.

"It's complicated. They think they saw something they didn't."

Her brother was being cagey, and she felt sure an officer was standing nearby. She glanced at Mike for some clue, but his gaze shifted between his compass and the way ahead as he led them through the trees and the undergrowth.

"Time," a male voice in the background said to Alex.

"Don't worry about me," Alex said, "but I'm sorry I'm not there to help you. Since it's Friday night, I'm going to be here through the weekend, at least, before I get a bail hearing. Do you still have that third-party service to get collect calls from the jail on your cell?"

"Oh, I must. I don't think I ever canceled that when you got out."

"I need you to hang up now, sir," the voice in the background said.

"I'll talk to you again as soon as I can, okay?"

"We'll stay in touch," Mike assured him.

"I love you," Alina said.

"I love you too," Alex replied.

The call disconnected.

Chapter Twenty-One

Alex hung up, relieved to have reached Alina and glad that Mike was with her but, for his part, the die was cast. He might have slowed Likho but, locked up now, there was nothing more he could do to help them against the other dangers out there. He could only hope Stribog would find his horn and then he and all his ilk could go back wherever they belonged.

Somewhere in the distance, probably the drunk tank, someone screamed mindlessly and incessantly: "I can't. I can't. I can't."

The booking procedure trundled slowly onward through the photo, fingerprinting, jail ID, issuing a jumpsuit, and classification to determine his section within the jail. He'd missed lunch today and dinnertime at the jail but, while in holding, a guard brought him a leftover lunch sandwich from the kitchen wrapped in a paper napkin. Alex forced his unsettled stomach to accept the food, balling up only one exceptionally stale corner in his napkin. In lieu of a trashcan he shoved it in his jumpsuit pocket out of habit born from his many years of not leaving food or trash in the woods.

Boredom seesawed with his abject fear over entering the system again; the one thing he had sworn to himself for three years that he would avoid at all costs. Finally, a guard arrived at his holding cell, handed him a pile of personal items, and guided him by one arm through a secure door and down a hallway. He stopped at a door near the end marked Pod D.

Inside the pod, the smells assaulted Alex, different from the other places he'd done time and yet the same bleach-covered filth. Free time had ended, and the inmates were in lockdown. Half an hour earlier and he would have been the new guy, led through a full dayroom carrying his bed linens and county-issued toiletries. Tomorrow, he'd still be the new guy—watched, inspected, quizzed, tested—but he'd start on slightly better footing. County jail wasn't new to him; he'd done nearly three months in Missoula before getting assigned to a prison, but it was Pelican Bay that would give him cred here.

In two and a half years behind bars he'd never indulged in the prison tattoo culture but other marks, more deeply engraved on him than ink on skin, kicked in on the walk to his cell. The muscles in his back and arms tightened—a dog with raised hackles; he held his head cocked differently, confident but not aggressive; his gait shortened, balanced and ready, though no one was near but his guard. A spontaneous metamorphosis back into a person he'd hoped he'd left behind forever.

He scanned the empty dayroom and spotted the large phone box bolted to the wall. Not a payphone—collect calls only back here, which cell phones couldn't accept.

"Could I make a quick call to check on my sister again?"

"Phone calls during free time only, nine to eleven in the morning, six to eight in the evening."

The guard followed him up the concrete stairs to the second floor and opened the industrial-mint-green metal door to his cell. With immense relief, he saw that he had no roommate, at least for the time being, though it was still early on Friday night. By the end of the weekend, one would be a near certainty. The door banged shut behind him and the sound of the key turning in the lock echoed in his skull. He stood motionless for a moment as the stark reality of his situation sank in: jail, parole violation, assault charges pending.

He unrolled his mattress and made his bed, leaving the top bunk mattress rolled tight, then paced his six-by-eight cell along the bunk beds, past the toilet, stopping at the solid door with the long, narrow, reinforced window. The window looked out on the wire between the second-floor balcony railing and the drop to the unadorned concrete dayroom below with a few long tables and one small TV mounted high on the wall. Paced back to the opposite wall between the beds and the TV-tray-sized desk with its attached metal stool across from the bunks. The claustrophobia of the small room and locked door pressed on him like he'd been buried to his neck in sand, but questions drove him to keep moving.

Questioning if his gamble had been right and his nephews really were at Dead Lake. Wondering if Alina and Mike had found the boys, or if Baba Yaga and the other things in the forest had found Alina and Mike instead. And beneath the more immediate concerns, wondering if his assault charges would stick. He'd been the only one to see Likho disappear into thin air while officers shoved him down onto the road, cuffed him, and read him his rights.

He'd told the arresting officers that he'd been searching for his nephews when he saw a kid run into the woods and thought it might be David. It turned out to be some youthful looking high schooler who'd been partying hard. The kid took a swing at him and they'd ended up on the ground. But between the assault the officers were sure they'd seen in the headlights, trespassing on state park land, and his prison record when they called in his ID, nobody was buying his story. He'd been questioned heavily about sexual interest in young boys and finally held on suspicion of assault with a deadly weapon.

The toilet contraption was the same tall, six-sided stainless cylinder as his Pelican Bay cell used to have, with a sink basin across the top and toilet bowl near the bottom. He pushed the button on the sink to receive a few seconds of lukewarm water and held the plastic mug he'd been given under the faucet. He sat on his bunk and drained the mug. The familiarity of it all increased rather than decreased his anxiety. He tried controlling his breathing to stave off panic. Finally, he lay back on his bunk. His feet might have stopped for the time being, but his mind hadn't, and stress chewed at his guts along with the stale ham and cheese sandwich.

When first released from Pelican Bay, he'd been afraid he would lie awake in his cell-sized cottage in Alina's backyard hearing in his head the clang of metal doors opening and closing all hours, guards talking as they made rounds. The incessant sounds of inmates verbally posturing, snoring, crying, yelling. Instead, three months in his own place on the dead-end street had reset his brain back to earlier times and to the silence he'd loved in his years at his Montana cabin. He'd slept deeply after the first week or so, and during the three months since his release, had felt like he'd begun to recapture a piece of his old self. And now he lay listening to catcalls of new "fish" being launched at him, along with the other familiar sounds he should have never had to know. And trying to relearn how to tune it all out.

The lights shut off suddenly in a series of loud clunks. Alex lay on his bunk in the dark, his claustrophobia wrapped around him like a blanket. The fears he'd pushed away—the personal ones he didn't like to admit—crowded in closer than the walls. He prodded at the limits of his tolerance like poking at a mouth ulcer with his tongue, while his questions shifted to darker and deeper musings: whether he should have made different choices and taken Likho's bargain. If he should have run again and saved himself, like he had that morning. If his choices and his consequences balanced in the scales.

If he could handle incarceration a second time.

Chapter Twenty-Two

"WE MUST BE there," Alina said when her shoe sank into wet, boggy mud. She pulled her foot free with a sucking pop, glad for her waterproof duck boots. She was chilled enough without sopping wet feet.

They had stopped yelling David and Jake's names half an hour ago with Alex's warning that the boys could be with Baba Yaga, and had been speaking in hushed tones. Now, certain her boys were near, her breath came shorter as if her lungs kept filling to cry out and call them home to her.

Mike turned off his flashlight, and she did the same. Darkness wrapped her eyes like a blindfold. It seemed impossible that it was only eight o'clock. Time seemed to have slowed ever since night fell, and she felt as if she'd been searching for half the night already. She pointed to the right, her night vision starting to kick in. Mike followed her lead as she took them north now instead of west.

Alex's certainty that the boys were here at Dead Lake had given her new energy. She had more focus and could think more logically. She'd called Dan to let him know that she and Mike were working their way north but hadn't told him about Alex's call or Dead Lake. If he raced up here and Alex's tip turned out to be wrong, she wasn't sure how he'd handle it. She'd called the police too, but they'd said the same as before, to go home and rest, and they'd restart the search in the morning. If she and Mike failed to find David and Jake near the lake, she'd tell Dan and the volunteers and the police and anyone else she could think of to canvas this entire area tomorrow.

The moon was a narrow sickle that cast poor light. She stepped carefully over the rough terrain, arms out to her sides. In the woods by her home, the redwood trees were widely spaced with an undergrowth of ferns and moss. Here, near the lake, the foliage grew thick and varied. Scratches laced her hands, wrists, and face from bushwhacking through dense shrubs, berry vines, and low, branchy trees. Scents of wild mint and pine, wet grass, late daisies, and decaying plant matter filled the night air.

A few hundred yards farther on, the ground dried and grew firmer under their feet, and they angled back toward the lake. The trees broke suddenly a few minutes later, and the black, eerie finger of water lay before them. Shadowy water lilies and marsh grass drifted on the surface at this southeastern corner, just above the true marsh. In the pale moonlight, she could see the opposite shore a scant couple of hundred feet away. The far end of the long, narrow lake would be about three-quarters of a mile to their right.

Like most locals, she'd heard the stories about the lake: That it maintained a constant level despite the fact that water flowed out of it, yet it had no inlet. That a Tolowa legend claimed the bottomless lake had swallowed their people, drowning them after an altercation among the tribal council. And, of course, the inevitable ghost stories that were bound to spring up around a place named Dead Lake. In actuality, with no inlet, it had probably been named for dead and lifeless water until the county stocked it with fish, reviving it. Either way, sections of it, like the one where they stood, felt creepy enough without the old rumors swirling through her memory and the new possibility of Russian creatures out of nightmare cavorting nearby.

The lake was deserted—day-use only and no campsites on either shore—not that anyone would have been likely to be here on a chilly November night anyway. She and Mike turned north and pushed on as quickly as possible.

Time lost meaning as she hyperfocused on every scent and sound for any sign of her boys. The thin strip of muddy beach came and went, forcing them to retreat often into the blackness of the trees and hazards of the undergrowth as they made their way up the shoreline. Worse still, when driven into the dense tangle of vegetation, branches rustled noisily and twigs and stems crunched underfoot. After stretches of walking on the sand, hearing nothing but the soft lap of water, she and Mike sounded as loud as elephants crashing through a jungle.

Relieved, at last, to see a glint of muddy beach again, Alina angled back down the embankment to the lake. Mike remained behind her, letting her lead. She had just reached the water's edge when a plopping noise froze her in mid-step. Adrenaline flooded her arms and legs, and her mind raced to locate the sound and frame it in some way that related to David and Jake.

"A fish jumping," Mike whispered in her ear.

Alina nodded. Of course. Once Mike said it, she recognized the wet splash she'd heard.

A pale, flat structure across the lake told her they were opposite the small parking lot, boat launch, and rickety fishing pier. She pointed, whispering to Mike, "We're about halfway up the lake."

Only the same distance again remained to find some clue to the boys' whereabouts, or they'd be forced to search hundreds of square acres around the lake step-by-step. She pushed the thought down and trudged up the muddy shoreline on legs that felt as heavy and boneless as sandbags.

Another plop, louder this time, a fish leaping higher or a larger fish. Fishing had never been her thing, but she'd heard the bass here could get pretty big. She walked on without turning. Mike's footsteps squished softly behind her.

A fierce splash and a yell from Mike broke the quiet. Alina spun with an involuntary cry of her own. Mike was nowhere to be seen. She ran calf-deep into the water, screaming his name from her raw throat.

A second later, Mike surfaced with a huge and desperate gasp for air. Between his dark skin, the lightless night, and a lake whose water was opaque even in day, she struggled to make out a shadowy shape behind him. Arms or tentacles or thick vines seemed wrapped across his chest, and an outline of what might have been a head and shoulders loomed behind his own. And then he was gone again, vanished beneath water as black as the mud she stood upon.

"Mike!" she yelled again. She waded into the lake, fumbling with her flashlight, turning it on just as a large shape flew over her head within inches of her scalp. With an almost soundless flutter, a huge owl flapped once more and stretched out for a lethal strike, talons extended, body back, wings out. The talons hit the water in front of her, and the bird beat its wings hard, leaning forward now and pulling what might have been marsh grass or might've been hair up into the air. More of the dark shadow rose from the water. A female voice screamed with fury. Mike surfaced with another gasp in front of the pair. Alina struck at the figure in the water and the owl with violent swipes of her flashlight. Coughing, he splashed in his heavy clothes toward the shore, pushing her ahead.

Alina threw her flashlight to the ground. She turned and lunged for his arm, nearly overbalancing. Grabbing the sleeve of his jacket, she hauled him onto the shore.

The owl and the thing in the water continued to fight but the owl seemed to have the advantage. The thing in the water took one last vicious swing, upended, and dove. Without pause, the owl streaked toward them.

Mike grabbed the back of her coat and thrust her toward the trees. Before they could reach cover, the owl's talons lanced into the back of her neck. Her jacket and hair provided some protection, but she felt claws pierce the skin, three spikes of fire knifing toward the vertebrae of her spine. Alina screamed and swatted behind her head at the bird. Mike launched himself past her, landing prone at the edge of the underbrush, scrambling and thrashing in the ground cover. He pushed to his feet holding a medium-sized stick. Spinning, he swung hard, as if about to behead her. Instead, she felt the thump of the impact on the owl's feathered body, and the tearing of her skin as he dislodged the bird from her neck. It fluttered up and circled above them.

"Go, Alina. Run!"

"No!"

Like Mike had done, she threw herself at the undergrowth. The knee she'd injured in her earlier fall ached. Her myriad scratches and cuts burned. Her neck wounds throbbed. She raked desperately through the grass and brush but found no other loose sticks. Patting the ground, she slapped down on the hardness of a palm-sized rock. Grabbing it, she twisted onto her back and heaved it, but the bird was so close to her face she missed. Mike, standing on the mud in a batter's stance now, swung at it again, but it lifted out of the way.

"It's trying to drive you away," he yelled. "It's me it wants. Go! Find your boys." Without another word, he sprinted away from her down the shoreline, then dodged into the trees. The owl stayed close behind him.

Alina stood shell-shocked as blood dripped from her neck, ran under her shirt, and trickled down her back like sweat. Even with adrenaline burning through her veins, she'd never catch up to Mike on her leaden legs. A soft splash from the lake shook her from her trance, and she ran into the trees, her arms in front of her face to protect her from the whipping branches and thorns. Surrounded by thick foliage, she finally stopped, shivering, and listened to the night sounds around her. Or, rather, the lack of sounds. Other than occasional sloshes from the lake and a distant whoosh of traffic and surf, the night was silent. Preternaturally silent, as if all the local wildlife had gone to ground in the face of the unnatural intruders.

It seemed a week, a month, a year before her heart and breath slowed to a rate they could sustain. She thought she'd cried all the tears from her body hours ago, but more came now. Russian lore had water spirits: vodyanoy, rusalka—probably others—and she'd likely never know what had grabbed Mike. The owl she could guess. He'd told her about the stryga when he filled her in on seeing Stribog and Koschei.

One thought overrode all the others, though. Mike was right. If her boys were out here, they could be the next victims of these horrible things. Still choking on sobs, she pushed off a tree trunk like pushing off a swimming pool wall, needing momentum to move forward. And she would keep moving forward, no matter what.

She no longer needed to move quietly. Mike had said the owl wouldn't follow her, and the two of them had already made enough noise to draw other ghouls and monsters for miles around. She yelled for her boys in a voice grown slightly stronger during their silent trekking and emerged back onto the shoreline, keeping well away from the water. She stopped again to listen for Mike, for sounds from the lake, for... she didn't even know anymore. A distant rustle of branches behind her might have been Mike, still headed away from her, but pulling her attention more strongly was a new scent ahead, drifting to her on the light breeze. Burning wood. A campfire.

"I WANT MOM," Jake said, again.

David didn't answer this time. He'd kept telling Jake they'd be found and things would be okay. He had to because Jake was just little and David had to be brave. Now it was dark, and they'd been with the weird lady since lunchtime, and his mom and dad and uncle hadn't come for them yet. Not even the one-eyed boy. The fear inside him whispered that they would never be found and nothing would be okay ever again.

The lady in the patched dress said something angry sounding, but she sounded angry every time she talked.

"You have to talk English," he pleaded with her.

She glowered like Mr Earnhardt did sometimes in science class and pointed away from the lake toward the trees with her walking stick, then stabbed at the pile of wood they'd gathered for the fire. The pile *he'd* gathered. Jake hadn't picked up more than a few twigs and he'd dropped most of those along the way.

The lady had shown him where to get the firewood at a downed tree. When they came back to the clearing by the lake, she'd made him stack some of it into a little teepee, with twigs and dry pine needles inside. When she'd started the fire, the house, standing behind her, had bent its skinny legs and sat on the ground behind the stick pile. Its doorway with no door looked like an open mouth and the windows on either side like eyes. David thought it watched him every time he moved, like the eyeballs on the paintings in the museum in San Francisco last summer.

Before collecting firewood, she'd shown them both how to fish in the lake by using strips of colored rags from her dress, a net of woven grass, and a sharp stick, but David couldn't catch any and Jake mostly just splashed around. Neither of them had eaten any lunch or dinner except for a few berries she pointed out. The lady had caught a fish, and she cooked it now over the fire she'd started. It smelled so good David thought his stomach might turn inside out.

Squatting on the other side of the fire, she used a forked branch to pull the fish from the small coals at the edge, then began peeling bits of flesh off with her hands. David watched her fingers go from the fish to her mouth, and his own mouth watered. She wiped the grease on the hem of her skirt and said more angry words, then picked up her long stick and shook it at him.

"Come on, Jake," he said.

"Where?" his brother said, sulking.

"To get more wood."

"I don't wanna get wood. I wanna go home. I wanna hotdog. And an ice cream sandwich. I want Mom."

The weird lady raised her stick again then went back to eating.

David wanted to eat too, and he didn't want to go into the woods in the dark just him and his brother, but his knuckles had already been rapped with that stick today. He took Jake's hand and pulled his little brother to his feet. Jake pulled back like he did sometimes when their mom tried to make him go to bed and he didn't want to.

"Come on, Jake," he said, sounding stern like his mom or dad would.

The lady hadn't hit Jake yet with that stick, but she didn't like them being loud and David didn't want her to hit either of them if Jake started yelling. More importantly, it was the first time she wasn't coming with them, and he had an idea. Jake stared up at the woman with large, wet eyes, but he followed David around the fire and away from the lake.

"Give me your hearing aid," David whispered to Jake as soon as they were out of sight. Jake stared up at him. David peeled the one closest to him off Jake's ear, pried open the battery compartment, and removed the small, round battery. He dropped the hearing aid and let it hang from the cord clipped to Jake's shirt, then pushed the battery deep in his pants pocket.

David had thought all day about running away, but he didn't know where he was or where to run to. Besides, he'd imagined that if he did, she'd send her creepy house after him and Jake to squash them. But Mr Earnhardt had said in science class that batteries could explode. If the weird lady and her weird house blew up, they could get away and find someone to help them.

He couldn't find the tree in the dark, so he just started picking up any sticks he found. Jake didn't help, but at least he didn't cry. A noise in the woods, somewhere farther down the lake, startled him. He imagined a hairy monster, bigger than the creepy house, crashing through the woods, coming to eat them. He ran through the scratchy bushes with the few sticks he had, Jake at his heels, though his brother probably hadn't heard anything.

The weird woman was standing on the other side of the fire now, looking down the lake. He dropped the sticks. She was still looking away, so he pulled the battery out of his pocket and dropped it in the fire. Just then, a distant shout came from the same direction as the other noises. Someone, a lady maybe, yelling "eye" or maybe "Ike," followed by a lot of splashing, loud enough even Jake heard it with only one hearing aid. The house stood up, smashing ferns and little bushes as it also turned toward the noise.

David snatched his brother's hand to run away from the explosion about to happen at the same time the weird lady lunged and seized them both, pulling them against her skirt. Jake planted his feet and tried to jerk away. "Mom!" Jake yelled.

The weird lady's hand squeezed so hard on David's upper arm it hurt. David heard a soft hiss from the fire. Panicked, he tried to twist out of her grip. A little flash of blue-orange flame, about the size of his thumb, flared and fizzed out in the fire, right near where he'd dropped the battery. Mr Earnhardt must be really bad at science.

"Mom!" Jake yelled again.

David wasn't at all sure the person yelling had been his mom. The voice had been scratchy, like he sounded when he got sick. Maybe it was the lake monster he'd seen earlier in the day when getting a bucket of water, a giant shadow under the surface that swam away when the weird lady shook her stick at it.

Then a man hollered something. They all stood motionless, him and Jake and the weird lady and the creepy house, like a game of freeze tag at school. All of them listening to the crashing and rustling in the trees far away. The lady kept squeezing his arm. David made a wish with all his heart that the man was his dad or Uncle Alex coming for them.

"David! Jake!" The lady yelled again, closer, calling their names. The voice still sounded scratchy, but this time he had no doubt. It *was* his mother.

"Mom!" he and Jake yelled together.

Now they both twisted and fought to get free. The weird lady's grip rubbed his skin till it burned. She dragged them step-by-step away from the lake and toward the woods. Jake kept screaming. David had to do something before she hid them from their mom.

As she yanked them past the fire, David lunged forward, jerking his shoulder. His fingers scrabbled at the unburnt end of a branch, thinking he could use it as a club, but the lady pulled at him and his grip slipped. He dug his feet in and lunged once more, hard enough to make her stagger. Seeing him fight, Jake fought as well and yelled again for their mom. While the weird lady shifted her hold on Jake and covered his mouth, David's fingers wrapped around another, smaller branch at the very outer edge of the fire ring.

She yanked him upright and this time his grip held. The little branch pulled free. He swung the stick awkwardly, one-handed, at her leg. He only managed to thump her calf and dress, but the impact knocked it from his hand. It dropped to the ground. She slapped her other hand over his mouth and dragged him by his neck.

A second later, she let go. Flames flared up her skirt, fanned from the singed cloth where the burning stick had struck her. The smell of fish and meat oils on the burning cloth filled the air. She let them go and beat at the dress with both hands.

David grabbed Jake's shirtsleeve and ran, as fast as he could, down the shore.

The lady fought the flames on her clothing, folding the cloth to smother them and trotting toward the lake. "*Molodtsy*," she called after them as they ran from the camp into the dark. For once, she didn't sound angry. "*Molodtsy*," she yelled.

Then he heard her laugh, loud and hard.

"Mom!"

When she heard both her boys yelling for her, Alina's heart squeezed so hard that she thought it would shatter. Acting on pure reflex and adrenaline, she waved

234

her flashlight beam ahead and ran. Her focus honed to a sharp, single-minded point. Her muscles burned. Conscious thought and logic were smothered by an avalanche of primitive maternal instincts.

"David," she yelled back, so loud it nearly tore her throat. "Jake!"

A woman's voice shouted something in Russian. *Fine lads? Good boys?*

It didn't matter. All that mattered was that someone else was near her boys. She ran faster still. The beach was a blur and her eyes teared in the cold. Around a slight curve of the beach, a small shadow appeared, moving toward her. It resolved in her flashlight beam into two figures holding hands, running.

"Mom!" David yelled again.

She rushed to them, not caring what, if anything, pursued them, though some small part of her registered that they appeared to be alone and unharmed. The last hundred yards were agony, waiting to sweep them up and protect their small bodies with her own. She reached them at last. Dropping to her knees, she pulled them to her, held them tight, and kissed their heads.

Her heart and breath took long minutes to slow, but the boys seemed less panicked than she'd been—Jake especially, who began talking excitedly about a lady and her house and the net he'd made.

Alina shone her flashlight up the beach, still seeing nothing. Pulling the boys away from the shore and under the cover of the trees, she phoned Dan. In the time it took for her to dial and him to pick up, she thought she'd burst with the news.

"I found them. They're okay. I need you to get the car and meet us at the fishing pier at Dead Lake as soon as you can."

Chapter Twenty-Three

MIKE RAN WITH the owl at his shoulder, clawing at him with its talons and striking with its beak. His soaking wet boots, jeans, and jacket chilled him and weighed him down. Branches slapped him in the face and roots and rocks tripped him in the dark. He wished yet again for his headlamp, lost somewhere in the lake. His foot sank into bog water and sucked loose, telling him he'd reached the marshy south end of the lake. He cut southeast, still running, headed for the redwood stand near Alex's house that would lead him to his car.

He tripped over a root and went sprawling, not for the first time. As before, the owl dived at him. He pulled his knife, rolled onto his back, and remained still, trying to lure it closer. It dived again. He stabbed up then slashed, but the owl evaded the knife and strafed a line of deep scratches across his wrist. It circled until he was up and running again, driving him in the direction he wanted to go anyway. More importantly, though, it continued to chase him, allowing Alina to escape.

He shoved a hand into his pocket and ran his thumb over the bullet cartridge once more. His gun was old and had been immersed in the lake too long. Water had gotten inside, and the bullets would be unreliable until the cartridge dried, which wouldn't be anytime soon.

The south end of the lake was less than a mile from his car, something he could run in a few minutes on a road. Over rough and brambly terrain, in the dark, pursued by the owl, it felt like running a marathon.

He pushed through the thickest barrier of branches and vines yet and suddenly emerged into tall, wide-spaced trees. Not far from his car now and with more room to maneuver, he stopped and looked back for the owl. The huge bird, on its silent wings, filled his vision. Feathers and the stiff quills beneath struck his face, and talons gripped his jacket. He threw his arms up and caught a beak strike on his left wrist instead of in his eye.

It was time to quit playing defense. He grabbed the legs just above the talons, trapping them against his jacket, and threw his right arm around the bird, pulling it hard into his chest. The raptor was light, only a few pounds, but strong, and the wingspan of four feet or more made it unwieldy. The talons punctured the heavy canvas of his jacket, the sharp nails piercing the skin of his chest like needles. He fought to control the head and that wicked, hooked beak—containing those unnatural rows of teeth—so near his neck.

The bird struggled. Mike twisted his head and hunched his shoulders to protect his throat and the vulnerable structures beneath. Crushing the bird to his chest, he let go of the legs. Ignoring the stabbing pain of the strikes, he pulled his knife from its sheath and plunged it hard up into the breast. The owl screeched and twisted its wings free. They beat at his face, blinding him. Mike released the bird and fell against the trunk of a tree at his back. The owl fluttered twice and dropped to the forest floor. It bled onto the pine needles and dirt, audibly sucking in air with the deep gasps of the dying. His own harsh breath drowned it out.

Mike leaned his head back, his heart thundering in his ears. In the distance, he heard a tenacious searcher calling the names of the boys. Pushing upright, he felt at his neck. His wounds trickled blood and he dabbed at them with his shirt. Adrenaline ebbed slowly and painfully from his muscles. With a hand that felt too weak for the task, he wiped the owl's blood off his knife and onto his jeans before re-sheathing the blade. He started walking on shaky legs, glancing back to make certain the owl was dead.

He didn't know these woods well but had seen from the map that they covered a small rectangular area bordered on three sides by roads. He was close to his car, less than half a mile for sure. All he had to do was keep straight south until he found the main path. He could drive to the parking lot at Dead Lake in minutes and find Alina.

He came to the trail about fifteen minutes later and turned right. His heart pounded less violently now, his legs felt steadier, and his wind had nearly recovered. A few minutes later, he was at his car. Relieved, he fished beneath the gun in his right jacket pocket for his keys. Then his left pocket. Panic surged, along with a sudden worry that they were at the bottom of the lake, until he found them in his jeans a moment later.

"Excuse me," a woman behind him said.

His hand dropped from the door handle to his knife as he turned.

She was maybe in her twenties, dressed in jeans and a sweater, with only a light rain slicker over the sweater. Her shoulders were hunched against the cold and her thin arms were crossed tightly over her chest. She held a flashlight in one hand, the beam turned away from them both.

"Were you out here looking for those boys?" she asked.

Her speech sounded stiff. From cold maybe, or from caution, approaching a stranger at night away from houses and people.

"Yes, I was."

"Did you see a man, about forty, wearing a navy-blue fisherman's cap?" She pantomimed a hat with a short brim.

"No. I haven't seen anyone else."

"Okay. Thanks." She looked around like the man might have appeared in the last few seconds. "I'm sure he'll be along in a while. I just hadn't expected to be out here after dark. I haven't seen him in the last hour or so but his car's still here." She pointed to an old Corolla on the street.

"Can you call him?"

"I'd love to, but I don't know his number. We work together at the boys' school. We spread out to search more area and I lost sight of him. I was staying close to the trailhead, hoping to catch him."

His hand relaxed on the hilt. He'd seen an unnatural dog, an unnatural owl, the creature in the water, and that weird Koschei thing with his nasty little attendants. Alex had even described Likho as either a goblin or a boy with no eye socket. She didn't fit the mold for a fairy tale monster.

"Is there someone else you can call?"

"No one that isn't away for Thanksgiving weekend." She gave a half smile.

He didn't have time to track her friend down for her. Alina was at Dead Lake on her own, a place where two creatures had attacked already, and another might be holding the children captive. His tension at the delay she was causing him must have shown.

"It's okay. I'm sure he'll be here soon. If not, I can just walk home. It's only a few blocks." She twisted and waved vaguely to the south.

The naval officer in him couldn't abide her walking home at night on her own because he wouldn't give her a ride. The crime rate in this town had soared as the local economy had plummeted.

"Where do you live?"

"Just past Washington."

He had to go south to Washington anyway to skirt the long, roadless tract below Dead Lake, before taking Riverside back up to the north end of the lake.

"I'll give you a ride if you want, but I have to get going. I've got somebody waiting on me."

"That would be great, thanks."

The moment she was in the passenger seat, he threw the car into gear and gunned the engine out of Alex's old neighborhood and down to Washington. She told him to go left, the opposite direction from Riverside. At Northcrest she told him to go left again, to the north.

"I thought you said you lived off Washington."

"Near it."

In a day filled with bizarre encounters, she'd seemed reassuringly normal. Now he was feeling less certain. He'd been too stressed and in too much of a hurry to realize she should have left a note on the car for the man who drove her here. Or to wonder why she didn't have his phone number if he'd picked her up at her house. He thought it now, though.

"Where are we going? Exactly."

"Just up there." She pointed ahead. Her jacket fell open when she lifted her right arm. Blood soaked her blue sweater to the hem. He grabbed the left lapel of her coat and yanked it aside. The heaviest saturation was near her heart.

Mike jerked the wheel and the front tire hit the curb. He braced against the steering wheel, but the woman rocked forward almost into the dash. He'd hoped she'd smash her head. Slamming the shifter into park with one hand, he pulled his knife free of its sheath with the other.

"That would not be good idea," she said, her English strongly accented now.

His hand remained where it was.

"I won't kill you," she said, the stiffness sliding from her speech as her native Slavic accent emerged. "Perun has bound me to his service, and he wants you whole. I can hurt you, though. You weakened me when you stabbed one of my hearts, but I found nice man near the road." She pulled a Greek fisherman's cap from her rain jacket pocket. "His blood made me strong again. Stronger than you."

He wondered if the man was dead or alive, and how long he might lie unnoticed in those woods. The woman looked down at the cap, running a finger over the braid at the brim. His hand tightened on his knife hilt and her gaze slid to his left arm. She shook her head in warning.

"I still have one heart left, and I doubt you could find it in time."

She smiled, showing her double row of teeth.

Chapter Twenty-Four

THE NEXT MORNING, following a six o'clock wake-up and roll call, Alex and his fellow Pod D inmates were herded to the mess hall for breakfast. He got in line near the back to have more choice over his tablemates, then took a seat at the far end of a table where only three other men sat.

"First time?" one of them asked finally.

Alex shook his head and kept eating.

"Where? Here?"

"Two and a half at Pelican Bay."

They left him alone after that, but he knew the respite wouldn't last. He didn't have the used-up look most of his pod-mates wore, the lines and scars that a life spent worn-out, worn-down, and living hard etched into a person. Sooner or later, one of the big dogs would shake him down to see how tough he was, or a few of them would corner him to make sure he wasn't a police plant.

After breakfast came chores: pushing a mop and rolling bucket around the second-floor balcony. It wasn't bad as assignments went, and neither was having a long-handled mop in his hands, just in case. He hated the constant fear and uncertainty here, just like he had in prison, and in the Missoula jail before that. Hated the noise and the smells and the food and the routines and a system that squeezed every drop of hope out of a person. He hated every second of life behind bars.

Finally, free time. As soon as the phone was available, he dialed Alina's cell and entered his old pin number for the debit account she'd set up three years ago. He waited through four rings, willing her to pick up before the voicemail did.

"Hello?" She sounded sleepy.

"Alina, it's me."

Her voice snapped to alertness. "Oh, my god, Alex. I wanted to come by first thing today, but they didn't have visiting hours this morning."

"Where are you? Have you found David and Jake?"

"I'm home, with Dan and the boys. They were there, like you said. I found them about half an hour after you called me."

"Are they okay?"

"A bit shaken up, but not hurt. We're all going to be okay." Alex sagged against the wall in relief while she continued. "I told the police last night that they'd wandered off and got lost up by the lake. But I'm not sure where Mike is, Alex. We got separated last night when something attacked him in the lake and... well, there's a lot to tell you when we get you out of there. I called him a couple of times last night and again this morning. There was no answer. I'm worried about him."

Now Alex was worried too, but he couldn't risk getting Alina involved again.

"He's a pretty capable guy. You focus on your family. Rest and take care of yourselves. Maybe you could keep calling him, though, and let me know if you reach him."

"I will. So, what's going on with you? What are you in for?"

He repeated the cover story he'd told the police last night. There was a pause as he waited for her to sift the bits of truth and interpret "the boy" to mean "Likho."

"Got it," she said. "Try not to worry. I'll call your lawyer and tell her what you told me. We'll get you out as soon as we can."

They signed off.

A few inmates approached him during the rest of free time and lunch. A couple to make sure he knew they were more badass than he was, but most out of curiosity. A few cautious ones kept their distance, which nearly made him laugh. By the time afternoon lockdown came, he felt exhausted, like he'd been up for days. He lay on his back in his bunk, one arm bent over his eyes to block out the light.

Since meeting Stribog on that stretch of road, the hits had kept coming, one after the other. Even if Likho laid low for a while, there'd be no peace or safety until the whole lot of them were back in whatever realm they'd come from. Once he knew the people in his life were safe, he could worry about himself.

Someone under his bunk spoke, a gravelly voice spewing nonsense words. Alex levitated up and across the cell, his hands balled into fists, his heart beating triple time. He pressed his back into the opposite wall and searched the shadows under the solid metal slab, imagining some psycho inmate hiding there since lunch. Or worse, a psycho roommate under there since last night.

Instead, the domovoi walked out from beneath the bed, not needing to duck to clear the frame despite his peaked hat.

"*Pochemu ty bespokoish'sya?*" he repeated.

Alex processed the Russian this time. The tiny man asked him why he fretted.

"Lots of reasons," he replied in Russian, his voice only slightly breathy.

"This place is bad," the creature said. "There's no hearth."

"Yes. This one *is* a bad place. Why are you here, Master Domovoi?"

"My place is in the home."

Alex hoped this didn't portend that Del Norte County Jail was to be his home for some significant span of time. Keeping his eye on the thing, he reached into his small trash can by the desk for the corner of the dry ham

244

sandwich he'd thrown out last night. A fire in a six-by-eight jail cell wasn't anything Alex cared to flirt with.

"Would you like"—he didn't know the words for ham sandwich—"food?"

It ate the chunk as greedily and noisily as it had eaten in his cottage on Thanksgiving night. Less than forty-eight hours ago. Hard to believe so much had happened in so little time. Alex sat on the edge of his bed and lowered his voice. Not that he was concerned anyone nearby would understand Russian, but in case someone overheard two voices where there should only be one.

"Could you help me to leave this place?"

The domovoi stared at the mint-green door. "I can unlock it if you've lost your key."

Alex pictured it unlocked, tonight, late. Then what? What if the domovoi could only open the cell door but not the door to his jail pod, or the door after that? And how could he hope to get past the guards and out to the street? What would it do to his sentence when he inevitably got caught?

"No. That's okay. Leave it locked." He tapped his fingers on the edge of the metal bunk. "How about Stribog? Do you know him?"

"Of course. I know all gods."

"Could you get a message to him?"

It eyed him disdainfully. "My place is in the home, not the halls of gods."

"Sorry. It's just that I need his help. There's a stryga after my friend, Mike, and Likho might still be after me."

"I know no Mike. Do you have straw? I need broom." He nodded toward the back wall under the bed.

"Uh, no. I'll see what I can do." Maybe break a few bristles off the pod's broom when he got his hands on it. "Remember my other home? The one where I'm happy? If you could help me get released—through legal channels," he emphasized, "we could go back there. Then I could help Stribog look for his horn."

"I remember this horn. I have seen it."

"Really?" he said, surprised. "When was that?"

The domovoi shrugged. "When days were young and gods were new. People too. He gathered up the winds and shaped them."

He was talking about the dawn of the Slavic nation. The beginning of their culture and folktales.

"He calls it a horn," the little man continued in Russian. "He blows it like a horn. But it's a brightness, a ray of sunlight on water. It quivers with the energy of a wild stallion roped. Feels warm, like a fire newly banked."

The lock clunked in his cell door. Alex panicked for a heartbeat thinking the domovoi had opened it. It swung back with a loud creak, and a guard stood in the doorway. Alex whipped his head to the domovoi, unable to stop the reaction or hide his fear of the guard seeing it. The little domovoi was nowhere in sight.

"Mr Orlov. Phone call," the guard said.

The guard placed him in handcuffs and led him out of the pod to a phone in the visitation area.

"Alex, Lois Tobares," his lawyer said when he answered.

The handcuffs forced him to hold both hands at his ear. "Ms Tobares. Thanks for calling me on a Saturday." He wondered what his sister must have done or said to reach her at the weekend.

"Tell me what's going on."

He related his cover story for the third time.

"So, basically, the only evidence the sheriff's officer and the park ranger have is what they think they saw in their headlights on a dark road?"

"Yes. That and the trespassing charge."

"But you were there because you followed that teenage boy out of concern for his welfare."

"Yes." The lie came more easily each time.

"And you can promise me that no boy is going to turn up at a hospital with a knife or whatever in his eye? The police aren't going to find any evidence of a crime at the scene?"

"I promise. Absolutely not." *Not unless Likho went back and planted it.*

"What is your parole officer's name again?"

"Jim Davenport."

"All right. Well, this sounds promising. Chances are I can't make anything happen until Monday at the earliest, though."

"I understand."

"By the way, I was going to call you next week. I managed to reach Julie Mosca the day after we last spoke. I didn't get the feeling anything was going to come of it, but then I got a call on Wednesday that she walked into the Bozeman Police Station and tried to recant her testimony."

His heart pounded in his ears. "That's huge." His next thought was to wonder how much being in jail again would fuck up this stroke of luck.

"Well, maybe. Or, like I told you before, maybe not. I sent the statement to your trial judge, but a clerk got back to me just before closing for Thanksgiving break. As I suspected, he's denied it as evidence. It's in the record now, though, so it may help if we get more evidence down the line."

"I see." And he did. The odds of Julie recanting her testimony had been long. The odds anything else would fall in his lap were astronomical.

The call ended with her promise to work on the current situation as soon as possible and the hope that she could make some positive headway before his bail appearance.

Alex hung up and signaled the guard. On the walk back to his pod, the tornado of emotions swirling around the fact that Julie Mosca had tried to change her testimony numbed his ability for coherent thought. The guard opened the door to Pod D and locked it behind them. Still numb, he registered a pool of sunlight on the floor of the common area, halfway between the door and the stairs to the upper level. It fell from a high window on his left and slowly dragged his attention back to the present. Sunshine was rare along this section of the coast, much less in November. He stared at the shimmering gold, mesmerized, as they approached it.

He missed Montana's wide blue skies of summer almost as much as he missed his few short months of recent freedom. It terrified him that he didn't know when he'd next walk free under the sun. He reached the puddle of light just as a cloud erased it, like some cosmic metaphor for Julie's recanted testimony being a ray of hope then meaning nothing.

And then it struck him. The domovoi's words: *It's a brightness, a ray of sunlight on water. Feels warm like a fire newly banked*. The blaze of heat he'd felt in the forest yesterday while looking for Koschei. The sensation like a shaft of sunlight hitting his skin in the damp coolness of the woods, cut off just before Koschei scrambled face-first down the tree.

The pieces all fell into place at once. Koschei had the horn. He must.

Hope swelled in his chest that maybe the sorcerer had found it yesterday and given it to Stribog. But Mike and he had spoken with Stribog on the road yesterday evening, just before he left to meet Koschei. If Koschei had handed over the horn, it would be done. They'd be gone now—the gods, Koschei, Likho... and the domovoi in his cell—back to wherever they'd come from.

Only one thing made sense: Koschei, the evil sorcerer—one who loved to hoard treasure, according to the tales—must have found the horn and planned to keep it for himself. He wasn't a deity; he wouldn't be tied to a homeland like the others. Maybe he planned to stay here with the horn. Alex needed to get word to Stribog as soon as possible, but how? He was stuck here in jail. Alina and her family couldn't get involved again. And Mike… Mike had gone missing.

Chapter Twenty-Five

ANGRY SHOUTING LIFTED Mike from oblivion to hazy consciousness. He blinked his eyes into focus to see a noon sun in a partly cloudy sky. Memories returned piecemeal. The woman last night, the owl thing. She'd forced him to drive out to Pacific Shores, a long-abandoned subdivision crouched along a strip of coast north of town, near Lake Earl. She'd bound him, hand and foot, and left him propped against a small tree on one of the undeveloped and overgrown housing lots. There had been others here too. His head ached trying to remember the details. A man he'd only glimpsed…

And Morana, he remembered with a start. Morana had been here, captive, burned alive, again and again. He jerked his head to the right. Pain lanced behind his eyes at the sudden motion and nausea tightened his stomach. Beyond explanation, she was still there, not far from him, burning in a bonfire. A fire that tormented her without killing her. For now, at least.

Her head tipped back in agony. She moaned in pain. Her white sweater and fitted jeans were unmarked by either ash or flames. She aged before his eyes again, maybe a year for every minute. Already she looked at least seventy, but her skin had not yet begun to burn. Soon, though, she would burn to ash, and somehow be brought back to start over. He tried not to dwell on what it must be like to suffer so intensely, for hour after hour. Few things in life had ever made him wince or turn away. This did.

"It's how the villagers used to kill her." A man strode toward him, the same one he'd seen briefly last night, with some kid stumbling along gripping one of his sleeves. "Some by fire, some by drowning. She is both Winter and Death, but they would kill the winter aspect of her at the start of spring, to keep her from returning and harming the newly planted crops."

The man appeared young, thirties maybe, though that was probably off by centuries, if not eons. He wore a costume, something like a traditional Russian dancer might wear. Tall, soft brown boots over ivory-colored leggings. A tunic of the same color, belted with thick leather and embroidered in brown and gold thread around the collar and down the center of the front. A hand-high, round cap of gold fur covered his thick, blond hair. The same outfit Alex had described when he'd told him about seeing Stribog fighting a younger man in a field near here. Stribog's enemy, Perun. The boy at his shoulder had to be Likho. A young boy, but instead of smooth skin over the right eye socket, skin now covered both eyes. It gave Mike grim satisfaction to know Alex had succeeded in his mission before he'd been arrested.

"Why hasn't the fire killed her then?" he asked.

"It tries but she can't be destroyed in the strength of her season. So she ages, as she does from the fall equinox to the start of spring, young woman to old crone. And because it is not her time to die, like a winter storm gone too briefly, she returns again in the fullness of her youth and strength. A nuisance, but true to her nature."

"So, why am I here?"

"Because Stribog has taken a special interest in your friend, Alex. The stryga could not bring your friend to me, so she brought you. If he contacts you with news, I want to know what it is." Perun reached down the front of his tunic to belt level and pulled out Mike's cell phone. Mike wondered if Perun had the first inkling of how to use it. "And when I can bring your friend here, perhaps

Stribog will come for him, if not for Morana. He's always been sentimental about humans. A failing of his."

He tossed the phone to the ground and lowered himself to sit cross-legged. Likho, still hanging onto him, stumbled. Perun roughly pushed the boy off. "Useless thing. Losing your eye to your silly game."

"Where's the strayaga?" Mike asked. He owed that one a little payback. He wished he could reach into his jacket pocket to see if they'd left him his gun and if his bullet cartridge had dried yet.

"The stryga?"

"Whatever." He couldn't care less what the thing was called. He just wanted it dead.

"She doesn't care for daylight. She'd fare less well in the sun than Morana does in her fire."

Mike glanced back to Morana. Like watching any horror unfolding, it was impossible for him not to stare, to take in every detail of her suffering. The brain trying to understand it at some instinctive level that craved the learning in order to avoid the same fate. She was elderly now, nearing the end of her years. She must've been through this cycle of aging and death at least a dozen times since last night.

He didn't know for certain because he'd been unconscious for most of it, though being close to her bonfire had probably saved him from hypothermia while spending the night outdoors in soaking wet clothes. What he could remember was that he'd fought the woman in the car. She'd overpowered him as easily as she'd threatened to do and had hurt him as she'd promised. With bruised ribs and blood running from teeth marks in his neck, he'd driven where she directed. When she'd tied his hands, he'd tried to run, and when she'd bound his feet, he'd tried to fight. The man in front of him now had taken his consciousness with a gesture. They hadn't bound him to the tree, but the rope at his ankles was pulled tight and fiercely knotted, and the rope around his wrists was a fiery hell. He waggled his fingers to bring circulation to them and they felt as nerveless and swollen as hot dogs.

Mike estimated they were near the middle of the subdivision, well hidden from both the coast and the main road leading here. The strange and empty acreage of Pacific Shores contained nearly thirty miles of paved roads and stop signs, fire hydrants and manholes. Within sight of this lot, old foundations jutted here and there from the trees and brush like discarded bones, and he knew a handful of run-down trailers and owner-built homes hid scattered among the native foliage and weeds. Half-buried and slowly decaying junkpiles dotted occasional lots. A few squatters held out with the aid of generators and septic tanks. More than six decades of dereliction and lawsuits over the wetlands property had left it a feral project, a ghost of itself haunting a thousand acres of otherwise unmarred coastline.

There was a rustling in the brush behind Perun. He looked casually over his shoulder and blind Likho, holding his sleeve again, turned as well. A barefoot young woman with soaking wet hair and a drenched shift approached him. She spoke to him in their language, but Mike caught Stribog's name.

He heard a low moan and looked back to Morana. She stood unbound but captive in the center of her fire. She stared at him from her old eyes and her now-flame-peeled face. Her hands clenched in fists of anguish. To his astonishment and horror, she spoke, though not aloud. She mouthed words slowly and clearly from lips that were losing small chunks to ash. *When I am young.* Then she nodded to her right. She was desperate to convey her message, and it sent a mirrored panic and urgency ripping through him when he couldn't understand what she meant.

Perun stood, pulling Likho up with him. Mike's attention whipped back to him, guilty that the exchange might have been witnessed but Perun's attention was on the girl. "When did the vodyanoy see him?" he asked the girl. "Which beach?"

When I am young, Morana mouthed again and moved her head and shoulder minutely to her right again. Was she indicating something to him? Some weapon? The direction of another enemy? His car parked on the other side of the fire—the one he couldn't reach with his hands and feet bound?

What? Mike said frantically and silently to Morana, but her gray hair had singed up to her blackened skull and her eyes had burned from her head.

She disintegrated in front of him. The skull crumbled and smashed to cinders at her own feet. Her blackened arms, bones showing, fell from her shoulders. The rest collapsed all at once, like a building demolished by explosives. Her empty clothes vanished. The air inside the circle of fire shimmered with the dust of her. When it cleared, Morana stood there again, dressed as before, stiff-legged, fists clenched in pain. Her skin was pale as milk. Her hair blonde and long. Her face and figure that of a lithe girl of perhaps eighteen.

Perun, back still turned, spoke again to the drenched girl. He sounded angry.

Mike had no idea if he was doing the right thing or not. He bent his legs for power and pushed his back into the tree, knowing he'd need to move quickly once he started. If his legs proved too numb from spending the night on the ground, this could end with him simply falling on his face. Either way, as soon as Perun noticed him, he'd probably be dead. Or worse.

Mike sucked in a deep breath, straightened his legs with an adrenaline-laced burst of energy to his thighs, and launched himself—hands and feet still bound—at Morana. If he'd misunderstood what she wanted him to do, he might accomplish nothing grander than catching his clothes on fire and burning to death next to her, while she continued to die and be reborn in agony.

The fire hadn't been made to hold him prisoner, though, and his clothes were still damp. He passed through the flames the same as he would a natural bonfire, and with the same consequences of heat singing his nerves wherever it brushed his skin. He held his breath to protect his lungs but felt his two-day growth of beard curl... his eyebrows... his short hair. He plowed into Morana with every ounce of strength available to him. His chest struck her left shoulder like a train hitting a deer. She flew out of the ring of fire. Her hip crashed into the front fender of his car and she spun to sprawl, face down, across the hood.

His collision with Morana had killed his forward momentum, so he twisted to land on the flaming wood with his left hip and shoulder, the side that had been farthest from the fire overnight and was still wet. Using the impact to keep moving, he shoulder-rolled for the first time in twenty years and emerged out the other side of the flames.

Mike lay on the ground, dazed with pain, as Perun turned with a look of surprise and anger contorting his face. His left arm stretched out, perhaps to Mike, perhaps Morana, fingers stiff and curled like the owl's talons. Mike braced for some magical impact.

Morana rolled off the car, and Mike saw an enormous orange-red bird rising behind her. It peeled up from the hood of his car, stretching and filling out from the two-dimensional gold firebird decal to a large three-dimensional creature as it rose. Its feathers were the intensity and color of the most brilliant red and orange and gold sunsets or sunrises he'd witnessed. They were as magnificent as a peacock's; the tail long and trailing, dripping flames and sparks like drops of water. From crown feathers to tail tip, the bird was as long as Morana was tall. It stretched its wings and flew like an arrow from a bow at Perun. Before the god could redirect his attack, the bird enveloped him with its fiery wings and he screamed. Likho fell to the ground and crawled blindly away, his clothing in flames. The drenched girl was nowhere to be seen.

"Hurry," Morana yelled.

She appeared to have aged up again to about the same as he'd seen her the other night at the motel. Moving stiffly to him, she yanked at his bindings so hard he thought his bones would break instead of the ropes. She froze or rotted or tore them somehow, then hurried the few feet to the passenger side of the car, now missing its gold firebird decal and leaving it a solid black Trans Am.

Mike pushed to his feet and fell again. Perun still fought with the giant bird and, in the scuffle, Mike saw his phone had been kicked in arm's reach. If Perun wanted it, Mike didn't want him to have it.

"Hurry!" Morana yelled again.

He threw himself flat on the ground and stretched one arm to its limit, scrabbling at his phone. Clambering to the car, he dove in. The keys were on the floor where he'd dropped them last night, hoping the owl-woman either wouldn't notice or wouldn't care. He turned the ignition, threw the car into reverse, gripped the wheel, and gunned the accelerator.

"What was that thing?" Mike asked, driving as fast as he could while trying to remember his way out of Pacific Shores.

"The Firebird."

The irony defied comment. "So you created it from that?" He nodded to the black hood of his car.

"No, it is something that has existed a long time. I only encouraged it to cross over here, like the other beings that followed us."

"Can it kill Perun?"

She shook her head. "The lesser beings can die, but another, just the same, will take their place in time. Perun cannot be killed, no more than I can. But we're weak from fighting each other this far from home, same as Stribog. The Firebird will be enough to slow him for now."

Mike turned right on Kellogg Road and saw their way out of Pacific Shores ahead.

"There was a man, last night. Someone helping search for Alex's nephews. The stryga told me she attacked him in the woods near Alex's house. I don't know if he's dead or alive. I need to see if I can find him." He slowed for the stop sign at Lower Lake Road.

Morana rolled down her window and craned her head to the sky. She yelled a long string of words in Russian. Mike crooked his neck to look up through the windshield and caught sight of bright plumage veering to the south.

"The Firebird will tell Yaga. If something can be done for him, she'll see to it. If not, she'll leave him where he'll be seen. We must find Stribog. Winter and Wind are a formidable combination. Better we're together in case Perun pursues us or the rusalka leads him to Stribog."

"The rusalka?"

"The girl he was speaking to. A drowned spirit. She and the vodyanoy watch the water for him."

Like Dead Lake, maybe? Mike recalled nearly being drowned by something there last night.

"Okay. Where do we find Stribog?"

"I don't know." She stared out the window, her eyes distant with pain or concern. "The rusalka said he was seen near the ocean recently. Wherever he is, hope that we find him before they do."

Chapter Twenty-Six

THE LOCK IN the cell door turned.

Alex jumped up and scanned the floor where the domovoi had been industriously scraping up crumbs and dirt with a lunch napkin. The small man was nowhere to be seen.

"Mr Orlov," the guard said, opening the door wide. "You're being released."

"Wha…?" The part of him that had learned in prison not to be gullible stamped down his rising hope, though not even the cruelest detention officer would joke about this.

"You're being released. Come with me, please."

The guard led him out of the pod to a holding cell in the processing area.

"Go ahead and get changed." He nodded to a heavy, clear plastic bag on the bench containing Alex's jacket and clothes. "I'll be back when your paperwork is ready."

Forty-five minutes later, a guard had him sign his release papers, then sign again for his wallet and phone. He shackled Alex's old ankle monitor to his left leg and escorted him beyond the final locked door.

Alone, Alex walked through the lobby and out the main door. Free.

He stood at the top of the front steps soaking in the foggy sunlight and reveling in the fresh breeze over his face. His confinement had lasted less than twenty-four hours, but the very real fear of imprisonment continuing for unknown years had etched into his nerves like an electrical fire. It wouldn't be smothered anytime soon.

Turning on his phone, he tried Mike first. To his relief, his friend answered immediately. The growl of the muscle car's engine in the background let Alex know he was on the road somewhere.

"Mike, good to hear your voice. Alina said she hadn't been able to reach you." He trotted down the steps and began walking aimlessly west to put distance between himself and the county jail building.

"Yeah, well, shit happened, but we're okay now."

"We?"

"Morana's with me. What about you? Sounds like you're outdoors. You get released?"

"Just now. Where are you guys? Tell Morana I need to find Stribog. I think I know where his horn is."

"Where—" Morana said sharply in the background, but Mike cut her off.

"We're on Lake Earl Drive. We'll come get you. Be there in ten."

Alex called Alina while he waited to let her know he was out and that he'd reached Mike. She filled in the details about his unexpected weekend release. Besides no evidence and no victim turning up, the sheriff's dashcam video had showed only grainy, nighttime footage from a bad angle. Alex and the boy on the road, then the boy jumping up and running into the woods. His lawyer had threatened legal action against the department for holding him on suspicion of assault with a deadly weapon with no evidence. She'd even lobbed the word "profiling" at them, for arresting an ex-con without probable cause.

Alex headed back toward the jail and a couple of minutes later Mike's car pulled up and rumbled at the curb. He assumed it was his car, anyway. The Pontiac Firebird was now a solid black Trans Am. He got in the back seat, feeling the chill emanating off Morana. She looked the same as always, but Mike's neck had bloody scabs, his hair was singed down to his scalp, and his jacket and pants were dirty and charred. Alex tried and failed to imagine what the hell had happened since last night.

"Are you both all right?"

"Where is the horn?" Morana snapped.

He summarized his conversation with the domovoi and his suspicion.

"I told Stribog Koschei was a traitorous creature, not to be trusted," she said. "Though this betrayal surprises even me."

"So you think I'm right?"

She nodded. "He has always been a collector of treasures and a thief. The horn would do him no good, but if he found it first, he might not have been able to resist, even at the risk of crossing Stribog. He'll have it well hidden. It would explain why Stribog couldn't find it. Koschei hid his own death centuries ago and none have ever found it."

"What do you mean he hid his death?" Mike asked.

"He embodied his death in a needle and hid the needle in an egg, then hid the egg where no one would find it."

"I thought you said you guys can't die."

"Koschei the Deathless is not an immortal, nor a lesser being that renews itself. He's a sorcerer, though a twisted and powerful one. A mortal man who bent the laws of nature to his will. Being here doesn't drain him in the same way it does Stribog, Perun, and me. It may be his plan to outlast us, to remain here with the horn once we have gone."

"So, what now?" Alex asked.

She shrugged with her hands, as if the answer had been obvious. "We go to Koschei. Stribog still meets with him once a day for information. If he is there, we can fight the sorcerer together. If he isn't, then I'll fight him as best I can."

* * *

ON THE WAY back to Jedediah Smith Park, Mike updated Alex—in his succinct way—on all that had transpired since he'd left Alina. Alex reassured him that Alina had made it home safe with the kids and Dan.

Mike skirted the road barrier, and Alex sent a wish out into the universe that no one had spotted them driving in. All he needed was to get turned in again less than twenty-four hours after he'd been arrested here.

They parked in the same place he and Mike had the day before, and the three of them followed what was becoming a beaten trail down the embankment and into the giant trees. Mike pulled his gun from one jacket pocket and a bullet magazine from the other. Examining the magazine, he gave a satisfied grunt and loaded it into the gun.

"Koschei. *Deathless*," Morana said, flicking a finger at the weapon. "That will do no good."

"Won't hurt," he replied, tucking the gun back into his pocket.

Alex spotted a flash of color overhead and glanced up to see a bird, twice the size of an eagle, with bright red and orange plumage and a long tail trailing sparks of flame down to the muddy forest floor. It said a lot about his past ten days that the fabulous Firebird of folktales elicited little more from him than acknowledgment of another fighter on their side. Getting the horn was all that mattered anymore.

One of Koschei's weird little attendants popped up suddenly from behind a fern. It bowed to Morana and ran off on its stubby legs. Alex scanned the crowns of the trees ahead. His forearms pricked into gooseflesh at the memory of the robed sorcerer scuttling down the tree headfirst. In a forest of nearly three-hundred-foot trees, he'd never be able to pick out the exact one, but he and Mike could track their footprints to where they had stopped and spoken with Koschei yesterday. As before,

Morana and the little gnome thing in front of him left no prints, making the job of tracking even easier.

"Wait," Mike said. Morana looked back at them.

Alex came level with him to see what had caught his attention.

Koschei, it seemed, did leave footprints, and Mike had found the spot where all three sets converged. Alex scanned up and slightly to the right. A glow of light had hit him in the face yesterday. From this angle, only one nearby tree would have been unobstructed by other branches.

"There." He pointed to the crown of the massive and ancient redwood. Morana's gaze followed.

The underbrush rustled just then, and a whole herd of little gnomes appeared, frantically tramping small plants to make a smooth path. Two more led Koschei by the hand. Alex suppressed the chill that ran up his spine again at the heavy folds of eyelids and the long beard of literal copper.

"Morana," Koschei said deferentially with a slight bow of his head, "it's been a while since you visited." His accented English had that same slow drawl as before. "And you." He turned his covered eyes to Alex. "You have brought my gold?"

The gold debt he'd promised that most likely bound his soul to this thing.

Morana shot Alex a look that said he was too stupid to live, then an icy look to Koschei. Alex wondered if the sorcerer might have had something to do with her capture and fiery ordeal. "If you have made a pact with this man, you must settle it later," she snapped. "Where is Stribog?"

"I haven't seen him since yesterday. I think he planned to search the ocean today."

"And his horn," she bit the words off. "Have you seen that?"

"I have not."

"You have always been and always will be a liar."

Right. Straight to it, then. At Alex's side, Mike slipped his hand into his jacket where his loaded pistol lay.

"Don't cross me, sorcerer," she continued. "You already have Stribog to answer to. Give me the horn and you can stay here if you like. Maybe you'll escape Stribog's justice that way."

One of the gnomes tugged at Koschei's sleeve and two of his attendants climbed his robes and hauled his eyelids up, hand over hand. The one tugging his sleeve pointed to the sky. Koschei looked up, not toward "his" tree, but straight to the Firebird perched above him. A spark fell to his shoulder and singed the deep blue velveteen.

Without warning, Koschei transformed. Alex had been looking directly at him, with his creepy eyelids and his emaciated face and his copper beard. And then he was looking at something out of a nightmare.

The heavy robe was gone, and a naked, skeletal thing stood in front of him. More bones showed than flaky flesh, but both were the dark-gray color of fire ash. The eye sockets were huge and elongated, the eyes bulging now that they weren't surrounded by skin. The cartilage of his nose and the bones of his toes were elongated, as were his fingers which looked to be made of iron. Light-gray hair hung long and sparse and the beard had vanished. No manhood remained between the pelvic bones. The monstrosity was a thing that had lived centuries beyond a natural life, preserved only by dark magic, and the sight of it sent ice sluicing through Alex's blood.

Mike stared at the creature, his gun hand paralyzed in his pocket.

In a flash, the monstrosity flew straight up into the air at the bird. The Firebird launched from its branch toward

Koschei, but Morana yelled instructions to it. She pointed emphatically to the tree Alex had indicated.

"She told it to find his treasure chest," Alex translated for Mike.

Koschei's skeleton—because that was the only way Alex could frame what he was seeing—attempted to pursue the bird into the air, but Morana thrust both arms out, hurling an arctic blast so cold that icicles coated his gray bones and pulled him to earth like a stone. The ice shattered on impact, but the bones didn't. The skeletal creature sprang at Morana, growing taller and wider as it neared. It stretched into a musty barrier of dark bones and thin membranes, with an incongruously unchanged and narrow skull perched atop. At the same moment, the little gnomes transformed into small black goblins with spindly arms and legs, and mouths filled with long teeth. Alex wondered if these were some of the lost souls in servitude to Koschei, and if he might end up the same by day's end if Morana lost this battle or left him to his promised debt.

Koschei reached Morana and wrapped her in a morbid embrace. His goblins attacked her legs. Chewing sounds filled the quiet forest, as if they all attempted to devour her. Morana made no sound, but ice suddenly coated the joints of her small attackers, freezing their biting jaws and clawing fingers. And something darker, more deadly, seemed to emanate from her. A darkness felt rather than seen. Alex had nearly died of cold once and recognized that darkness for what it was: wintery death. The little goblins fell from her legs and lay rigid and dead, but she was weak and had fought too many battles. Neither her cold nor death seemed able to stop the sorcerer.

Mike aimed his gun at Koschei.

"You might hit Morana," Alex said.

"She can't die." He placed the barrel directly against the sorcerer's skull and pulled the trigger. The report echoed in the quiet forest.

Koschei retracted back into the tall skeleton. Iron finger bones grabbed either side of its head. It turned to Mike, jawbones agape. If a bullet hadn't stopped it then not much would, but Alex had to do something. He picked up the largest rock he could find at his feet and swung it at the back of the skull, impacting with a deep thud but little effect.

A thumping noise came from above.

Alex looked up. The Firebird was high in the tree, repeatedly flapping back then flying forward to strike hard at something. There was a loud creak and scrape. Alex could make out the treasure chest now, sliding from the crook of a wide branch toward its tipping point.

The skeletal thing screamed and peeled away from them.

One final thump and the chest fell. The four of them stood motionless as it tumbled through the air. The size of a large chest or footlocker, maybe iron-banded. A metal hasp on the front. It fell more than two hundred feet, smashing into the ground with a thunderous crash. It exploded into splinters, the contents detonating in all directions. A dragon's hoard scattered across the ground: gold and gems, a sword and crown. Coins and trinkets and lockets and fine jewelry. And among the vast treasure, a curved horn, the color of ivory but gleaming like the sun. The flash of light and wave of warmth from it hit Alex like a physical blow. A muted murmur drifted to him from the bell of the horn. A susurration. A fugue of barely audible sound that fell somewhere between whispers and whistles.

Still screaming, the skeletal sorcerer ran in lurching strides toward the items, grabbing them and clutching them to its hollow chest, coins falling between its fingers.

Morana, bleeding from half a dozen wounds, limped rapidly behind it, closing the gap. She reached out with one hand and grabbed Koschei by the vertebrae of his neck. They both stood still as statues, another invisible but mighty struggle taking place between the Goddess of Winter and Death and Koschei the Deathless.

The Firebird swooped then and struck Koschei with dazzling speed and strength, but it cried out in pain, caught in some violent flow of magic, and retreated to a branch, long silver hairs clutched in its talons. It remained on its perch, watching, as if afraid to approach the pair again.

Alex and Mike ran for the treasure. Alex sprinted past a fortune on the ground with eyes only for the horn. Mike stopped short and bent to grab another item, oval, as large as a big goose egg or a small ostrich egg, painted and gilded with gold trim.

Alex reached the horn, and the beauty of it stunned him. About the length of a trumpet, shaped and curved like an old Viking war horn. A golden braid ran from below the mouthpiece to a small gold ring on the underside of the bell. The whispers coming from it were like music now; a tune his ears or his soul registered but his brain couldn't hold. He lifted it reverently, feeling its weight. Warmth seeped into his hands and flowed straight toward his heart, filling it with emotions too large and wild to contain.

Koschei cried out, snapping Alex back to himself.

With a massive effort, Koschei shrugged off Morana. She fell to the ground and lay motionless; her youthful face held a grayish cast. The sorcerer-monster ran for Mike in great leaping strides. The big man raised the egg over his head in both hands and smashed it into a rock on the ground. It didn't even crack. He stuffed the egg inside his jacket and pulled his gun as Koschei reached him. He fired point-blank into the skeleton's eye socket. The trigger clicking was the only sound in the otherwise still forest. The gun had misfired.

Mike changed his grip to pistol-whip his attacker, but Koschei enveloped him as he had Morana, in musty and flaky gray. Mike would never survive an assault that had incapacitated a goddess. Alex slung the braided cord of the horn over his shoulder and grabbed the hilt of a heavy and ornate longsword from the ground. He ran to Mike. A stench of decay filled the air, making it hard to breathe. Thin bones gripped Mike's neck and pulled his head further into Koschei's essence that was neither flesh nor bones. Mike flailed but couldn't break free.

Alex swung at Koschei's back, hitting bone. The sorcerer arched, loosening his grip. Suddenly the Firebird was diving from above, huge, fiery talons aimed again at Koschei's head. The Firebird struck, sinking burning talons into the skull, and dragged the monstrosity away from Mike. The big man stumbled to his knees, and the egg fell free of his jacket. The Firebird and Koschei thrashed together on the ground. Flames danced along the sorcerer's bones.

The gray monster rolled and spread across the beautiful bird like an eclipse across the sun, expanding, pressing, squeezing until nothing of it could be seen. Alex stabbed the sword into the monster's side, but Koschei only flinched. A predatory screech under the gray mass became a muffled caw, and then a choked and distressed cry. A few fiery feathers drifted from beneath the burning mass of bones and leathery tissue.

Still on his knees, Mike had thrown the egg onto the ground and fought to extract the dud bullet from the pistol. Koschei pushed away from the bird, the life crushed out of it, and crouched to spring at Mike. Alex swung the sword in a wide, high arc. He'd hoped to break the neck bones and decapitate the sorcerer but hit his moving target on the shoulder instead. With the sword embedded in its upper arm bone, Koschei threw Alex aside. From the ground, he saw Morana roll to her hands and knees and crawl toward Koschei. Relief coursed through him at seeing her alive and fighting again, however weakened.

Before Alex could get up, Mike had cleared the bullet and now aimed his gun at the egg. Alex prayed it wouldn't be another dud. It wasn't. The bullet tore a hole front to back and the egg jolted with the impact, landing with the wide holes showing. Through the gaping rent in the egg, Alex glimpsed a long, thick piece of metal, like an oversized sewing needle. With an earsplitting wail Koschei flung himself at Mike's back. Mike tucked his head as the sorcerer grappled to get his hands around the big man's throat.

Alex struggled to his feet, the horn slung over his shoulder and the sword still in his hand. Morana beat him to the fight. She grabbed Koschei's head from behind. Her fingers pressed into the sorcerer's oversized eyes. Alex watched them ice over. With Morana behind Koschei and Mike in front, Alex had little room to maneuver the sword. He heard Mike praying aloud, something about giving his hands strength, as he shoved his fingers into the egg's ragged holes. He strained, ignoring the monstrous thing trying to choke him. Alex chopped the sword down in a short arc between Koschei and Mike, striking at the bony wrists. Koschei's grip loosened. Mike grunted with effort and strained harder. With a cry of exertion, the egg tore apart.

Mike pulled the long, silver needle from the shards with bloody fingers. Morana held Koschei's head tight. Mike turned in Koschei's slackened grip and plunged the needle between the ribs at the level of the thing's heart.

With a screeching wail, the skeleton fell to dust.

Mike dropped to his knees, gasping for air. Morana, also breathing raggedly, approached Alex. Her wounds healed as he watched, but she moved slowly and stumbled. She reached out a hand, and he passed the horn to her. Energy and light drained out of his world as it left his grasp.

"Mike, you hurt?" he asked.

The big man grunted and shook his head, panting for air. With an effort, he pushed to his feet and came to them.

"What do we do now?" Alex asked Morana.

"We need to take it where the winds blow the strongest."

"What about waiting for Stribog?"

"He'll feel the horn now that it's been freed from the chest. He'll come to us."

"The lighthouse," Alex said. "The winds will be strongest at the lighthouse."

Chapter Twenty-Seven

"WANT ME TO drive?" Alex offered when they reached the car.

"I got it," Mike said.

He got behind the wheel stiffly, protecting his ribs on the right side. His neck wounds from last night were bleeding again, along with his fingers. He still carried a faint smell of woodsmoke and scorched hair, and all three of them had brought the musty stench of Koschei's ancient bones into the closed car. Mike rolled down his window.

As before, Morana sat up front and Alex took the back seat. He stared at the horn in her lap. Its simple beauty and soft glow still mesmerized him. Its susurrations called to him.

"Do you think Perun is still after you?" he asked once they were out of the park and headed for the lighthouse.

"Without doubt," Morana said. "Hopefully Stribog will find us first." She sounded weak and looked worse. Unlike Mike, she bore no visible wounds now, but she moved slowly and her pale, cool skin held a sickly grayish cast. He wondered if Stribog would be equally frail by the time they found him.

They parked in the designated lot across a channel from the lighthouse on its island bluff. At low tide, the two-hundred-foot channel crossing below the parking lot was a rough, sandy beach cluttered with driftwood and rocks. At high tide, though, it became part of the ocean. Alex could see from where he stood that the tide was coming in. Both an advantage and a disadvantage. Battery Point Lighthouse, built in the mid-1800s, still functioned. The beacon was automated now, but the small building, which doubled as a museum and tourist attraction, was staffed year-round by monthly resident volunteers for tours given at low tide. They'd have to wade the channel, and it wouldn't make for a quick escape, but at least there'd be no tours or tourists there.

They set out on the path from the parking lot, down a zigzagging boardwalk, to the edge of the swirling water. The sun to their left peeked under the clouds; a large reddish-orange ball of flame kissing the ocean at the horizon line.

Morana, carrying the horn, strode into the chilly water without hesitation. Mike followed. Alex came last. Seawater flowed into his boots with his first step, chilling his feet with fifty-five-degree ocean water. He picked his way carefully, feeling for rocks and driftwood along the bottom. Halfway across, the water came to his calves, pushing and sucking at his legs and splashing up to his thighs. Mike, in front of him, scanned side to side as if he expected a shark to appear at his feet. Or maybe the thing from Dead Lake Mike had told him about.

On the far side of the channel, a wide, paved sidewalk spiraled up the small bluff to the lighthouse at the top. The sun was half doused in the ocean by the time they reached the crest. The bluff stretched maybe one or two hundred feet across in either direction and stood about the same height above the waves. The elevation allowed the lighthouse to be a squat structure, barely two floors high, with a beacon at the top.

The security floodlights and lighthouse beacon had already turned on, but Alex saw no lights inside the museum or residence quarters to indicate a volunteer on site. With his soaked legs and feet, Alex shivered in the chill air as he scanned the outcrop for Stribog.

Mike walked a large elliptical around the lighthouse, checking the area and looking over the bluff in all directions, then returned to the lighthouse and peered in the windows. Morana moved to a small bench under the tree and sat heavily.

"Is there anything I can do for you?" Alex asked. She shook her head.

"How long do you think we'll have to wait?"

"As long as it takes for him to get here."

The quiet of anticipation had fallen over their little group. Alex wandered to the south side of the bluff, near the path. He'd been here before, had taken the kids through the bottom-floor museum and up to the beacon. But the features that had previously struck him as artsy or interesting now seemed strange, almost grotesque, while sharing this small outcrop in the last of the daylight with a Slavic goddess and a magic talisman.

South of the bluff, the jetty stretched away; a long, narrow breaker with scores of the weird tide-breaking gray dolosse at the end scattered like giant concrete jacks in a children's game. The lone windswept tree to his right had survived so many storms off the ocean that its branches grew mainly to the east. The low branches were festooned with an odd assortment of old net floats: foam, wood, cork, and plastic ones—from rolling pin size to the size of a child's beach ball—perhaps forty or fifty of them, cracked and weathered. A broken tree trunk nearby held a scoured carving of a gnarled, bearded fisherman's face. And the lighthouse itself was said to be haunted by the ghosts of the old keepers.

The sun dipped below the ocean. The temperature felt as if it dropped ten degrees in an instant. A few moments later, a grunt came from the west and they all turned. Stribog's head and shoulders appeared as he climbed the last of the cliff from the ocean side. He stood dripping wet in his dark-gray suit, much the same as the first day Alex had seen him in the field, flying his kite. Seawater ran from his beard, and small shreds of yellowish seaweed clung to the weave at his shoulders. Alex had thought Morana said he was searching along the coast for the horn. He considered now that maybe he'd been searching the seafloor.

Stribog's eyes swept past Alex to Morana, who sat on the bench cradling the Horn of the Winds in her lap. His gray eyes lit with joy.

"Ah, and here we all are, together once again." The deep voice came from the other direction as four newcomers reached the crest of the path.

Like Stribog and Morana, Perun wore the same cream and gold outfit Alex had seen him in earlier. Blind Likho, in his boy form, stood at Perun's side, holding a pinch of the god's sleeve between his fingers. At Perun's other side was a woman Alex didn't recognize. She wore jeans and a light rain jacket. The jacket hung open, revealing a sweater beneath crusted with dried blood. Behind them came a dark-haired woman, this one wearing only a light shift, as sopping wet as Stribog's suit.

Perun was one of the most powerful gods of the Slavic pantheon. Likho might be blind, but Alex would never assume him harmless. Whoever the two women were, they weren't likely to be good news either. Morana looked spent, Stribog not much better. And in a battle between gods, he and Mike would be as useless as a parachute full of holes. Now that all the gods were here and the horn had been found, he and Mike could probably leave unmolested and put this mad circus in the rearview mirror. Why should it matter to him if Perun won today or Stribog? He'd be rid of them all either way.

But that's what his first arrest had done to him. Made him not want to take a stand, not care about what was right, not get involved. He had gotten involved, though. He'd fought both Likho and Koschei for coming after his family and friends. Even the idea of Perun burning Morana galled him. And if Morana and Stribog lost, there was no guarantee Likho wouldn't hang around or come back again someday to exact vengeance for his eye. Useless to them or not, Alex would be staying to fight with Stribog.

Bad luck that Morana had chosen to sit under the tree. It put the path between her and Stribog. Perun and his entourage stood slightly downhill from them. Still, Alex saw no way for Morana to get the horn to Stribog before Perun could intercept.

Everyone else on top of this little island must've been thinking along the same lines. Morana stood from her bench, tense as a soldier before battle. Stribog watched everything, waiting to see which way the dice would fall. Mike, near the front of the lighthouse, had one hand in his jacket pocket and the other fingering the empty knife sheath at his belt.

Fortunately, Perun looked rough around the edges too. He was stuck in this foreign country like the other gods, weakened by using his magic as well as having been captured first in the kite, then imprisoned inside Alex, and then attacked by the Firebird.

Morana moved first.

Alex watched in awe as her body stretched, growing as tall as the highest floats in the tree, then taller. She lost substance as she grew until he could see the tree behind her. Skeleton bones replaced her fingers. Her clothing morphed from contemporary to bell-shaped, layered robes in the varied shades of snow and ice, from pale blue to icicle gray to snow white. A tall headdress of black spanned the crown of her head, with a lacy black veil falling behind and strange embroidery across its front that drew Alex's eye and sent thoughts of death shivering down his spine. Her face remained youthful but gained an aspect of terrible power—a cold and emotionless visage—and her blonde hair came unbound and floated on a chill breeze. He would have dropped to his knees before her and thought her invincible except for the cost of the transformation showing in her tired eyes. Still growing, she reached across the lighthouse to pass the horn to Stribog, who had remained in his human form.

But Perun had also changed. He stood now as tall as Morana, garbed in a thick, flowing tunic of royal blue, elaborately trimmed in gold, and wearing a golden crown. His arms were banded with gold and one hand held the haft of an enormous silver axe, finely worked and etched in symbols. Alex swore he saw gold lightning flash in the god's blue eyes. A black storm cloud gathered above them, pulled from the gray fog and distant rain clouds to the west.

They stood like that for a loaded moment before Perun hurtled into Morana's side like a charging bull. Her ephemeral aspect did nothing to protect her. He sent her flying and grabbed for the horn that dropped from her hands. As he lunged for it, Stribog hurled a narrow gale of wind that knocked Perun to his knees and sent the horn skittering over the ground toward Morana.

Morana struggled to rise and Stribog ran for the horn. Alex wondered if maybe Stribog no longer possessed the strength to throw off his human form. Perun swatted Stribog to the ground with one huge hand and lifted his axe above Stribog's neck. Morana flickered to human size, then back into her goddess aspect. She struggled to her knees and grabbed the horn from the ground. With no hope in her expression, she lifted it to her lips and blew.

No sound emerged.

Perun slammed his enormous axe down into Stribog's neck. The blow should have severed his head and sunk the axe blade a foot into the rock of the bluff. It didn't, but it left a deep and bloody wound across Stribog's neck. Alex's hand went to his own throat in horror and empathy as the old man failed to stir. Perun rose and again headed for Morana. Lightning crackled in the black clouds and rain fell among the increasing gusts accompanying the growing storm. Blasts of cold and even a few flakes of snow pushed back at the rain, but Morana looked near the end of her strength while Perun seemed to grow only larger, stronger.

They were done, then, Alex realized, Stribog and Morana. He and Mike could do nothing against enemies like these, and if they tried anything, the two women looked more than eager to stop them.

"Orel and Orlov," Stribog croaked, lifting his partially severed head to stare straight at Alex. Perun hefted his axe for a second blow.

Stribog had said the same once in the motel. The evening Alex had gone to Morana when Perun was trying to tear out of his belly and Stribog had confessed who he and Morana really were. *Orel and Orlov, he'd said of himself and Alex, one with the strength to capture Perun, the other with the strength to hold him*. How? Alex wondered again. How had he had the strength to hold him?

He didn't know, but there was only one thing he could think to try.

"Morana," Alex yelled, and held his hands up like a wide receiver.

She looked down to the horn, uncertain, and then tossed it high in the air, arcing over the kneeling Perun. Perun raised his free arm and a bolt of lightning shot out to knock the horn to earth, but a strong gust just then carried it to Alex. Stribog's head dropped back to the ground.

Alex caught the horn, its warmth and weight filling his hands, its music filling his ears.

The two women immediately surged toward him. From the corner of his eye, he saw the one in the bloody sweater shrink down and sprout gray wings, then spread them in a huge wingspan. He took a deep breath and pressed the gold ring of the mouthpiece to his lips. He blew as hard as he could.

A small, tremulous sound emerged. A sound that might come from a cheap toy horn stuffed with cotton.

The owl swooped at him, grabbing with its talons for the wide bell of the horn. Four bullets peppered the owl less than a foot above Alex's head, the loud report of Mike's gun ringing in the silence that followed. The owl fell at his feet, dead and bleeding profusely from only one of the four wounds.

Morana rushed Perun, who was headed for Alex.

Alex ran from the god and the girl in the wet shift, sucking in the deepest breath he'd ever taken in his life. Likho, standing alone, turned his blind eyes toward him and Alex tripped on a rock and stumbled. Alex tightened his chest and puffed out his cheeks, bracing himself to hold the breath no matter what as he hit the ground. He tried to stand but made it only to his knees before the girl landed on his back. Her wet fingers wrapped about his face and head. He felt as if he'd been immersed in a lake. He heard another report from the gun and saw a hole appear at her shoulder, but the bullet had no effect. It seemed to pass through her the same as it would through water.

With his held breath, with every shred of strength in his body and air in his lungs, Alex brought the horn to his lips again, passing through her fingers without resistance. He placed the cool smoothness against his mouth. He blew the horn a second time with every ounce of strength in him, exhaling the last breath he would likely ever take.

A sound vibrated on the air. A low humming. A droning vibration like a village child might make blowing the clan leader's war horn—but still, the true and musical tone of the horn.

A hiss sounded in the distance. The woman in the wet shift dropped her hands and swiveled her head, scanning the horizon. Perun froze, still a stride away from Alex.

The winds came.

Alex could feel them whistling across the ocean waves and the land. They came rushing and roaring from the eight directions to converge on this small promontory. The leading edges lifted his hair, and the floats in the tree rattled and thumped together. The tree's branches began to sway. A hiss and roar of increasing gusts hit the white siding of the lighthouse and the lamp turret. Alex knew it was the barest hint of things to come when the body of them arrived.

From the north, Alex felt a cold and deadly blast. An arm of wind to strike and smite. A wind that could take a person to the ground and freeze them in place, struggling to breathe against its icy fingers. Morana lifted her head from the ground at the touch of that wind.

From the northeast came a biting wind. A Siberian wind with teeth that could chew down to the bones of a person.

From the northwest came a howling wind with a cry as empty and lonely as only vast stretches of nothing could be.

From the west came a traveler. A foreign wind that began in other lands before racing to the ancient and widespread Slavic lands that had created Stribog and Morana.

From the east came a wind bitter and salty, though from where Alex stood now, the ocean lay to his west. An east wind rolling off the Bering Sea with the strength to smash ashore as a hurricane.

From the southeast came a wind warmer, but no less ferocious. A heavy, laden chinook wind.

From the southwest came a wind with terrible speed, as if it had rolled down great mountains, like a roller-coaster car hurtling at them.

And from the south came the strongest wind of all. A powerful howling from grassy plains and rocky steppes and great, rugged expanses.

The eight winds sang together in their wild voices, each different from the other. Before humans walked the land, these winds had whipped up devastating tides and waves. They had felled swaths of forest with straight-line blasts, laying trees down like stalks of wheat before a thresher. They had blackened the sky with tornadoes and pulled oceans and lakes into swirling waterspouts hundreds of feet tall. Animals had run before them and hidden from their wrath in caves and dens. And when humans had come, they had been as helpless before these winds as the animals. Gales had blown down huts, made kites of teepees, reached their tendrils into the cracks of homes and roofs and torn them asunder. They had sunk boats and blown apart brick and cinderblock. Tossed semitrucks like children's toys.

The eight winds swirled around Alex. He could feel they hadn't yet reached their full strength and he despaired its coming. He crashed to his hands and knees, clutching the horn under his body with all his strength. The winds shoved at him harder, forcing him down to his face and stomach. He lay in the wailing, shrieking ferocity with the horn pressing into his chest.

He'd managed to summon the winds but had no idea how to control them now that they were here. His hair whipped in all directions at once. His jacket lifted as if a giant hand grabbed the cloth to pull him from the ground. He could only catch his breath in small sips as the wind raced past his face so fast that it either sucked all his air away or suffocated him with too much at once.

The tree behind him cracked and splintered. The white siding pulled from the lighthouse in chunks and sailed through the air like streamers. Spray from tall waves crashed against the bluff. And still the winds strengthened.

Tall boots of soft leather appeared in his field of vision and his heart sank. He could barely move, much less fight. A hand gripped his arm and rolled him easily onto his side so that the west wind battered the back of his head. It plowed into his back like a train, thrashed against his butt and legs, flapping any fabric not already tight to his skin. The east wind did the same to his face, chest, thighs. He rolled his eyes upward, blinking against dust and dirt hitting like tiny missiles, expecting to see Perun. Instead, he saw Stribog.

Larger than life, the god's hand covered Alex's upper arm and shoulder. He glowed with health and strength and vitality. His suit had become a long, gray tunic intricately embroidered at the sleeves and hem and worn over leggings. His ushanka hat and eagle pin were gone, but the emblem of an eagle blazed across his chest in blue and gold thread. His silver beard was now pure white and flowed halfway down to his tooled leather belt. His long white hair, held with a band of etched gold encircling his head, barely stirred in the chaotic winds.

He gently took the horn from Alex, and without appearing to change, it now matched his gigantic size. Standing straight, so tall his head seemed to brush the clouds, he lifted the horn to his lips.

A symphony of sound boomed across the bluff. Eight notes played at once: deep and high and musical and strident. The resonance of a cello, the song of an oboe, the whistle of a flute, the smooth tone of a trumpet. Over it all, binding them all, the call to arms of a war horn.

The winds responded eagerly. They swirled like a tornado forming, spinning the last few tangled floats into a swirl and tearing the ropes from the remaining branches of the tree. The pressure on Alex's body eased and he sat up.

He rubbed grit and tears from his eyes in time to see the dead body of the owl and the rusalka girl caught in a swirl of wind. They were torn from the bluff and hurled into the air, higher and higher, until they vanished like Dorothy spun away to Oz.

Stribog turned next to Perun. Likho fumbled away from him, crawling toward Stribog until he held a fold of his leggings in his fingers. The winds encircled Perun without lifting or moving him. They spun faster and harder. Perun turned from solid to translucent to transparent. His fine clothing pulled into ghostly shreds. Then his axe did the same. Then his body and face. He dissipated until flimsy bits of him twirled in the cyclone, coloring the swirl of air deep blue and silver and gold. The powerful whirlwind spun off the edge of the bluff and away, up and to the northwest, taking the storm clouds and rain with it, and leaving the bluff in sudden stillness.

Alex stood. Mike clung to the doorframe of the lighthouse as he pulled himself to his feet. Morana remained in her immense goddess form, but she had solidified now, and her cold face held a beauty almost too wonderful to look upon. She walked to Stribog's side.

A white mouse ran across the ground from the west and climbed onto Stribog's boot.

"You're late," he said sternly, looking down at it.

The mouse peered up at him, tiny pink paws folded at its chest and whiskers quivering. The next moment it was an attractive young woman—human sized, pale skinned, and white haired—standing in front of Stribog.

"I'm sorry," she said in Russian. "Something prevented me from crossing over."

"Eh, Perun, no doubt," Stribog said. "No matter, you're here now and I have a different task for you. For you and Likho." The woman bowed her head in acknowledgment. Likho shifted his grasp from Stribog's leggings to the woman's skirt. "And you, my friends"—he turned to Alex and Mike—"I owe you my thanks."

"How did I do it?" Alex asked. "How was it that a goddess couldn't blow the horn, and I could?"

"Orlov, son of Orel. Both eagles." He touched the eagle embroidered across his chest. He shrugged his hands. "Not a son. A great, great, something-great result of a tryst long ago. I believe it's why, when I threw the horn as far as I could from Perun, it came to this ancient forest for its magic and near to you for your blood. When I followed it here, I felt your presence and knew you for what you were. You and your sister, but her fainter as we pass traits father to son and mother to daughter, so I drew on your heritage to trap Perun inside you. I had hoped you would also be able to sense the horn and help me find it. After a fashion, you did."

"So they're gone now?" Mike asked. "The stryga and that water monster?"

"Yes. The stryga, you killed. Another will take her place and fill her role soon enough, but not here in this land. And the rusalka too, I have sent her home."

"Did you have the power to do this all along?" Alex gestured to Stribog's immense form.

"I had to conserve what strength remained to me until the very end. I knew I'd need it to win my battle with my brother. And now I have. And now we must go as well. I've healed, and the winds have helped Morana, but she's still weak."

Without another word, Stribog and Morana, Likho and the mouse woman, vanished into a gust of wind and were gone.

Chapter Twenty-Eight

ALEX WOKE FROM a sounder sleep than he'd had in nearly two weeks. Unsure what had woken him, he opened his eyes to bright sunshine streaming in the small windows of his cottage. Standing on his chest, fists on hips, was the gnarled little domovoi from his jail cell. Alex jerked so hard in surprise, the little man nearly fell off. He jumped onto the bedclothes and Alex sat up.

"Stribog says his debt is paid," he said in Russian.

The hammering of Alex's heart pulsing in his neck and ears ebbed slowly as he stared at the thing, processing its reality. "What debt?" he said finally. "I thought he already took Likho and the rest back to Russia, or wherever it is you're all from. That's all I ever asked of him."

"He made a pact. If you helped him find his horn, he would take care of all your problems. Stribog kept me here to tell you when it was done. Likho and the Dola returned to him this morning, and he instructed me to let you know the debt has been paid. He also sent the Dola to find this for you." He fished in a large pants pocket and pulled out the amulet Alex had lost up by the Oregon border. "He thinks you should wear it."

Alex took the pendant from him and slipped the chain over his head, still confused. "When what was done? I don't understand." He wondered if he was translating the words correctly.

"And if you don't know, how could I? This is not good place. You have no hearth."

"It's in the main house," Alex said distractedly, but the

little man had already vanished, leaving only dust motes swirling in the sunlight.

He got up and dressed. Nervous, he crossed the lawn and climbed the back porch steps, unsure about the reception he'd receive from Dan and Alina, having not seen them since the search for the boys had begun. Last night he'd talked a long while with Mike as they debriefed each other and processed the weirdness over a few beers, and then he'd crept home to sleep without disturbing the family.

Apparently, he wasn't the only one who'd slept in. It was after ten, but Sunday morning pancakes, bacon, and eggs were in full swing in the kitchen. Dan's eyes hardened for a moment when he first spotted him in the archway of the living room, but his brow smoothed and he pulled out a chair at Alex's usual place.

"You're just in time," he said. "Everything's still hot. Want some coffee?"

"God, yes," Alex said, and crossed to the chair.

David and Jake both started talking at once about their day in the forest with the weird lady. Bonkers snuffled at the edge of the table, nearest the plate of bacon, and drooled from the numb side of his mouth.

Alina turned and gave Alex a smile that said things were okay and they would catch up on everything later. Alex stabbed a fork into the stack of pancakes she pulled out of the oven and poured a mug of coffee from the pot Dan handed him.

ALEX SAT IN the recliner after breakfast, facing Dan and Alina on the couch, exhausted from his retelling of the last two days' events. Upstairs, the boys played some noisy game of hide and seek. Bonkers lay at the side of Alex's chair and Alex petted him absently. The dog had been home longer than any of them, pacing in the backyard, waiting for dinner when Alina and Dan had returned home with the boys.

Alex had been beyond relieved to see the boys bouncing back so well from their encounters. As Alina pointed out, to them it hadn't been an abduction. It had been a boy their age who led them to a woman who put them to work for a day until their mom came and got them. The creepy hut had given them both nightmares, as had the woman striking David like an angry nun, but Alina planned to schedule them both with a counselor first thing on Monday.

Dan and Alina had listened with rapt attention to his adventures. The relief on their faces at learning that all the creatures were gone for good was the best homecoming Alex could have asked for. He told them about the domovoi's cryptic message this morning, but they understood no more than he had. Together they looked up the Dola on his phone, and found it was a creature of fate or perhaps good fortune.

Alex's cell phone rang. "It's Lois Tobares," he said to Dan and Alina.

"Your lawyer's calling you on a Sunday?" Alina said.

He shrugged and put it on speaker.

"Alex, I wanted to tell you right away. There's been a break in your case. Steven Fabick, the man you were convicted of assaulting in Montana, apparently managed to lose some more of his drug supplier's money. He was murdered last night. And in the weirdest twist of fate I've seen in twenty years as a defender, the man who killed Fabick got hit and injured by a drunk driver in an auto-pedestrian accident just outside the apartment. Paramedics and police found him with a bloody crowbar in his jacket about the same time police were arriving at the apartment for the noise complaint and discovered

Fabick dead. The assailant plea bargained his murder charge by giving up the drug supplier this morning. He said in a sworn statement it's the second time he was hired to beat Fabick with a crowbar. The date he gave for the first assault is the attack you were convicted for. Once forensics matches the DNA, you'll be cleared. Considering Julie Mosca's recent statement recanting her testimony, it wouldn't surprise me if the courts overturn your conviction first thing tomorrow. You might not get anything more than an apology for your time served, but I'll petition for lost wages. The main thing is, they'll clear your record the minute the court overturns the ruling."

He slumped back in the armchair, stunned. "I can't believe it," he said.

But he could believe it. The domovoi's words made sense now. The God of Wind, known also as a spreader of fortune, had told Alex if he helped find his horn that he'd take care of all his problems. And now, the debt had been paid. Stribog had sent Misfortune and Fate to Montana on his behalf. Fabick hadn't stood a chance.

Alina and Dan were grinning almost as broadly as he was himself.

Epilogue

ALEX PULLED HIS phone from its belt holster, surprised to have reception in this part of the forest. The screen showed the call was from Mark Fenster.

He'd kept his longtime friend up to date on the good news as it'd happened over the past six weeks: the overturning of his conviction, the freedom to return to a state or federal enforcement job, his applications to various openings. And, finally, the acceptance a month later at his first-choice job, Olympic National Park, on the gorgeous peninsula west of Seattle. A million acres of wilderness and seventy miles of coastline.

The peace and serenity of living in the forest again had begun to heal a lot of wounds; being back doing the job he loved more than anything after three years in hell, even more so. But between the reception out here and in the forests of Montana, he and Fen had connected only by text for the two weeks since his move.

"Hey, Fen, how you been?"

"All good. How you doing, buddy? How's the Seattle area treating you?"

"Really well. Like, so well it's kind of amazing. It's nice to have the convenience of a big city so close on top of everything else out here, Rainier, St. Helen's, the San Juan's. Honestly, though, they're just icing on the cake. This park, the national forest around it, the ocean… it's pretty incredible. So, when you coming out to visit?"

"I was calling to ask you the same thing. Turns out Ken finally got his transfer to Florida. He heads out for Ocala next month. That means there's a job opening up if you want to come back to Montana. And besides, I still owe you that dinner at The Anvil."

Alex chewed his lip. "You know, as much as I miss Montana and Lolo, after everything that went down there, the truth is, I don't think it would feel the same anymore."

"Yeah, I guess I get that. Besides, I wouldn't sell your cabin back to you anyway."

Alex laughed. "You know, even if the last three years hadn't happened, I wonder if this is where I was meant to end up. It's early days still, but I think I could see myself staying here for the long haul."

"Wow. It all sounds pretty great."

"Get this. I even got set up on a date already. A gal in Seattle. A friend of someone at the information desk."

"And?"

"It was nice. She was nice. She's a marine biologist doing a long-term study on ocean temperatures and migration patterns. I'm seeing her again for dinner tomorrow."

"How about your sister? How's she doing now you've moved?"

Alex hadn't told Fen about his and Alina's bizarre two weeks, fighting creatures out of folktales and myth. But Fen had known him for many years. He knew that Alex had been Alina's guardian when he was still a teenager himself, and that she'd been there for him like nobody else had been while he was in prison.

"She's good. Now that I've moved away, she and Dan are thinking about maybe going back to the Eugene area. They've been looking into job offers there, and Eugene to Seattle would only be a four-hour drive. We could even make it a day trip and meet halfway in Portland."

"Didn't your friend Mike end up moving to Portland?"

"He did, yeah. His youngest son moved there recently. Mike turned down his crabbing job and moved there to try and build a closer relationship with him. He landed a job as a shipyard supervisor. I helped him move and a month later, he helped me move up here. Last week he told me he'd bought a small boat to live on."

"Sorry. You cut out on that last bit. I'm on Highway 12."

Fen sounded choppy as well. "No matter, I was just rambling. Sounds like I'll lose you soon. Hey, it's good to hear from you, Fen."

"You too, Alex." The reception suddenly became crystal clear. "I hope you'll come and visit sometime. But I gotta tell you, it's really good to hear you happy again. Happier than here, I think, even before everything went down. It sounds like that place is going to be good for you."

"I think it is too." Through his shirt, Alex fingered the lucky amulet his grandfather had given him. "It's been nice to have a little good luck again. I feel like maybe this time it'll last."

THE END

Acknowledgements

MANY THANKS TO the wonderful friends, all authors in their own right, who have helped in various ways with this book, including my long-standing Elementals critique partners: Laurence Raphael Brothers, M. E. Garber, S.H. Harrison, M V Melcer, Sandy Parsons, and Lettie Prell, and to friend and coffee buddy Sam W. Pisciotta for the writing chats and moral support. My gratitude also goes out to the friends who availed themselves for cultural advice: Leonid Korogodski for his input, Oleg Kazantsev for his feedback throughout the novel, and Alex Shvartsman for both his advice and the wonderful introduction. Any inaccuracies in this novel are entirely my own, whether intentional fabrications for story purposes or due to unintentional misunderstandings or errors on my part.

About the Contributors

ALEX SHVARTSMAN (BROOKLYN, NY) is the author of *Kakistocracy* (2023), *The Middling Affliction* (2022), and *Eridani's Crown* (2019). Over 120 of his stories have appeared in *Analog*, *Nature*, *Strange Horizons*, etc. He won the WSFA Small Press Award for Short Fiction and was a three-time finalist for the Canopus Award for Excellence in Interstellar Fiction.

His translations from Russian have appeared in *F&SF*, *Clarkesworld*, *Tor.com*, *Analog*, *Asimov's*, etc. Alex has edited over a dozen anthologies, including the long-running Unidentified Funny Objects series.

Alex's story "Whom He May Devour" is currently in development as a live action TV series.

His website is http://www.alexshvartsman.com.

L. D. COLTER HAS farmed with draft horses and worked as a paramedic, Outward Bound instructor, athletic trainer, roller-skating waitress, and concrete dispatcher, among other curious choices. She's an author of contemporary, epic, and dark fantasy novels, a WSFA Small Press Award finalist, and a two-time winner of the Colorado Book Award for science fiction and fantasy.

You can find a list of her published works and more at ldcolter.com or her newsletter at Speculations.

FIND US ONLINE!

www.rebellionpublishing.com

/solarisbooks   /solarisbks

/solarisbooks   /solarisbooks.
bsky.social

SIGN UP TO OUR NEWSLETTER!

rebellionpublishing.com/newsletter

YOUR REVIEWS MATTER!

Enjoy this book? Got something to say?

Leave a review on Amazon, GoodReads or with your
favourite bookseller and let the world know!